D1159867

The New World

ALSO BY MATT MYKLUSCH

The Jack Blank Adventures

The Accidental Hero

The Secret War

The End of Infinity

Order of the Majestic

Order of the Majestic

Lost Kingdom

ORDER OF THE MAJESTIC

The New World

MATT MYKLUSCH

Outreach - Bookmobile
Fountaindale Public Library District
300 W. Briarcliff Rd.
Bolingbrook, IL 60440

ALADDIN
NEW YORK LONDON TORONTO · SYDNEY NEW DELHI

This book is a work of fiction. Any references to historical events, real people,
or real places are used fictitiously. Other names, characters, places, and events
are products of the author's imagination, and any resemblance to actual events or
places or persons, living or dead, is entirely coincidental.

ALADDIN

An imprint of Simon & Schuster Children's Publishing Division
1230 Avenue of the Americas, New York, NY 10020
First Aladdin hardcover edition August 2021
Text copyright © 2021 by Matt Myklusch
Jacket illustration copyright © 2021 by Owen Richardson
All rights reserved, including the right of reproduction in whole or in part in any form.
ALADDIN is a trademark of Simon & Schuster, Inc., and related logo
is a registered trademark of Simon & Schuster, Inc.
For information about special discounts for bulk purchases, please contact
Simon & Schuster Special Sales at 1-866-506-1949 or business@simonandschuster.com.
The Simon & Schuster Speakers Bureau can bring authors to your live event.
For more information or to book an event contact the Simon & Schuster Speakers Bureau
at 1-866-248-3049 or visit our website at www.simonspeakers.com.
Jacket designed by Karin Paprocki
Interior designed by Mike Rosamilia
The text of this book was set in Goudy Old Style.
Manufactured in the United States of America 0621 FFG
2 4 6 8 10 9 7 5 3 1
Library of Congress Cataloging-in-Publication Data
Names: Myklusch, Matt, author.
Title: The new world / by Matt Myklusch.
Description: First Aladdin hardcover edition. | New York : Aladdin, 2021. |
Series: Order of the Majestic ; book 3 | Audience: Ages 8 to 12 |
Summary: Joey Kopecky and his friends Shazad and Leonora have one last chance to defeat the Invisible Hand.
Identifiers: LCCN 2021007341 (print) | LCCN 2021007342 (ebook) |
ISBN 9781534479401 (hardcover) | ISBN 9781534479425 (ebook)
Subjects: CYAC: Fantasy. | Magic—Fiction. | Adventure and adventurers—Fiction.
Classification: LCC PZ7.M994 Ne 2021 (print) | LCC PZ7.M994 (ebook) |
DDC [Fic]—dc23
LC record available at https://lccn.loc.gov/2021007341
LC ebook record available at https://lccn.loc.gov/2021007342

FOR MY READERS.
THIS BOOK WOULDN'T EXIST
WITHOUT YOU.

Contents

Prologue
Power and Responsibility

"Ladies and gentlemen, our time together is nearly at an end," Joey announced. "For my final trick, I need a volunteer to join me onstage. Somebody special," he added, raising a finger in the air. "Preferably someone with a touch of magic in their soul. I don't suppose anyone here tonight fits that description. . . ."

The floorboards creaked beneath Joey's feet as he waited for an answer that wouldn't come. He looked out to where the audience should be. But there was no audience. The seats were all empty, and Joey was alone on the stage. He was wearing a tuxedo and standing beside a table with his old magic set, Redondo's Mystery Box, resting on top. Joey had no idea how he'd gotten there. The situation didn't make any sense.

Despite his young age, Joey Kopecky was a master magician, but he wasn't a *stage* magician. It was true he spent nearly all his free time in the Majestic Theatre, but he never performed there. No one did. The Majestic was more of a clubhouse. It was a treasure trove of magical objects that had been left to Joey and his friends by their former mentor, Redondo the Magnificent. Magic shows had been Redondo's stock in trade, not Joey's. He had no plans to become a world-famous magician. He had actually taken great pains to avoid the spotlight, but there he was, dressed up like he was trying to be Redondo for some reason. Even the words Joey had used to address his nonexistent crowd were not his own. He remembered hearing Redondo recite those lines the last time he ever performed in public.

"What am I doing?" Joey wondered aloud.

"It looks like you're doing my act," a familiar voice called out behind Joey. "You seem to have stolen everything except my mustache."

Joey turned around and saw Redondo standing at the edge of the stage. In that instant, he understood what was going on. "I get it now. This is a dream."

Redondo walked over to where Joey was standing. "That's

one way of looking at it. I prefer to think of it as a special appearance. One night only."

Joey smiled, glad to see Redondo, even if he was just a manifestation of Joey's subconscious, sleeping mind. Redondo was exactly as Joey remembered him. Stylish and confident, he was the classic stage magician. Redondo was dressed, as usual, in a black tuxedo with a white dress shirt, vest, and bow tie. His stark white hair was combed perfectly, and his pencil-thin mustache completed his polished look. "Aren't we a pair?" Redondo asked, noting their identical outfits.

"I don't know why I'm dressed like this," Joey said. His own standard uniform was a T-shirt and jeans. The only jacket Joey ever wore was a hoodie.

"I like this look on you," Redondo told him. "Imitation is the most sincere form of flattery. Can I tell you a secret, though? I always hated these things." He untied his bow tie and let it hang loose around his collar. "There. That's better."

"You? Telling secrets?" Joey said. "Now I know I'm dreaming."

"If you say so. I hope I'm not intruding."

3

"No way," Joey told Redondo. "I wish you were here for real."

Redondo furrowed his brow. "Who's to say I'm not?"

Joey hiked his shoulders an inch. "I don't know. You *are* dead."

"And?" Redondo asked, as if death were a small matter, hardly worth mentioning. "When magic is involved, not to mention a magician of my caliber, nothing is impossible. I stuck around to say goodbye *after* I died, if you recall."

"Exactly," Joey agreed. "You died. You said goodbye. That was over a year ago."

"And what a year it's been," Redondo replied, beaming. "You've been busy. I said you flattered me before, but the truth is, you've put me to shame. I've been watching. You've discovered secrets even I never knew. The secret history of the world! You found out what happened to rob the earth of its magic all those years ago, and now you're in a position to do something about it." Redondo pointed an aiming finger at Joey. "That's the part that's got you worried, I expect. What comes next?"

"I'm not worried," Joey said a little too quickly.

"Really?" Redondo's lips curled up in a knowing smile,

not fooled at all. "I heard you ask for volunteers just now." He looked around the empty theater. "So far I don't see anyone raising their hand. You're all alone, young Kopecky. Why is that?"

Joey said nothing.

"It's got to mean something. Could it be because you *feel* like you're all alone, up against impossible odds?"

"This is just a dream," Joey maintained. "I'm not alone in real life. I've got friends. Shazad, Leanora, Janelle . . . they're with me. We're the new Order of the Majestic."

"That's good. That's important. The purest, most powerful form of magic cannot be created alone, but there's no getting around the fact that you're the one with the wand. When the time comes, *you're* the one who has to say the magic words."

Joey looked down and realized he was holding the wand. Had it been in his hand this whole time? He didn't remember having it earlier.

Redondo held out his hand. "May I?"

Joey gave him the wand.

It was made of polished black wood and had white silver tips at each end. The average person probably would have thought it was a prop from an expensive magic set or a high-end Halloween costume. Only a handful of people knew what it really was. Most of the world's magical objects were enchanted relics that had survived through the ages. They were ancient artifacts that had been infused with a finite amount of power long ago. The wand was more than that. It was a conduit for pure, undiluted magical energy and could be used to do almost anything. It could literally bring imagination to life. Redondo waved the wand in the air as if to cast a spell. Nothing happened. He lowered his hand, disappointed.

"If I could take this back, I'd do it in a heartbeat, but that's not in the cards for either of us. Everything's been building up to this moment. It's your wand now. Your turn."

"That's what I'm afraid of." Joey took the wand back. Even in a dream, it could have only one master at a time. Right now that master was him.

"Why don't you tell me what's on your mind," Redondo said. "Say it out loud. Make it real. Then we can deal with it."

Joey held up the wand, seeing it for what it truly was—a double-edged sword. "A thousand years ago, Merlin used this wand to save the world from a tyrant, a mad emperor deter-mined to wipe magic off the face of the earth. He almost did it, too. Merlin stopped him, but after the fight was over, he didn't use the wand to set magic free. He used it to hide away whatever was left."

"He created a refuge for magic and more," Redondo said, defending Merlin's choice. "A hidden country where fantas-tic, unbelievable things could thrive in secret. Merlin saved magic by making it disappear."

"And that's what killed him," Joey countered. "The wand killed Houdini, too. It killed you."

Redondo scoffed. "The wand didn't kill me. I sacrificed myself to keep it out of the wrong hands. It was terribly heroic," he added, sounding slightly wounded, as if Joey wasn't giving him the credit he deserved.

"It was definitely heroic," Joey agreed. "But you were already dying by then. That was because of the wand, wasn't it? It was too much . . . too much power."

Redondo nodded, a grim look on his face. "As far as I know, that wand has zero limits. People are a different story. Even people like us." He turned his palms up. "You once told me that you wanted a magical life. There's no free admission to this show. If you fly too close to the sun, eventually you're going to fall. But still . . . you get to fly. Most people never get that chance."

Joey grimaced. Redondo was confirming his worst fears, which wasn't surprising. If this was a dream, he wasn't even talking to Redondo. He was talking to himself. But that didn't mean he shouldn't pay attention. Like Redondo had said, nothing was impossible. What if it was a dream, but at the same time, it was also something more? Joey couldn't pass up the chance to ask the old man for advice.

"Is it worth it?" he asked. "Using the wand to do something big like that? Like, *really* big?"

"That depends on what you have in mind. It could be, but you have to wield the wand wisely. Don't try to do too much at once. You need to make your actions count." Redondo shrugged. "On the other hand, you could choose to do nothing at all. That's an option as well. You could hide the wand away, keep your head down, and live your life. A very comfortable life, too, I might add. It wouldn't take much. Just a touch of magic here and there whenever you felt the need."

"No," Joey said. "I can't do what you did." Redondo had

spent twenty years living off the grid, mired in depression as he and the wand gathered dust in the Majestic Theatre. He changed course at the end of his life, but Joey didn't get the impression that he had ever been comfortable.

"My situation was different," Redondo argued. "I had the Invisible Hand after me. You don't have that problem anymore. No one can make you do anything you don't want to do. You're not pressured by anyone."

"Except by me," Joey replied. "I can't just sit on the sidelines when I have the power to make the world a better place. Also, Janelle would never let me get away with that. This wand is like a weapon of mass creation. I've got to do something with it."

"I understand." Redondo nodded. "Where there is great power, there is also great responsibility."

"You stole that line from Spider-Man."

"Actually, I was quoting Winston Churchill, but you make a good point. This is no comic book. In real life, heroes often pay a very high price. I've been there." The expression on Redondo's face had turned very serious.

"I don't want to go there," Joey said. "I'm not looking to be a hero. I just want to make a difference. I don't want to . . ." Joey's voice trailed off as the Majestic Theatre started to wither, aging rapidly from the restored, grand palace he knew and transforming back into the ruined, abandoned wreck it had been when Joey first found it. In the blink of an eye, it changed from a vibrant, glamorous venue into something that was, for all intents and purposes, dead.

"Do I have to end up like you?" Joey asked.

"You already have." Redondo took in the sight of the decrepit, burned-out husk the theater had become. He nodded to the wand. "You inherited the Majestic Legacy, just as I did, and Houdini before me. But you're different, young Kopecky. You and your friends have a chance. You might be the ones to complete Merlin's last great trick."

Joey scrunched up his face. "What do you mean complete it? What trick?"

"Merlin left behind unfinished business. His story isn't over yet." Redondo opened the Mystery Box and found his old deck of fortune-telling cards inside. "Every magic trick, big or small, is like a story. And, like any good story, it has three parts, or acts. The first of these is called The Pledge." Rather than drawing his customary three cards off the top of the deck,

Redondo took only one. It had the image of a heart icon with a hand placed over it. The words on the card read THE PLEDGE. "This is *our* pledge to the audience that something incredible is going to happen. That what we plan to do is worth their time. We present them with something: an object, a scenario, or sometimes with nothing at all. Even nothing can be something if you look at it the right way. Nothing *now* represents the possibility of something later." He ripped off a corner of the card and gave it to Joey. "Hold that."

Joey took the torn piece, and Redondo flipped the card over. The other side had a bent arrow symbol like a U-turn sign. Below that it read THE TURN. "Our second act is The Turn, in which we deliver on our promise. We take our ordinary something and do something extraordinary with it. Or, more precisely, we begin to. The possibilities here are endless, but it could be as simple as making the item disappear." Redondo snapped his fingers and the card vanished from sight. "But that alone is not enough. People make things disappear all the time. They lose them, hide them, waste them, and forget about them. Making something disappear does not qualify as magic. More is required."

Redondo's eyes went up to the ceiling of the dilapidated

11

theater, which had several large holes in it. A bird had swooped in through one of them. They watched as the bird flew a wobbly path around the theater. Something was wrong with one of its wings. Redondo held out his hand to it. The tiny bird came down and perched on his finger. "It's not enough to change something or make it disappear. The real magic comes in the third act, The Prestige—when we bring it back."

Redondo cradled the bird with the injured wing in his hands, hiding it from sight. When he opened them back up, the bird was gone and the card had returned. This time it had the image of a twinkling star on its face. The words at the bottom of the card read THE PRESTIGE. Redondo retrieved the torn piece from Joey and put it back into place. It reattached seamlessly, as if the card had never been ripped off at all. "Do you understand what I'm telling you?"

Joey took the card from Redondo and stared at it. "I think so."

Redondo's trick was an analogy for Joey's dilemma. The severed corner of the card was like the wand, something magical left in his care. The card and the bird with the busted wing were like the world. They were both broken, and Joey had the power to make them whole again. At least, the wand had that kind of power inside it. Joey wasn't sure if he had it inside him. He could finish Merlin's final act, but he worried that if he did, it would also prove to be his own.

Joey shuffled the full deck of cards in his hand. Over the last year, he had gotten in the habit of pulling three at a time, just as Redondo had often done when he was alive. The pictures on the face of each card were always different and always offered cryptic messages about the future. This time, when Joey drew three cards off the top, there was nothing on them. He turned the deck over and fanned the cards out.

"They're all blank."

Redondo stroked his mustache, thinking for a moment. "What do you suppose that means?"

Joey grimaced. "No future."

Redondo seemed unconvinced. "That's one possibility. You can't change the cards you're dealt. Only how you play the hand."

"Bringing magic back to the world is a pretty big deal. Tell me the truth, Redondo. You think I can do it without dying in the process?"

"The truth?" Redondo thought for a moment. "No. But everybody dies. The question is, what do we leave behind when we go?"

Joey looked up, upset that Redondo was speaking so casually about his impending death. "I was hoping you might have a better answer."

"Oh, I do," Redondo assured him. "But it's not my place to say." He patted Joey on the shoulder. "This is your time in the spotlight. I have every confidence in your ability to put on an unforgettable show."

It suddenly felt like Redondo was saying goodbye again, and Joey wasn't ready. He still had so many questions. "You're not going to help me?"

Redondo laughed. "Help you? How? According to you, I'm not even real!"

"Yeah, but—"

"You don't need my help. Not anymore. You've got everything you need right here." Redondo tapped at his temple. "Think about it, young Kopecky," he added with a wink. *"Where's your imagination?"*

1

Showtime

The roof of the Majestic Theatre was Joey's "go-to" spot when he needed a quiet place to think. He had a bit more on his mind than the average fourteen-year-old boy, so he needed a place like that pretty often. Joey spent a lot of time up there with a foot on the ledge, staring out at the city in silence. In that one respect, the night was no different from any other, but the night was still young.

The theater was not as tall as Joey's apartment building across the river in Hoboken. At home, he had a clear view of Manhattan's iconic skyline, but he preferred to be on top of the Majestic. The city had grown on Joey. The neighboring buildings towered over the theater like an urban forest, and Joey liked being in the thick of it. He liked the city's energy. Tonight, however, that energy was noticeably absent. It was eleven o'clock on a warm October evening, and New York was eerily quiet. The streets should have been bustling with activity as the nearby theaters released their audiences and the sidewalks filled with people, but that wasn't going to happen. The lights had all gone out, and not just on Broadway. An invisible enemy had swept across the globe, shuttering businesses, taking lives, and forcing everyone into isolation. It wasn't an evil scheme by dark magicians that had done it, but a virus. The latest crisis in a world filled with problems that were spinning out of control. For Joey, it was the final straw. People everywhere were desperate for the pandemic to end and life to return to normal, but Joey took a different view. In his mind, normal life wasn't enough. Normal didn't work, and the truth was, it never had. Joey was after something better.

"You finished brooding up here, Dark Knight?" Janelle asked him.

Janelle liked to tease Joey for spending so much time up on the roof looking serious. She was convinced that he secretly wanted to be Batman, but really, he was more of a Spider-Man/Winston Churchill type.

"I'm not brooding," Joey said. "I'm thinking. You hear that?"

Janelle paused a moment to listen. "I don't hear anything."

"Exactly. It's like some kind of post-apocalyptic disaster movie out there. Only it's real."

"I know," Janelle agreed. "It's scary how fast everything changed."

"You know what's scary? How much I miss going to school. I never thought I'd say *that*." Exemplar Academy, the school for gifted students that Joey and Janelle both attended, had switched to all-virtual classes when the pandemic began. Only the students who were working on a vaccine were allowed back in the building. Joey and Janelle were not part of that effort, but they had their own plan to make good on the school motto and change the world for the better.

"Are you ready?" Janelle asked Joey.

"I'll be down in a second. I'm just taking one last look."

"At what?"

"A world without magic."

Janelle joined Joey at the edge of the roof. She nudged him with her elbow. "Was that your Batman voice? Because if it was, it needs work."

"Stop it," Joey complained. "I wasn't doing a Batman voice." He narrowed his eyes, trying to look tough. "*This . . . is my Batman voice*," he rasped in a gravelly tone.

Janelle laughed. "That was even worse."

"No way. That was quality. I stand by it."

"Can we stand somewhere besides the roof? Shazad and Leanora are downstairs in the Map Room. Their parents just got here."

"They're here? Why didn't you say so?"

"I just did." Janelle gave Joey's arm a tug. "Let's go, Boy Wonder."

"Did you just demote me from Batman to Robin?" Joey winced, stung by the comment. "That's cold."

Joey followed Janelle down to Redondo's old office. Having never met Redondo, she always called it the Map Room, which made sense because one of its walls was covered with a giant interactive map. It was a mural of the Secret Map of the World. Leanora and Shazad had painted it using magic brushes, and the map moved just like the original had done, allowing them to zoom in on lost realms and magic gateways that led all over the planet. This was the room where Joey, Shazad, Leanora, and Janelle made all their big plans.

A year of talking, researching, plotting, and scheming—not to mention a whole lot of rooftop thinking—had finally led to a breakthrough. The Order of the Majestic was ready for action.

"You found him," Leonora said to Janelle as they entered. "Where was he?"

"In his office." Janelle smirked.

"The roof again?" Leonora asked. "Pretending to be the DarkBat?"

Joey snorted, trying to keep a straight face. "Exactly. That's one hundred percent right. How's it going down here?"

"Everything's fine," Leonora's mother said, smiling warmly at Joey. "We're just mapping out our plans for the evening."

"For the hundredth time," Shazad's mother added. "How are you, Joey?"

"I'm good, thanks," Joey replied. "I'm ready."

"Hello, Joey," Shazad's father said from a few feet away, where he stood studying the map alongside Leonora's father. Both men waved to Joey and went back to strategizing. "I think we need more people at Stonehenge," Shazad's father said.

"*Da*," Leanora's father agreed. "My cousins can join you there. The rest of our family will be here, here, and here," he added, tapping spots on the map.

Shazad's father rubbed his chin, staring at the map. "Yes, this is good. This can work."

"How is everyone else doing?" Joey asked. "All set?"

"Just about," Shazad said. He spun the Staff of Sorcero around in one direction, extending it to the size of a bo staff, then twirled it back the other way to shrink it down to the length of a ruler. He handed it to Janelle, who thanked him. "Are you sure you don't want to take anything else with you?"

"I'm sure," Janelle said. "I like this one. It makes sense to me. Somewhat."

"Good thing Hypnova brought it back to us," Shazad said.

"It was the least she could do," Shazad's mother said. "After keeping the Caliburn Shield for herself."

"She needed it more than we did," Shazad told his mother.

"I know. And you left it in good hands—that's the important thing. But I would have liked you to have it tonight. For protection."

"I'll be fine," Shazad reassured his mother. "I'm ready for tonight."

"Are you ready?" Leanora asked Joey. "Everything taken care of at home? Your parents all tucked in, safe and sound?"

Joey nodded. "That tea you gave me worked like a charm."

"That's because it was one." Leanora grinned.

Leanora's mother said something in Russian. Joey didn't understand the words, but he knew a reprimand when he heard one. From the way the grin slipped off Leanora's face, Joey knew he was right.

"What?" Leanora said. "Dreamleaf is a natural sleep aid. It's harmless." She had given Joey and Janelle a special blend of enchanted tea leaves that her family kept in their pantry. It was amazing stuff, guaranteed to put anyone who drank it to sleep within minutes, but only if they were in a safe place. Also, they would wake up immediately if they were in danger.

"My parents had two cups each, they liked it so much," Janelle said. "They should be out for the next forty-eight hours at least."

"Same here," Joey said.

"And while they sleep, everything's going to change,"

21

Leanora's mother said. "They're going to wake up in a whole new world."

Joey shrugged. "More like the old world back again, but yeah. That's the plan."

"You're not concerned about what they're going to say?" Leanora's mother asked. "It's going to be quite the rude awakening. And then, when they find out *you* are responsible?"

"*Mamushka*," Leanora said. "If Joey has to explain himself to his parents when this is over, that would be a very good thing."

"I'm just worried about all of you," Leanora's mother said. "Our plans tonight are dangerous. Joey's and Janelle's parents deserve to know the truth of what you are doing."

"They can't handle the truth," Joey said, making a rare, non-comic-book movie reference.

"You never know," Leanora's mother said. "They might surprise you. We've faced our share of difficult audiences over the years, and always, we've been able to reach them. My daughter might disagree, but not everything has to be a fight."

"We've been through this," Leanora said. "And tonight does."

Onstage, Leanora's family was known as the Nomadiks. They performed all over the world, hiding magic in plain sight and inspiring a belief in the impossible. Their shows helped keep magic alive in people's hearts, but their influence was always limited to a single town or village at a time. The act had never been enough for Leanora. She wanted to take on the forces that held magic back directly. Getting her parents to come around to her way of thinking had not been easy, but she had done it. Convincing Joey's parents to do the same was out of the question.

"Mrs. Valkov, my mom and dad would never let me go ahead with this," Joey explained. "They wouldn't understand. They can't understand. Not yet."

"They will . . . in time," Shazad's mother said. "It's all right," she added to Leanora's mother. "Sometimes people need to be shocked into seeing things differently. Look at us. Before Camelot, we never would have approved of this crusade. Now we're lending the children magic artifacts to take with them into battle. Speaking of which . . ."

Shazad's mother placed one last item into Joey's overstuffed backpack and handed it to him. Joey peeked inside and thanked her. It was loaded with enchanted objects.

For generations, the Hassans had acted as the guardians of rare and powerful magical items. They traveled around the world, collecting them and keeping them out of the wrong hands. Up until now, that had been as far as they were willing to go, but the secrets that Joey, Shazad, and Leanora had uncovered in Camelot had changed everything.

"A pity the rest of the world didn't learn from Camelot," Leanora's mother said. "If they had, we wouldn't have to do this."

"We got the crowd warmed up," Leanora told her mother. "Tonight we hit them with the showstopper."

Joey was inclined to agree. Camelot had been a good start, but it was only a start. The lost kingdom's inexplicable return had led many people to conclude its existence was magical in nature. Before the pandemic had curtailed travel, millions of visitors had journeyed from all over the world to see the castle with their own eyes. Most of them went back home open to the idea that magic was real. However, for every new believer, there were countless others who refused to entertain the possibility. It wasn't hard to see why. The modern world, with its many problems, beat magical thinking out of people, and powerful forces conspired to push them away from the truth. Well-funded social media campaigns and dubious news organizations spread misinformation and lies, claiming that Camelot was a publicity stunt for an upcoming movie, or some kind of elaborate prank. People accepted these ridiculous explanations because they understood them. They fit with a picture of reality that the general public already knew and believed in.

Joey saw Ledger DeMayne's handiwork in all of it. As the leader of the Invisible Hand, DeMayne had connections everywhere. His considerable resources, plus the natural suspicion that people held for things they didn't understand, made for a powerful combination. That was how the Invisible Hand had kept the world's magic to themselves for so long. By leveraging the twin powers of manipulation and denial. After Camelot, there had been flare-ups of magical happenings all around the world, but they were quickly swept under the carpet and pushed out of the news cycle. For example, Janelle and Joey's alternative energy project at Caltech had been taken over by the government and shut down. They were told it was due to safety concerns and national security interests, but Joey knew it was just more behind-the-scenes maneuvering by Ledger DeMayne and the

Invisible Hand. That setback, over a year ago, had lit the fuse for tonight's mission. The Order of the Majestic couldn't beat the Invisible Hand inch by inch, one step at a time. They had to do something big. Something no one could explain away, deny, or cover up.

"It was always going to come to this," Joey said. "It's why the Order of the Majestic exists. It's why I have the wand."

Joey stopped short of calling it destiny, but there were definitely times when it felt that way. This night had been a thousand years in the making. Ever since the mad emperor of a lost, forgotten country had decided there was too much magic in the world. Joey joined Leanora's and Shazad's fathers at the map. It told the story of a great injustice and what could be done to set it right.

"In the beginning, there were three cursed objects strategically placed at key points around the world," Joey said, running through their plan of action one last time. "Three dark magic markers that blocked the flow of magical energy. We destroyed one of them at Camelot last year. The other two are here and here." Joey pointed out targets in the North Pole and somewhere between Hawaii and Japan. "If everything goes according to plan, Shazad and Leanora will take them both out tonight."

"Don't say 'if,'" Shazad said. "There is no 'if.' We're doing this. Security around the dark markers was on high alert after Camelot, but now?" He shook his head. "It's a skeleton crew. They're not ready for us."

"The next twenty-four hours are going to be very interesting," Leanora said.

Her father chortled. "You don't have to tell us." He and Shazad's father stepped away from the map so everyone could see what they had done to it. Using the magic paintbrushes, they had marked up the map like two generals laying out troop positions in a battle plan. Nomadiks and Hassans were stationed all over the world in places that were strong in magic and steeped in lore. "We'll be there to greet the new world when it gets here."

"And we'll make sure everyone gets to see it," Joey added.

He kept his eyes on the map, tracking the Imagine Nation as it moved slowly across the Atlantic Ocean. A year ago, the magical, roaming island had vanished from the map by the time the paint on the wall had finished drying. It had been gone most of the time since then, but it had recently resurfaced without warning or explanation. Joey and his friends took it as a sign. Another reason to believe it was time for them to act and give magic back to the world.

"I can't believe this is actually happening," Janelle said. "No more planning and waiting. We're going to change the world—tonight."

"No sense in putting it off any longer." Joey took the wand out of his sleeve. "I haven't used this thing all year, I've been saving it for this. Chances are, after tonight I'll never use it again."

Everyone got quiet when Joey produced the wand. His choice of words was a sobering reminder of the dangers associated with its use.

"I think I speak for everyone when I say the restraint you've shown with the wand has been remarkable," Shazad's mother said to Joey a few moments later. The adults in the room all nodded in agreement. Joey felt a "but" coming on. He was right. "But are you *really* sure you want to go through with this plan? All of it? Surely it's enough just to destroy the dark magic markers?"

Joey shook his head. "This wand has unfinished business in the Imagine Nation. A thousand years ago, Merlin used it to hide the island away from the world. I'm going to bring it back. I know it's hard to understand, but it's something I have to do."

"I understand why you don't want to tell your parents," Leanora's mother said with grudging approval.

"I'll be the first one to tell them when it's over," Joey promised. "I'm not looking to sacrifice myself for the cause. On that note . . . check it out." He pulled up his sleeve, revealing a green rectangular mark on his inner forearm. Everyone leaned in for a closer look.

"You got a tattoo?" Janelle asked. "When did this happen?"

"Five minutes ago, up on the roof. It's not ink. I used the wand to do it."

"Joey!" Janelle gave him a shove. "You can't be using the wand on pointless stuff like that."

"It's not pointless," Joey said. "It's like a power meter in a video game. This mark lets me know exactly how much energy I have left. Every time I cast a spell, the green bar goes down based on how much magic I used. See? It's not quite a hundred percent full."

Upon closer examination, everyone saw there was a black border around the green bar on Joey's arm. The color measured how much Joey had used the wand, going almost to the top of the rectangle, but not quite.

"So, when the power runs out . . . ," Shazad prompted.

Game over, Joey thought.

He pulled his sleeve back down. "The idea is for it not to run out."

The room got quiet again. Everyone knew what it meant if Joey pushed himself too far with the wand.

"Stick out your hand," Leanora told Joey. He did as he was told. She put her firestone pendant in his palm. "I want you to take this."

Joey looked down at the priceless magical weapon. He was stunned. Leanora's firestone was a Valkov family heirloom that had saved their lives on more than one occasion. Giving it to him was an incredible gesture. "Lea, this is too much. I can't."

"I'm only *lending* it to you," she said. "The idea is for you to bring it back."

"Right. I knew that," Joey said, feeling a little foolish. He should have known she wasn't giving him the stone. She probably wanted to hand it down to her children one day. "I appreciate the offer, but I already have this whole bag of tricks." He lifted the backpack that Shazad's mother had packed for him.

"So? Now you've got one more," Leanora said. "Between that and what's in the bag, you've got no excuse to use the wand. Not unless it's absolutely necessary."

"Don't you need the stone? What if I lose it?"

Leanora's eyes narrowed.

"You'd better not," her father said. "Then *she'll* kill you."

Joey put the pendant around his neck. "Thank you. I'll put it to good use." He held up his right hand as if swearing a vow. "After I use the wand to get everyone where they're going, I'll put it away. Emergencies only from now on. I promise."

"Be sure to hold him to that," Leanora's mother told the children. "Fortunately, you don't need to send us anywhere," she added to Joey. "We made our own travel arrangements."

Leanora's father flashed his palms. At first they were empty, but the second time he opened them, a golden door-knob with a red ruby in the handle appeared in his hand. It was another prized Valkov family possession, this one with the power to turn any doorway into a magic portal. "Can we help you get where you're going?" he asked Shazad's parents.

31

"No, thank you," Shazad's father replied. "Shazad's brother is waiting for us at home. That's our first stop. We'll collect him and depart from Jorako."

Leanora's father offered his hand. "Good luck."

Shazad's father gave it a hearty shake. "To all of us."

The grown-ups said their farewells, first to each other and then to their children. As Joey watched everyone embrace and tell one another not to worry, he wished he could have had a proper goodbye with his parents, but he also knew leaving things the way he had was the only option. The number of red eyes in the room confirmed even families who understood magic as a daily reality couldn't help but worry at a time like this. But they let their children go and left to do their part.

Eventually, only the four children were left in Redondo's old office. Everyone looked at each other. The awesome scope of what they were about to do hung heavy in the air between them.

Janelle broke the silence. "Everybody ready to make history?"

"Ready or not, it's showtime," Leanora said.

Joey held up the wand. "Guess I better say the magic words."

"What do you have in mind?" Shazad asked. "Anything special?"

"Let's see. . . ."

Joey never planned out what he was going to say before he used the wand. It was always something that came to him in the spur of the moment. Either a single word or a turn of phrase that signaled what he wanted to do, captured how he felt at the time, or had real meaning for him. Past choices had been old-timey, modern, and everything in between. Movie quotes and tag lines were not out of the question. Joey's spontaneous method had not been Redondo's approach to wielding the wand, but it was his way of making magic and bringing his imagination to life. As he and his friends prepared to embark on the adventure of a lifetime, there was only one thing he wanted to say.

"You guys are the best friends I've ever had." Joey waved the wand. "Godspeed."

A light appeared at Leanora's and Shazad's feet. It swirled around them as if it were alive, growing brighter with every revolution until it was so intense that Joey and Janelle had to shield their eyes. When the light blinked out and they lowered their hands, Shazad and Leanora were gone. The world's last night without magic had officially begun.

2

The Thirteenth Floor

"How do you feel?" Janelle asked Joey.

He checked his arm. The green power meter glowed as it went down a tiny, almost imperceptible amount. "I'm fine. See?" He held his arm out for her to see. "That was hardly anything."

"Good." Janelle rubbed her hands together, eager to follow in the others' footsteps. "Our turn now."

"Right." Joey tucked the wand up his sleeve and strapped his backpack on his back. Rather than use the wand to send them on their way, he used a cane to hook a latch in the attic door above their heads. A set of stairs folded out from behind it. Joey and Janelle went up through the opening and came out through a trapdoor in the stage floor down below. After that they lowered themselves into the orchestra pit and walked up the aisle toward the lobby. When they got there, Joey paused a moment, struck by the sight of the old posters of Redondo that still hung on the walls. He needed a second to psych himself up before he took another step. At that moment, Shazad was hiking across a city-size iceberg in the Arctic Ocean and Leanora was climbing an active volcano in the North Pacific, but he and Janelle had the most perilous journey of all. They had to cross the street.

For Joey, it meant going back to where it all began. The place where he had first encountered magic and the Invisible Hand: the headquarters of the National Association of Tests and Limits. Joey's life had changed in so many ways since that fateful day. He had learned about the world and how it really worked—or didn't work—and what the people in the building across the street had to do with it. Joey had extensively researched Ledger DeMayne's day job at the NATL, where he went by the alias Mr. Black. In the course of his investigation, Joey discovered that the NATL was not a private company, but rather a subsidiary of a much larger entity called Consolidated Global Interests. CGI was a sprawling corporate empire, the biggest and most powerful company in the world. It was also a front for the Invisible

Hand, which explained why it was almost impossible to find anything written about it anywhere. What Joey was able to find confirmed that the NATL building was actually the CGI building, and the man in charge of it all was responsible for a lot worse than manipulated test scores. Joey and Janelle were going to break into his office, and the plan couldn't have been simpler: They were going to walk in the front door.

"It's funny," Joey said as they approached the dark tower. "The first time I saw this place, it made me think of a super-villain's fortress."

"Very perceptive of you," Janelle replied, reaching for the door.

"Comic books taught me well."

The main entrance of the CGI building was locked, which came as no surprise. There was a security guard at a desk behind the glass doors. She wasn't terribly interested in Joey or Janelle and barely looked up from her phone when they tried to get in. "I was hoping I wouldn't have to use this thing," Joey said, making a face as he took the Hand of Glory out of his backpack. It was the severed left hand of a thief, mummified and bloodless, but no less disgusting for all that. Joey had first come across the item in Transylvania a year ago. He and his friends had gone back to retrieve it after their quest for Camelot had ended. Joey hated it there, but going through Dracula's castle was much easier the second time around, once they knew there were no real vampires inside. Unfortunately, touching the Hand of Glory never got any easier for Joey. It was wrapped in a cloth. He had wanted to use a ziplock bag for it, but Janelle was dead set against single-use plastics with no exceptions. "Ugh," he said, wrapping his fingers around the wrist like a handle. "So gross."

Suddenly, he could see as clearly as if it were 10:00 a.m., but that wasn't why Joey needed the hand. In addition to granting its holder the ability to see in the dark, a Hand of Glory had the power to unlock any door. Joey tapped the fingers of the hand against the pane of glass in front of him and heard a latch click. He and Janelle pushed through the revolving doors and strolled into the lobby.

Now the security guard took an interest in them.

"Excuse me! The building's closed. You kids can't come in here," she said, striding toward them. As Joey wrapped the hand back up, the guard pushed past him to inspect the door. "How'd you even get this open? It was locked. I know I locked it."

She was a tough-looking woman who clearly took her job seriously and would have been intimidating under normal circumstances, but these were anything but normal circumstances.

"Don't worry about it," Janelle told her. "We're just here to pick something up."

"Pick something up? What are you talking about?"

"We'll be in and out. Ten minutes tops."

The security guard snorted out a laugh. "Try ten seconds tops. Play time's over kids. Let's go. You can't be here right now."

"Yes, we can," Janelle said, polishing a red ruby brooch that was pinned to the lapel of her jacket. A crimson glow appeared on the guard's face. "It's okay, really."

The more the guard stared at the jewel, the more her eyes went blank. Eventually, a red glow appeared in the center of her pupils, and she said, "It's okay." Her voice was completely monotone. Any trace of confrontation had been drained out of it.

"We have an important meeting on the thirteenth floor," Janelle told her.

"You . . . have a meeting upstairs."

"And we don't want to be late."

The guard nodded slowly, staring at the jewel. "You'd better hurry," she said. She gestured toward the elevator bank with a sweeping motion. "This way, please."

Joey and Janelle followed the guard to the elevators. She kept looking back at Janelle's red ruby brooch as she walked, unable to take her eyes off it for more than a few seconds at a time. The enchanted crystal, which made people very susceptible to suggestion, was another new addition to the Order of the Majestic's arsenal. It had previously belonged to a woman called Scarlett, who had been part of the Invisible Hand. She had used the sparkling relic against Shazad in Transylvania, but lost it after a confrontation in the Amazon on the road to Camelot. By the time that adventure was over, Scarlett would suffer more grievous losses, including the ability to do magic altogether. She had no further use for the ruby, so Joey, Shazad, Leanora, and Janelle had made a special trip to South America to find it. It took the better part of a week and an exhaustive grid search of the area surrounding a village that had been completely swallowed up by the jungle, but in the end, they'd reclaimed the magic item from the rain forest. Janelle was the one who had found the gem, and she had taken quite a shine to it. So had the guard, but in a very different way, and not one that she would ever understand.

When they reached the elevator, Janelle told the guard to stay in the lobby. "You're doing an excellent job," she added.

The guard lit up, clearly very proud of herself. "I'm doing an excellent job."

"As soon as these doors close, you're going to forget about us and go back to your desk."

The security guard nodded as if accepting an order. "As soon as these doors close, I'm going to—"

The elevator doors shut, cutting her off midsentence. Joey hit the button for the fourteenth floor. "Nice work with the Jedi mind trick. That couldn't have gone any better."

"I'm not using the Force," Janelle said with a little side-eye. "It's hypnosis. I did the research on this. The induction phase—flashing the ruby—quiets the part of the brain involving sensory perception and emotional response. The suggestion phase—telling the guard what to do—counteracts unhelpful and unwanted behavior."

"Janelle, just admit it. You're using a magic ruby."

"I'm using it as a catalyst for a well-studied and legitimate form of treatment by medical doctors and therapists."

Joey had to laugh. Despite everything Janelle had seen and been a part of, her scientific instincts died hard. Over the last year, she had been able to use a variety of magical objects, but only when she was able to view them through the lens of some kind of scientific principle. "You might have to rethink the way you look at magic before this is all over."

"I don't have a limited view of magic," Janelle argued. "If anything, I have a bigger view. My view *includes* science. I don't see them as opposites. Magic is just science we don't understand yet."

Joey put his hands up. "If that helps you." He had heard this argument before. "Go with it until it stops working."

Joey stared at a digital screen on the wall in front of him. It was installed just above the buttons for each floor and cycled through images, stats, and corporate slogans while he and Janelle debated the fine line between magic and science. It was all public-friendly PR stuff from the many businesses CGI owned and operated. As usual, there wasn't a single mention of CGI to be found in any of it. Even in their own

41

building the company kept a low profile. CGI was a massive conglomerate that spanned every major industry on earth, including financial services, energy, media, education, transportation, aeronautics, technology, and arms manufacturing. They were so big that in some countries, it was hard for Joey to tell where the national government ended and CGI began, but somehow, they managed to fly almost completely under the world's radar. Consolidated Global Interests was not a name people knew. It was a holding corporation that owned a lot of other companies, including the bank that had acquired the accounting firm where Joey's father worked. When Joey thought about the motives behind that transaction, he was grateful that Ledger DeMayne no longer knew who he was. There was no business reason for an enterprise the size of CGI to buy Joey's father's tiny firm. It could only have been done to gain leverage and influence over Joey. That was how Ledger DeMayne stayed on top of the world— by exercising influence from the shadows. He was always two steps ahead, pulling strings from behind the scenes to manipulate events to his advantage. CGI was a far-reaching spiderweb that covered the globe, and DeMayne sat at the center, connected to everything. Wherever and whenever magic appeared in the world, he and his Invisible Hand cronies would skitter across the web to get there first, wrap it up, and vanish before anyone knew what had happened.

Ironically, it was the acquisition of his father's firm that had tipped Joey off to CGI's existence. That and the fact that the company's corporate headquarters had the same address as the NATL. Once Joey started digging, he even found an article that mentioned Ledger DeMayne by name, or more accurately, his fake name. It was buried in the middle of a news story about another one of CGI's curious acquisitions. The article had credited "John Black" as the force behind several unconventional business decisions that had paid off surprisingly well and noted that he was rarely seen outside his thirteenth-floor office, where he was always hard at work plotting the company's next big move.

The elevator bell dinged, announcing the fourteenth floor. It was an unwritten rule that no building in New York should have a thirteenth floor. The numbers in every elevator Joey had ever been in skipped from twelve to fourteen because of pure superstition, and everyone just accepted it as normal. Joey viewed it as proof that people still had the capacity for magical thinking. Even the most pragmatic, fact-based designers and architects understood that no one wanted to live or work on a floor with such an unlucky number, and they constructed the world accordingly. At least, that's how it was in Western culture. Joey wondered if buildings in China skipped the fourth floor, which was an unlucky number in Chinese culture. Either way, Joey understood that a belief in unknowable, unprovable things impacted people's lives and behavior every day all over the world, and that knowledge gave him hope.

When the elevator doors parted, Joey and Janelle stepped out into a dark and quiet space. The lights flickered on, triggered by motion sensors, revealing an open office floor plan with rows of empty desks and blank monitors. Private offices and conference rooms lined the perimeter of the floor. They all had glass walls that offered no privacy. Joey and Janelle took a moment to survey the scene. It was all very corporate, sterile, and boring. "I expected something different," Janelle said.

"Me too," Joey said. "I was here before, back when this was a testing center. It didn't look anything like this."

"They could have renovated."

"Maybe." Joey pictured the floor filled with employees during the day. He couldn't imagine Ledger DeMayne spending any amount of time crowded in with the people who worked here. He was the kind of guy who would have wanted his space. And the glass-walled offices were a non-starter. DeMayne was allergic to transparency. Joey knew right then and there he was in the wrong place. DeMayne's office, assuming he really had one, would be something fancier. More exclusive. Special. He returned to the elevators and hit the call button.

"What's wrong?" Janelle asked as the doors opened up.

"This isn't it."

Back in the elevator, Joey hit the button for the lobby, taking the car down. "Don't worry. We're not leaving. I've got an idea." As soon as the digital display with the floor numbers started to change, he activated the emergency brake. Joey did it right after the number fourteen dimmed out but just before the number twelve lit up, effectively halting the car in between the two floors. He hit the "doors open" button a few times, but nothing happened.

"Need a hand?" Janelle asked. It took a split second for Joey to realize she was talking about the one in his bag.

He groaned, forced to use the Hand of Glory a second

time. Joey took it out and tapped it against the elevator doors. They opened immediately.

"Whoa," Janelle said, her lips forming a surprised O.

"Whoa is right," Joey agreed. "*This* is the thirteenth floor."

Outside the elevator was an impossibly large space with a fifty-foot ceiling, which was especially noteworthy as the floor they had just left was fifteen feet away at most. A jet-black bridge ran out from the threshold of the door, extending at least a hundred yards. Beneath the bridge, there was darkness, smoke, and as far as Joey could see, no floor. Across the room, a series of massive beams rose out of the abyss, curving over the bridge to form a partial tunnel. At the end of the tunnel was a door.

"Where did all this come from?" Janelle asked.

"Don't ask me. All I know is that's where we've got to go." Joey pointed to the door. "It's not that far."

As soon as they set foot on the bridge, there was a sound like a giant switch being thrown from "off" to "on," and the whole room lit up with an ominous red glow. Joey and Janelle froze in place.

"So much for sneaking in unnoticed," Janelle said.

Joey looked around to see if anyone was coming to get them. There was no one there, but there was also no way out. The elevator doors had closed behind them and faded away, becoming part of the wall. *No turning back*, Joey thought. *What else is new?* In the crimson light, he scanned the room for threats. Joey couldn't put his finger on it, but something about the walls bothered him. He ran his hand over the smooth, shiny black stones that the elevator doors had transformed into. They were the size of shipping crates. Stacked with geometric precision, they covered the room except for one spot. One of the stones was missing. Joey was so busy staring at the hole in the wall, he almost didn't see the stone that had recently vacated that space. It was barreling down the bridge, about to run him over.

"LOOK OUT!"

Janelle leaped forward and swung the Staff of Sorcero into the giant block. Sparks flew as she cleaved it in two, saving Joey's life.

"Every action has an equal and opposite reaction," Janelle said, citing Newton's third law of motion. "This staff, whatever it's made of, absorbs kinetic energy and redirects it. The more things you hit with the staff, the stronger it gets. Right?"

"Right!" Joey said distractedly. He wasn't sure if Janelle's explanation was scientifically accurate, or just a rationalization on her part, but he wasn't complaining. "That works. Let's go with that."

He took a deep breath, still processing his narrow escape as Janelle spun the staff around, ready for the next assault. As Joey watched the two halves of the block fall away and disappear into the darkness below the bridge, he shared Shazad's gratitude that the staff had been returned. He and Janelle were going to need it.

All around, Joey saw the mighty stone blocks that made up the walls rattling in their sockets, getting loose. This was the building's real security system, and he had a feeling it was far more effective at stopping intruders than the guard in the lobby, however tough she might have been. They were going to need more than Janelle's red ruby to cross the bridge. Joey gripped the orange gemstone Leanora had given him tight in his fist, hoping it would be enough.

"Ready?"

Janelle moved aside as Joey charged up the firestone. "After you."

With his fist glowing like the embers of a fire, Joey

stepped forward. He didn't get two feet before another black stone broke free of the wall and swooped down to the bridge, headed straight for him. Joey planted his feet as the block closed in and fired a blazing punch into its center, blasting it to bits. His fist still crackling with energy, he shuffled to the left and threw his arm out to the right, backhanding a second stone that was already upon him. Rock fragments, big and small, flew out in every direction. Joey had to turn away to shield his eyes, and when he looked back, a third stone was seconds away. He wasn't ready for it. Fortunately, Janelle was. She darted ahead of Joey, stabbing the end of her staff into the stone, destroying it before it reached him.

"That's two you owe me," Janelle said.

"Something tells me I'll get the chance to pay you back." The next salvo of large stones was on its way.

Janelle's eyes widened. "Go!"

They took off running down the bridge. The blocks came down with a vengeance, coming at them from all sides. Joey and Janelle fought their way forward, covering each other's backs as they went. Joey drove his fist through block after block, and the Staff of Sorcero became a blur as Janelle swung it back and forth, obliterating every obstacle in her path. It was a tough slog, but they were making progress, and Joey felt himself getting the hang of it. He was just hitting his stride when the room tilted sideways. After that, it went upside down.

"Talk about an unexpected twist," Joey said, surprised to find his feet still anchored to the bridge. "You okay?" he asked Janelle.

"Trying to concentrate here," she answered, slicing through a stone the size of a buffalo. From Joey's point of view, the broken pieces of the stone seemed to fall up, rather than down. It was a disorienting optical illusion, which of course was the whole point of flipping the room. Joey forced himself to stay focused on the blocks and keep going. It wasn't easy fighting while inverted, but he took some solace in the fact that it was nearly over. The wall was running out of stones to throw at them. Soon there was nothing left but a couple of rows of stone blocks on either side of the bridge. Joey breathed a sigh of relief, but that feeling was short-lived.

A sound like a freight train running over tracks at a high speed echoed through the room as the wall rebuilt itself. Stonework unfolded like an accordion, and within seconds, a fully replenished wall was ready to start over at square one.

"I can't keep this up forever," Janelle said to Joey. He could hear the strain in her voice.

"I don't think we're meant to," Joey replied, also running out of steam. He felt like a character in a video game moving up to a more difficult level, but he and Janelle didn't have three lives. He thought about using the wand, but he didn't want to go there yet. He had to use its power sparingly, or he wouldn't live through this adventure. Of course, he wasn't likely to live through getting crushed or knocked off the bridge either. He was still going back and forth on what to do when every piece of the wall came alive at once. The giant stone blocks hovered in the air, poised to overwhelm Joey and Janelle in a simultaneous barrage. The two friends looked at each other in terror.

"RUN!" Janelle screamed.

They made a break for the tunnel covering the door at the end of the bridge. Joey sprinted after Janelle, finding cover just in time. The blocks rained down like a meteor shower, crashing against the beams and breaking apart. Fragments shot through the gaps in between the beams, pelting Joey and Janelle with rock particles and covering them in dust. Joey fumbled in his bag for the Hand of Glory as he ran. He no longer cared how gross it was. In fact, Joey couldn't wait to slap the dead hand's palm against the door. Unfortunately, a chunk of rock the size of a bowling ball came through at the last second to knock his backpack out of his hands. Joey's stomach lurched as he watched the bag, and the many magical items it contained, go over the side of the bridge.

"Shazad's going to kill me."

"I don't think he's going to get the chance." Janelle wrestled with the door. Naturally, it was locked.

This time Joey didn't hesitate. He pulled the wand out of his sleeve and thrust it forward.

"No!" Janelle shouted, stepping into Joey's path. She swung the Staff of Sorcero as hard as she could. Sparks flew and the door splintered around the doorknob. She pushed it open and reached for Joey's hand. With no idea what they were getting into next, they dove for safety as the walls came crashing down.

3

Office Party

Joey and Janelle landed in darkness. Outside on the bridge, the tunnel was still getting shelled, so Janelle kicked out with her foot to close the door behind them. After that, everything went quiet. The bombardment finally stopped. Exhausted from their ordeal, Joey and Janelle allowed themselves a moment to lie on the floor in silence. It seemed they were out of danger. For the time being, at least.

"You were going to use the wand," Janelle said to Joey after she caught her breath. It was an accusation.

He sat up and put the wand away, guilty as charged. "I know."

"You said you wouldn't do that. You promised."

"Emergencies only, I said. You don't think the situation qualified?"

"'Emergencies only' means last resort. It doesn't qualify unless you try every other option first. You weren't going to try any."

"Did you see me lose my bag out there? That could have been my head. Or yours! I didn't want to find out the hard way that the staff wouldn't cut it. Fortunately, it did." Joey stood up and looked around. The broken door let in a little light but not much. "Let's not argue about it. It's over, and I didn't have to use the wand." He reached out a hand to help Janelle up. "Thanks to you."

Janelle took Joey's hand. "Nothing's over. We're just getting started. You need to be more careful."

"I know. Let's get some light in here," Joey said. He flipped the light switch, and the office building's modern, corporate environment returned. They were in a posh executive suite with an incredibly soft gray carpet. Joey could feel its cushion and bounce through his sneakers. It was like standing on a pillow. The room had a minimalist design. Black walls with dark wood accents and no artwork hung anywhere. Floor-to-ceiling windows that wrapped around the office gave its occupants something better to look at. The scene outside the windows was not one that could be found outside the thirteenth, or even the fourteenth, floor of any building in Midtown Manhattan. Somehow their vantage point was higher, looking down on the spire of the Empire State Building and all the way out to the Freedom Tower at the southern tip of the city. Odd as it was, Joey didn't give it a second thought. There was magic at work, and he'd seen stranger things. Much stranger.

He gravitated toward the desk, which was empty save for a blank notepad, a paperweight, some papers, and a business card holder. A wall of flat-screen TVs filled the space behind the desk, which Joey found excessive. He couldn't help but notice the office was twice the size of his living room back home with a much nicer sitting area. Leather couches and comfortable chairs were arranged around a coffee table on the far side of the room. In the corner, a bar tray shaped like a globe was stocked with what Joey assumed were very expensive bottles.

"Nobody home," Janelle said. She spun the Staff of Sorcero around counterclockwise, shrinking it back down to the size of a baton. Joey didn't ask Janelle what the science behind that move was. If she overthought it, she might not be able to do it again. She took a shiny black bag the size of a pillowcase out of her inside jacket pocket and shook it out. "Think we'll be able to get what we came for?"

"We'll get our chance. Just don't let your guard down," Joey warned. "Stay frosty." He had put the firestone pendant back around his neck, but he stood ready to grab it at a moment's notice.

"Stay frosty?" Janelle tried out the phrase with a smirk. "What movie is that one from?"

"Not everything I say is a line from a movie."

Janelle raised an eyebrow and waited.

Joey sighed. "*Aliens. Battlestar Galactica. Call of Duty.* Take your pick."

Janelle snickered. "I like how you mixed in a video game reference this time."

"This *is* the boss level."

Janelle walked past the couches, glancing at the business magazines and financial trades on the coffee table. "It's not what I expected."

"Not at all," Joey agreed. "You have to run some kind of extra-dimensional gauntlet to get here, but then once you're inside . . . ," Joey trailed off, shaking his head. "I thought it would look like Dr. Strange's mansion in the village or a

Death Eater's lair, not some boring banker's office."

"The wall of TVs is kind of Bond-villain-esque," Janelle said.

"I guess." Joey found the remote and hit the power button. The TVs flickered on, but Joey muted the screens before the volume kicked in.

"What are you doing?"

"I want to see what he watches." The TVs were each set to a different news channel. The stories that flashed across the screens were all too familiar. Wildfires in Australia and California. Red skies up and down the West Coast, which made it look like Mars. Polar ice caps melting. Oil spills and pollution. Hurricanes, tornadoes, droughts, and floods, and that was just the tip of the rapidly disappearing iceberg. Everywhere Joey looked, the planet was dying, and no one was doing anything about it.

He shut the TVs off. He had seen enough.

The world needed saving, and not just from the Invisible Hand. Magic was the key. Joey thought about all the polluting industries people tolerated . . . the fossil fuels that the world couldn't live without . . . By this time tomorrow, they would all be made obsolete. After all, who needs oil when you've got magic? It was the ultimate sustainable solution. Limitless, clean energy, just waiting to be tapped. There was only one catch. People had to believe in it.

That was where Joey and his friends came in. They were going to shake the world out of the state of learned helplessness it was in and introduce new possibilities. New wonders. Like Shazad's mother had said, people needed to be shocked into a new way of thinking. As far as Joey was concerned, it was the only way to save the world from itself. People needed change they could believe in. The Order of the Majestic was going to give it to them, but they couldn't do it alone.

Janelle crossed the room to the desk and picked up a business card from a stack in a silver container. It identified Ledger DeMayne as CGI's executive vice president of strategic development, operating under the alias John Black. "Why not CEO?" she asked, showing the card to Joey.

"Not his style. He'd rather be the guy behind the guy. The power behind the throne. From here, he pulls CGI's strings."

Joey continued to explore the room. There wasn't much to see. There were no trophies or bookshelves with interesting relics placed among the books. There was nothing that seemed to be of any real value to them in their quest for information. Nothing they could learn from. DeMayne didn't even have a computer.

Janelle went through the desk drawers and found a black leather journal. She took it out and started looking through it.

"Anything juicy in there?" Joey asked after a few seconds.

Janelle bunched up her lips, scanning the pages quickly. "Nothing we didn't already know or suspect. It *does* confirm that DeMayne had a hand in the NSA and DARPA taking over our energy project at Caltech last year. And, he's got 'Fixed News' media running counterprogramming against Camelot, calling it a hoax."

"No surprises there," Joey said.

Janelle kept reading. "Listen to this: 'Blackhart Protection, a subsidiary of CGI Military Solutions, to recall ten thousand private security contractors from assignment in the Arctic Ocean and North Pacific due to inactivity and reduced threat level at target sites.'" She closed the book. "That's good news."

"Nice to know we were right about that," Joey said. "It should make Shazad's and Leanora's lives a lot easier tonight."

At the moment, Joey and his friends had the element of surprise on their side. Hypnova had erased DeMayne's memory of them outside Camelot, and for the last year, they had been free to do as they pleased without drawing the attention of the Invisible Hand. That advantage had been a game changer, allowing the Order to mount an offensive for the first time since Houdini.

Joey spotted a game board set up on a small table behind the desk. He had missed it on his first lap around the room, but now it stood out to him as an item of interest. He approached the board. It was a thick, round slab of dark marble with concentric circles growing out from the center in fading shades of gray. There were five tokens on the board, each about the size of a standard chess piece. They were carved out of different materials and came in different colors. Two of them, the red ruby and gray stone pieces, had been set on their sides as if lost or captured. Joey wondered if they represented Scarlett and Grayson Manchester. The remaining pieces were black obsidian, white ivory, and what to Joey's untrained eye appeared to be a flawless diamond. Joey picked up the crystal and ivory pieces and studied them closely. Ledger DeMayne had once referred to the struggle for control over the world's supply of magic as "the great game." Joey assumed the black piece was DeMayne, but these other two were question marks. He wondered who they were.

Joey set the pieces back down, but unfortunately, he wasn't careful to put them back where he found them. He placed them in the center circle, and suddenly there were two new people in the room. Janelle hit him in the shoulder, her eyes the size of gobstoppers.

"Joey. Heads up. We've got company."

Joey took a step back, but there was nowhere to go. He had the window behind him, and the two men who had just materialized out of thin air were standing in front of the office door, blocking the only way out.

Joey, Janelle, and the two strangers stood there in silence. Everyone seemed equally surprised to be there staring at each other. Joey didn't know who the two men were, but he knew they were trouble. He got a bad vibe from both of them. One of them was six feet tall, muscular, and well dressed, sporting a shirt, a tie, and a stylish patterned vest. He wore a flashy watch, some large rings, and had a little pouch at his waist attached to a thin gold chain. He was bald but had a thick, well-groomed beard. He was handsome but intimidating. His sleeves were rolled up to the elbows, and his pink skin was covered with tattoos. The other man wore a heavy coat with a fuzzy collar and a scarf that was wrapped around his neck and tucked into a sweater. Joey thought he looked like he belonged in a ski lodge. His face was thin, and his skin was pale, almost to an unhealthy degree. He had light blond hair that was so fair it was almost white and striking blue eyes, but the dark circles underneath softened their glow. Joey noticed a bracelet on the wrist of his left hand with a single clear stone.

"Mr. Ivory?" the man in the winter coat said to the man with the beard. When he spoke, Joey saw his breath form an icy white vapor.

"Mr. Clear," the bearded man replied, recognizing his counterpart. "This is a surprise." He eyed Joey and Janelle with an air of reserved curiosity. "I was just about to say I hate when the big man calls us in like this, but the big man's not here, is he? What's this about? I wonder."

Joey looked back and forth between the two men and the game board. Hearing them say their names out loud, he knew he had messed up big-time. They were part of the

Invisible Hand, and he was responsible for bringing them there. He was about to move the pieces back to their original places when the man in the parka, Mr. Clear, stopped him.

"Freeze."

He reached out a hand, and the stone on his bracelet sparkled with light. The next thing Joey knew, his own hand was encased in a block of ice. It fell heavy to his side before he got near the board.

"Don't do that," Mr. Clear said in what sounded to Joey like a Norwegian or Swiss accent. Maybe it was German. He didn't know. Mr. Clear cursed and zipped up his coat, muttering, "Unbelievable. I was just starting to warm up."

"Why don't we all take a step back from the game board?" said the larger of the two men, Mr. Ivory. He motioned with his hands, and Joey and Janelle did as they were told. "After all, we just got here. You two called us here. You can't go pulling the rug out from under our feet without even saying hello. That would be rude."

Janelle and Joey huddled close together. She looked at his hand in concern and asked him with her eyes if he was all right. He nodded. His hand was freezing, but he didn't want to do anything rash. Not until he knew more about

Mr. Ivory and Mr. Clear. They weren't part of the plan.

Mr. Ivory went to inspect the pieces on the game board. He pointed at Joey, assuming he was the one who had moved them. "You moved the pieces and brought us here," he guessed. "How did you know how this worked?"

"I didn't," Joey said. "I was just . . . I was standing there and . . . I don't know what happened. I . . ." He was rambling, trying to figure out what to say and how to play this. Eventually, he went with the truth. "I was wondering who those game pieces were supposed to be. I put them in the center and boom. There you were. Just like that."

"Just like that." Mr. Ivory nodded. "Very interesting. Who are you? If you don't mind me asking." He looked at Janelle. "I heard you call him Joey, but I didn't catch your name. What are you two doing here?"

Joey and Janelle said nothing.

"Are you lost?" Mr. Ivory pressed.

Mr. Clear opened the door and looked outside. "They broke in."

Mr. Ivory took a peek at the wreckage out in the hallway. "Look at that. You came in the hard way. That's impressive. But, again . . . I'm wondering what you're doing here. Why would you go through all that? Do you have any idea where you are right now? Whose office you're in? What do you think this place is?"

Joey shot a quick look at Janelle and gave a tight, almost imperceptible shake of his head. He didn't want to give up any information if he could help it. Maybe they could play dumb and talk their way out of this.

The subtle exchange between Joey and Janelle didn't go unnoticed. "Look at you two, being all sneaky." Mr. Ivory laughed. "Come on, you obviously know something about magic. My friend here turned your hand into an ice cube and you didn't bat an eye. The question is, what do you know about us? Because you definitely know *something*. It's all right. You can tell me," he said, his tone softening as if he were trying to put them at ease. It wasn't working. "Here's what I'm thinking: Maybe you heard rumors about this place, found out a few secrets, and wanted to learn more. Maybe you came here to join up and be Company Men like us. And Company Women," he added, nodding to Janelle. "That wouldn't be the worst thing in the world. We could use some new blood. But, then again, it could be you're here for a different reason." Mr. Ivory's eyes narrowed. "It could be you're the people we've been looking for. The ones who caused all that trouble last year. The big man's been working awful hard trying to figure out who dropped Camelot smack-dab in the middle of an English meadow. Maybe there's a reason he missed you." Mr. Ivory tapped Mr. Clear on the shoulder. "Just a theory, but I think we've got some new players in this game. Very new by the looks of it."

Mr. Clear shook his head. "That can't be. They're just . . . children." His tone and expression changed midsentence, like he'd just realized something.

"What is it?" Mr. Ivory asked.

"That ruby she's got on her lapel there . . . Scarlett had one just like it."

Mr. Ivory's eyebrows went up. "I remember Scarlett. Haven't seen her in a while."

Mr. Clear made a fist. The stone on his bracelet lit up again, and the red ruby froze and cracked in place. Janelle let out a yelp as she brushed frost off her shoulder, and fragments of the ruby fell to the floor, ruined.

"Nice work, Mr. Clear," said Mr. Ivory. "You're two for two."

Mr. Clear seemed to derive no pleasure from his partner's compliment. He just shivered and blew on his hands, trying to warm them up. He looked very uncomfortable.

"I should have known," Mr. Ivory said. "Never underestimate children. It'll be the death of you. I ever tell how I got started in this business?" he asked Mr. Clear. "Wasn't much older than they are at the time."

"I think there's some mistake here," Joey said. "I don't know . . . We don't know what you're talking about."

Mr. Ivory put a finger up. "I wasn't finished." He took a breath and went on in an even tone. "Please don't interrupt. It's not polite."

Mr. Ivory crossed the room to the bar in the globe. "Where was I?" He removed the top from one of the bottles and sniffed at it. "Oh yes, how I got started. I was young and foolish like you. Back in those days, kids used to bully me. Picked on me something terrible. I was a scrawny child. People are always surprised to hear that, but it's true. When I stood sideways, people thought I disappeared."

Mr. Ivory put some ice in a tumbler glass and poured himself a drink. "One day a bunch of kids were taking a hike in the woods near the place where I grew up. When they asked me to come along, I was thrilled. I was over the moon." Mr. Ivory raised his tumbler to his lips and took a sip. "I should've known better."

"What happened?" Joey asked, trying to buy time. He knew the story wasn't going to have a happy ending, but Joey wanted to keep Mr. Ivory talking while he thought about his next move.

"They ditched me. That was their plan from the start. Fun, right? They left me out there. I got turned around trying to find my way back, and I had to spend the night alone. I was wandering around lost and scared, and someone found me, just like we found you. It was a woman. This old lady of the forest people talked about. She took me back to a shack, deep in the woods. Deeper than I'd ever been before. Problem was, this particular old lady was a witch, and wouldn't you know it, she was fixing to eat me. Being skinny saved my life, because she wanted to fatten me up first. It was a real Hansel and Gretel situation. Difference was, her house wasn't made out of candy." He paused and took another sip of his drink. "Her house was made out of bones.

"Of course, I knew from the start something was wrong, but what was I gonna do? I couldn't get away. I couldn't get home by myself. Almost a week I was there, with this woman doing her best to turn me into a decent meal. She had her eyes on me every second. I couldn't get free, but I kept my eyes open too. I was looking for something I could use to save myself, and I found it. No spoilers there—I wouldn't be standing here otherwise. But here's the twist. You might be wondering why I'm Mr. Ivory and not my pasty friend here. It's because of my teeth." Mr. Ivory smiled wide, showing off a bright, flawless smile with the exception of one empty space. He was missing a tooth. A big one right next to his two front teeth. "The old lady had a whole bag of teeth. A special bag. I stole 'em. And I used 'em. Had to pull one of my own teeth out first. I didn't think I was strong enough for that, but you'd be surprised what you can do when your life is on the line."

Janelle covered her mouth, clearly disturbed by the story. "That's . . . horrible."

Joey shuddered, trying not to picture the gruesome, desperate scene from Mr. Ivory's childhood. He didn't want that image in his head. At the same time, a morbid sense of curiosity compelled him to find out how the story ended. "I know I'm going to regret asking this, but what do you mean you used the teeth? Used them to do what?"

"I'm getting to that." Mr. Ivory set his drink down on the desk and reached for the small pouch at his waist. He unhooked it from his belt and fished around inside until he found what he was looking for. He removed a long, sharp tooth from the tiny bag and held it up so everyone could see. "This one's a crocodile tooth." He opened his mouth and pressed the tooth into place, filling in the gap in his smile. "Wait until you see what it does."

The transformation that followed was terrifying, even for people who were used to seeing magic in action, as Joey and Janelle were. They watched as Mr. Ivory's skin hardened, turning green and bumpy. The pupils of his eyes narrowed into slits, and his jaw grew wider to accommodate a mouth full of pointy teeth. He didn't get any bigger, but he was already big and frightening. Now he was downright gruesome.

"Funny thing about that tooth—it tastes like Captain Hook's hand." Mr. Ivory laughed, smacking his lips. "But enough about me. I want to hear about you. Let's start with your names and what you're doing here."

Mr. Ivory took a step toward Joey and Janelle. Janelle reacted quickly and spun the Staff of Sorcero back out to its full length and shifted her feet, adopting a fighting stance. Joey grabbed the firestone with his left hand, charging up his right hand with enough heat to melt and split the block of ice. There was no point in hiding what they could do anymore.

"Ha! What'd I tell you?" Mr. Ivory said to Mr. Clear. "These two came to party."

"Stay back," Joey said.

"What is *that*?" Mr. Clear asked, fascinated by the sight of the firestone, which seemed to be the exact opposite of the gem he carried on his wrist, bringing warmth instead of cold.

"You don't want to find out," Joey warned.

"I think I do," Mr. Clear said with a jealous look in his eye.

"Don't get your hopes up," Mr. Ivory told him. "Big man gets first dibs on anything new. You know that."

"The big man's not here."

"Not yet." Mr. Ivory pointed at the game board.

Joey turned and saw the black obsidian piece moving all

by itself. His stomach tightened as it slid slowly across the marble, inching toward the center. In just a few seconds, the black piece—and the person it represented—would be standing alongside the white and the clear. The fire in Joey's right hand flickered and dimmed. This was *not* how he'd hoped the night was going to go.

The black game piece stopped moving, the office door opened, and in walked Ledger DeMayne, aka Mr. Black, leader of the Invisible Hand. Mr. Clear and Mr. Ivory stepped aside, making room for their boss as he entered and took stock of the room without a word. If he was surprised to find such an eclectic group waiting in his office, he didn't show it. He was unflappable as ever, looking like an evil corporate raider in his million-dollar suit with his wavy blond hair and youthful good looks. His eyes settled instantly on Joey.

"You," he said, squinting, as if he recognized Joey from somewhere but couldn't quite put his finger on where. "I know you . . . don't I?"

Joey didn't like hearing that. He wasn't ready for DeMayne to remember him just yet, and he didn't like to think about what might happen if he stuck around much longer. He wanted to get what he came for and get out of there as fast as possible. There was only one way to do that. He let go of the firestone pendant and went for the wand.

"Don't get mad at me, Janelle, but this is a definite emergency."

4

Surprise Guests

Joey cast two quick spells, and he and Janelle were gone from Ledger DeMayne's office. They blinked out of sight, teleporting away from New York City and out of danger. Seconds later, they materialized on the deck of a strange ship floating in an even stranger location—the sky. Joey had no clue where they were, but when he saw the Caliburn Shield hanging over the door to the captain's cabin, he knew he was in the right place. After all, he hadn't asked the wand to bring him somewhere. He had asked it to bring him to *someone*.

Joey put the wand away and looked around, astounded by the sight of the vessel they had just boarded. The large wooden ship looked like a prop from a pirate ride at a theme park, but it was real. It also had a giant hot air balloon where the mast and sails were supposed to be. The balloon was stitched together from an assortment of fabric patches, covered over with a network of ropes, and strapped to the railing. A large iron cauldron at the stern of the ship blazed with purple flames, filling the balloon with hot air and keeping it aloft.

It was quiet on deck as the ship drifted slowly through the night sky. An endless landscape of dark gray clouds surrounded them, obscuring the ground below.

"Before you say anything, I was always going to use the wand to get us out of there," Joey told Janelle. "It was the only way to get here."

"I'm not complaining this time," Janelle replied, clearly very happy to be far away from the CGI building. "That was a bad scene back there."

"It was about to be." Joey touched a hand to his chest. His heart was racing like a hamster on a wheel. Seeing DeMayne again after all this time had freaked Joey out more than he had expected. He told himself to get it together. "It's okay. We're safe now." He pointed to the shield over the door. "The only thing that can get past that shield is this wand. No one's coming after us."

"That's a relief." Janelle held up the shiny black bag she had pulled out of her pocket back in DeMayne's office. Something was moving around inside it. "I'm going to keep a tight grip on this, just in case."

"Good thinking."

"Any idea where we are?"

"If I had to guess, I'd say someplace very high." The ship passed through a heavy cloud that covered them in a thick mist. "High and foggy," Joey clarified.

Janelle let out a terse laugh. "Glad we've got that sorted out." She looked over the side of the ship, trying to see what she could see. "Not much of a view, is it?"

"Depends on what you're looking at," Joey countered. "This ship is incredible."

"Thank you," said a voice in the fog. "I like it too." Janelle tensed up and moved closer to Joey as a hooded figure came up behind them. "Of course, I should feel that way. It's my home. You two are the first guests I've had in quite some time." The mysterious person pulled back her hood, and Janelle relaxed her stance. "Welcome. I've been expecting you."

"Hypnova," Joey said, relaxing a bit himself. "It's good to see you."

"It's good to see you too. And I don't say that very often."

Joey smiled. In addition to the sense of safety he felt on board Hypnova's ship, he felt a touch of pride knowing he was part of an exclusive club of people who had been allowed to retain his memory of her. Ledger DeMayne had gotten his mind wiped clean after meeting Hypnova, but not Joey. She was exactly as he remembered, dressed in a stylish green and gold outfit with a golden saber on her hip and a cloak on her back. Hypnova had dark brown skin, hazel eyes, and long hair that fell down around her shoulders in thick braids. Janelle went quiet, staring at Hypnova like she was a superhero. Joey understood completely. As far as he was concerned, she basically was a superhero.

"Well? Are you going to introduce me to your friend or not?" Hypnova asked.

"Right! Sorry, this is—"

"Janelle Thomas," Hypnova cut in. She reached out to shake Janelle's hand. "I'm only teasing. I know all about you, Janelle. You're going to be instrumental to our plans this evening."

"Thank you." Janelle reached out to shake Hypnova's hand. "Thank you. It's . . . nice to meet you," she sputtered, no doubt surprised to learn that Hypnova not only knew her but held her in high regard.

For his part, Joey wasn't the least bit surprised. Hypnova had known all about him, Shazad, and Leanora long before they had met too. Hypnova knew things. It was what she did. She was the one who had set everyone on the road to Camelot and helped them understand their true mission as the Order of the Majestic. Joey wondered how much of what they had planned for tonight was his idea and how much of it came from Hypnova. They had not spoken since Camelot, but they had never been fully out of touch. Over the past year, she had left notes for him at the Majestic Theatre, as well as a few helpful items, such as the Staff of Sorcero. Shazad had accidentally left the staff behind in the Himalayas after their first meeting with Hypnova, but she had dropped it off at the theater a few nights later.

Janelle held up the staff. "Shazad wanted us to thank you for bringing this back," she said. It seemed to Joey that Janelle's natural confidence was returning now that the initial shock of meeting Hypnova had worn off a bit.

"Where is Shazad?" Hypnova asked. "And Leanora? We're going to need them tonight too."

"So you know about tonight, then," Joey said, confirming what he had already suspected.

"I have an idea," Hypnova replied.

Joey nodded. "I figured you would. We got here using the memory you gave us. Shazad and Leanora painted the Secret Map of the World on the wall in the theater. The Imagine Nation was on it. The island that Merlin broke off from the lost continent and turned into a refuge for magic."

"Magic and more," Hypnova said.

"It disappeared from the mural after we were done, but it came back a couple of days ago," Joey said.

"That was my doing," Hypnova admitted. "I wanted you to see it. To know it was out there, but I didn't want you to go. Not until it was time."

"You put the image in our heads," Joey said. "Did you put tonight's plan in there too?"

"I don't manipulate the minds of friends," Hypnova said. "I simply gave you access to information. What you do with it is up to you, but I know you well enough to guess your choices. I know what we *want* to do. What I don't know is how we're going to do it. That's your department. Aren't you the creative problem solver?"

"It's not just me. It's all of us." The alarm on Joey's phone started ringing. He took the phone out of his pocket and silenced it. "Speaking of 'all of us.'" Joey pulled the wand back out of his sleeve and waved it at an empty space on the deck of the ship. "Together again."

With that, two tiny balls of light the size of marbles appeared, hovering in midair. They quickly grew to the size of softballs as they went swirling around each other like playful birds. Soon Joey had to squint, the light was so bright. There was a brilliant flash, and he covered up, turning to avoid the glare. When Joey looked back, Shazad and Leanora were standing two feet away.

"There you are," Hypnova said. "What have you two been up to?" She smiled as if she could guess the answer.

Shazad looked like a human Popsicle. He was rubbing his arms to warm up and stamping his feet to shake snow off his body. Leanora took a deep breath and let it out slowly. Her face looked flushed, and she smelled like roasted marshmallows.

"How are you both doing?" Joey asked after everyone said hello. "Leanora, are you okay?"

Leanora straightened up and pushed her hair out of

her eyes. "Of course I'm okay. Why wouldn't I be?"

Joey shrugged. "I don't know. Are your boots supposed to be on fire?" He pointed to the magic footwear Leanora had on her feet. The Winged Boots of Fleetfoot gave her super-speed and let her take up to three steps in the air at a time. At the moment, the soles were blackened and burnt. Tassels on the boots glowed like lit fuses.

"What the—" Leanora twisted around with a jolt and fanned the red-hot boots with her hands. "I had to run across lava," she explained once the amber glow on the tassels faded. "Can you believe it? Lava! I did it, but the boots were ruined. They ran out of magic."

"Looks like you got out of there just in time," Janelle said. "Both of you. How did it go in the arctic?" she asked Shazad.

"M-mission a-c-c-ccomplished." Shazad shivered. "Is that a fire? Do you mind if I just . . . ?" He trailed off on his way over to the blazing cauldron. "That's better," he said a few moments later, warming himself near the purple flames. "How did it go with you two?" he asked Joey and Janelle. "Did you have to use the wand?"

"How did I know you were going to ask me that first thing?" Joey had to laugh at how his friends went straight to business. Nothing ever fazed them, not even the sight of Hypnova's flying ship. "I did use it. Just a little bit. I had to."

Shazad frowned. "How much is a little bit?"

"Not a lot." Joey held out his arm, showing off the green energy bar. It had gone down again as a result of his recent spells, but only a little. It was still very full. "See?"

Leanora looked at Janelle, clearly hoping to get the full story from her. "What happened? What did he do?"

"He hardly used it," Janelle said, backing Joey up. She counted off the moments Joey was forced to use the wand, putting up a finger for each: "He used it once to take us here and once to bring you guys here. . . . He was *going* to use it one other time, but I stopped him, and he used it right before we left to get us out of trouble. However, that was an extreme situation, so I can't fault him for it."

"I can." Leanora folded her arms and lectured Joey with her eyes. "That's four times you used the wand now?"

"Three times," Joey corrected her. "Don't look at me like that. We had the dangerous job, remember?"

"What happened?" Shazad asked. "Are you guys all right?"

"We're fine," Joey said. "But I didn't have a choice. Really. Everything I brought in there . . . all that stuff your mom gave me so I wouldn't need to use the wand? Gone. It fell off a bridge into some kind of void. I've never seen anything like it." Joey held out his arms. Except for the wand, his hands were empty.

Shazad and Leanora went quiet. That got to them.

"Your backpack's gone?" Shazad asked with a pained expression on his face. "You lost everything?"

"I did manage to hang on to this." Joey lifted the firestone pendant, holding it by the string around his neck. Leanora closed her eyes for a second, relieved that the firestone had not also been lost.

Joey felt terrible. He didn't have the heart to tell Shazad that he never even got to use the magical objects in the bag. The priceless collection of items on loan from Shazad's family were not only gone, but they had gone to waste. Joey kicked himself for not using the wand to get across the bridge. If he had, maybe he wouldn't have lost everything else. With the bag gone, he would be forced to rely on the wand more, not less. On top of that, he was dreading Shazad's reaction to the news.

"I don't know what to say," Joey told his friend. "I'm so sorry."

Shazad took a deep breath and let it out. Joey could tell that his friend was trying to remain calm. "It's done. Forget the backpack. I'd rather lose that than lose a friend."

A wave of relief crashed over Joey. He was grateful to Shazad for understanding and genuinely touched by his concern. "I'll make it up to you. I promise. I'll tell your parents what happened. I'll take full responsibility."

"They are going to be . . . quite upset," Shazad said, dreading his parents' reaction. "No!" he added quickly, shaking his head. "I'm not going to worry about that now. You made it out of there safely. That's what matters. I'm just glad you're both okay."

"Thanks, Shazad," Janelle said. "I'm glad we're okay too. All of us. The good news is, Joey didn't lose everything." She held up the shiny black bag. It jumped around in her hands. Something inside it clearly wanted out.

"A Bag of Holding?" Hypnova observed, suddenly very curious. "What have you got in there?"

Joey grinned. "It's a surprise."

Hypnova didn't return the smile. "I don't like surprises, Joey. I like figuring things out. I like knowing things. For example, I know where they were tonight," Hypnova said, indicating Shazad and Leanora. "The dark magic markers vanished from the map shortly before you arrived. I assumed you were all going after them together, but clearly that's not what happened. If they were fighting their way across fire and ice without you, what were you two doing? What was 'the dangerous job'?"

Joey felt that swell of pride again, pleased to discover that some things were beyond even a Secreteer's knowledge. That boded well for the future. "Janelle and I broke into the Invisible Hand's headquarters."

"What?" Hypnova was taken aback. "Why would you go there?"

"We had to pick someone up."

Janelle turned the bag over and dumped it out. Hypnova actually gasped as a grown man fell out of it. He was way too big to fit inside the bag, but that wasn't what shocked her. The bigger surprise had to do with who the man was. He hit the deck of the ship face-first and looked up with murder in his eyes.

"You remember Ledger DeMayne."

5
The Man Who Stole the World

Shazad and Leanora were ready with a rope the second DeMayne came out of the bag. Working together, they wound it around his body, tying his arms to his sides and binding his legs at the knees. Naturally, it was no normal rope they used to restrain him. It wasn't Redondo's old length of Gordian rope, either, which looked impossible to escape but could be easily shrugged off by those who knew how to do it. Instead, they used a shining golden string that reminded Joey of Wonder Woman's lasso. It was called Gleipnir, and it was another treasure borrowed from the Hassan family vault. Gleipnir was an ancient relic of Norse mythology that had once held the great wolf Fenris—or so the story went. The line glowed brightly in the fog, it was stronger than any chain, and it was as thin as a silk ribbon.

According to Norse legend, it was constructed from a list of impossible ingredients, including, among other things, the sound of a cat's footsteps and the breath of a fish.

DeMayne was momentarily disoriented after being held captive in the bag, which allowed Shazad and Leanora to get the drop on him. Hypnova was speechless, watching with her mouth open as they moved quickly to secure him. By the time they were done, DeMayne was bound from head to toe, and Joey felt much more comfortable knowing DeMayne couldn't possibly get free.

"What's going on?" DeMayne slurred as Shazad and Leanora eased him into a sitting position with his back up against the ship's railing. "Get this off me!" he demanded. The group stood over him, looking down as he struggled in vain to free himself. "I'm warning you, release me now or I won't be responsible for what happens next. I swear, I'll kill every last one of—"

DeMayne paused as he seemed to notice for the first time the ambient light on his restraints. He stopped struggling.

"Is this Gleipnir?" he asked.

"You know your relics," Shazad said. "Good. That should save us some time. If you recognize that rope, then you understand the situation you're in. You can't break free, so don't bother trying."

DeMayne ignored Shazad and strained against the glowing rope once more for good measure. It was no use. "I understand the situation," he growled. "Do you?" His eyes shot up with renewed vigor, studying his captors. "If you did, you wouldn't let me see your faces. You'd run. You'd throw yourselves off this ship to escape the punishment you've got coming to you after this . . . I don't even know what to call it. I want to say 'outrage,' but it doesn't seem like a strong enough word." The longer DeMayne went on talking, the more the edge went out of his voice, but Joey knew he was raging beneath the surface. DeMayne was a proud man. Being trapped like this had to be killing him. "I'll tell you what I'm going to do." DeMayne checked his temper and put on a fake smile. "I'm going to be magnanimous. I'm going to give you a chance to reconsider what is clearly the worst decision anyone's ever made. This is a onetime offer. Whoever you are, whatever it is you're after . . . leave it alone. Walk away. Let me go and it's *possible* I could be persuaded to forget what happened here tonight. However, that's if—

and only if—you release me and beg my forgiveness now. Right now. This second. After that, I make no promises, except to say that you have no idea who you're dealing with, and you don't want to find out."

"Actually, we know you better than you think," Joey said. "You may not know who we are, but we know you. That was a pretty good monologue though. Was that your bad-guy intimidation speech? You have that all rehearsed and ready to go?"

DeMayne clenched his jaw. "You really shouldn't taunt me."

"I'll take my chances," Joey told him.

"Chances with your life?" DeMayne snorted. "Such bravado, all of a sudden. You didn't have much to say back in my office with Ivory and Clear."

"We're not in your office anymore, are we? As for your generous onetime offer, we'll pass. You're going to forget about this whether you want to or not."

Joey could sense DeMayne's frustration as he tried to figure out where he knew him from. It was clear he still had no memory of Joey or anyone else on deck. "I want answers and I want them now," he said, still trying again to take control of the situation. "Why did you bring me here? *How* did you bring me here? What's going on?"

"That's what I'd like to know," Hypnova said.

"This is your absolute last chance to untie this rope, or I'm going to—"

"Oh, be quiet."

Hypnova twirled a finger at DeMayne. His head went back as if he'd been hit in the forehead with a tennis ball, and he coughed out a plume of purple smoke. When he finished hacking it up, he had a vacant look about him as if his brain had been emptied completely. "It seems I don't know you as well as I thought I did," Hypnova said to Joey. "Why is he here?"

"What did you do to him?" Janelle asked. She waved a hand in front of DeMayne's face and got no response. His eyes were open, but it seemed as if he couldn't see a thing.

"He's in a trance of sorts, unable to retain memories from moment to moment," Hypnova said. "He'll stay this way until I release him, which I will do," she promised. "I wouldn't leave even this awful man in such a state, but first I want to know what you're doing with him."

"We're getting to that," Joey said.

"Get there quickly, please. I spent the last year keeping the Invisible Hand away from you. Day after day, I covered up your tracks as you sought out how to destroy the dark magic markers. All of this, while on the run from the Secreteers for telling you the truth about the secret history of the world. I've been sleeping with one eye open. If not for the Caliburn Shield, I would never sleep at all. Now I see I put my life on the line to keep you hidden from Ledger DeMayne and his thugs only to have you seek him out. Why?"

"He's got a secret," Joey said. "A big one. Something even you might not know."

"About what?"

"The Imagine Nation."

"Something *I* don't know?" Hypnova was skeptical. "I don't understand. If the dark magic markers have been eliminated, magic is free to come back to the world. Why do we need him?"

"So magic can stay," Joey told her. "We're not done yet. People still have to believe."

"We have to *make* them believe," Shazad added. "That's where he comes in."

All eyes turned to DeMayne, who was still in a daze, oblivious to the conversation going on around him.

"Bring him around so we can talk." Joey said. "Don't you want to find out what he knows?"

Hypnova raised a finger toward DeMayne, ready to snap him out of his trance. Her curiosity was clearly piqued, but still she hesitated. "Are you sure about this? You want to put yourself back in his crosshairs?"

"You can always wipe his memory again after we're done," Janelle said. "Right?"

Hypnova nodded but still looked concerned. "I hope you know what you're doing," she murmured. She snapped her fingers, and DeMayne's consciousness returned. Joey watched his eyes clear as he shifted in his bonds. "Still here," he said flatly, as if he'd just remembered his predicament. "I'm going to kill you for this. All of you. I'm going to kill you twice."

"Nice to know we made an impression," Joey said.

"Who are you?" DeMayne asked. "How do you know me?"

"We're the people you've been looking for all year. The ones who found Camelot?" Joey gave a little wave. "That's us. The Order of the Majestic."

DeMayne laughed derisively. "Don't be ridiculous. You're just children."

"Sure we are," Joey said. "You got captured by a bunch of random children. Not sure how that makes you feel better, but what do I know?" DeMayne looked down. Joey knew he had struck a nerve. "How do you think we got you in that bag? I used this."

Joey held up the wand so DeMayne could see it.

DeMayne leaned forward, blinking in disbelief. "The wand," he whispered. "You are the Majestic."

"Told ya," Joey said. "But we're not the Order of the Majestic you're used to dealing with. We do things a little different."

"Obviously." DeMayne eyed Hypnova, who stood out as the only other adult. "I take it you're their leader? You let these children throw their lives away like this?"

"At the moment, I'm following their lead," Hypnova said. "Think of me as more of a trusted compatriot. We've met before, by the way. Not that you would remember."

"This is Hypnova," Joey said. "She used to be a Secreteer."

"A what?" DeMayne coughed, producing more purple smoke. A fine mist hovered around his nose. It almost made him sneeze, but the sensation went away, irritating him further. "What magic did you use on me? How did you do that?"

"It's not magic," Hypnova told him. "That power comes from me. Memories are mine to control. All Secreteers have that ability. As for who the Secreteers are? Well, they're not that different from you and your lot, unfortunately. Secreteers work to keep magic hidden away, protecting fantastic and unbelievable wonders from a world that once tried to destroy them. The Invisible Hand keeps magic under wraps simply to restrict supply and consolidate power. Over time I came to understand it's a distinction without a difference. Regardless of intention, the result is the same. Both parties deprive the world of something it desperately needs. A vital resource." Hypnova pointed to Joey and the others. "They take a different view. That's why I'm helping them change the world."

"We've already changed it," Shazad said. "The dark markers that hold magic back are gone."

"Your days of manipulating the world and keeping magic to yourself are over," Leanora added.

DeMayne said nothing, but Joey could see concern

94

behind his eyes, wondering how he and his friends knew so much. "Dark markers? I don't know what you're talking about."

"Are you sure about that?" Leanora asked. "We just got back from the coldest place on earth and a tropical island that doesn't exist. That's not ringing any bells?"

DeMayne's face fell as the realization sank in that Leanora and Shazad weren't bluffing. "The frozen heart of the frost giant?" he asked.

"Melted," Shazad said proudly.

"The root of the molten mountain?"

"Also known as the root of all evil?" Leanora asked. "I threw it into a volcano."

"*Lord of the Rings* style," Joey said, bumping fists with Leanora.

DeMayne was staggered. There was no getting around the fact that the world had been irrevocably changed, and at this point, there was nothing he could do about it. Joey could tell DeMayne had never imagined this day would come. "This can't be," he said in a bewildered voice. "It's not possible."

"Nothing's impossible," Joey said. "You of all people should know that."

DeMayne's expression turned to rage. "You're mad," he spat. "Do you have any concept of the power you've just unleashed? Not all magic is good magic. With those markers gone, there's going to be doors opening all over the world. Ancient doors to places with dangerous people . . . dangerous things. The world isn't ready!"

"We're ready," Shazad said. "Where do you think our families are right now? They're all over the world, in places where magic is strong, guarding lost doors and waiting on old roads, making sure nothing bad comes in."

"They're also making sure you and your friends can't take control of anything good that happens to appear," Leanora said. "We're not going to let you sweep it all under the carpet or carve it up for yourselves. What we're doing is for everybody."

"Your families . . . ," DeMayne repeated, looking back and forth between Shazad and Leanora. "I remember now," he said, slowly putting together who they were. "The Hassans and the Nomadiks. I don't recall your families ever being this bold before."

"I thought he wasn't supposed to recall anything," Janelle said.

"This conversation is triggering his memories," Hypnova explained.

"He definitely looks triggered," Janelle agreed as DeMayne made yet another attempt to break free of Gleipnir, really giving it everything he had. He had to know it was pointless, but he wasn't going to give up without a fight.

"Let me go!" he shouted, breathing heavily, full of fury. "What do you think is going to happen here? Are you going to keep me tied up forever? Is that your plan? You think my people are just going to sit on their hands while you turn magic loose on an unsuspecting world?"

"The world isn't going to be unsuspecting much longer." Joey pointed out into the murky fog that surrounded the ship. "Somewhere out there is a place—a secret place where impossible and unbelievable things are daily realities. A lost island that roams all around the world. It's the last remnant of an ancient magical land. People call it the Imagine Nation. Hypnova showed us a glimpse of it. We're going to show everyone. That's what's going to end the Invisible Hand's stranglehold on magic once and for all. The return of the Imagine Nation and everything in it . . . That's something you can't cover up or put a spin on to make people doubt and disbelieve. *That's* the plan."

DeMayne looked like he had just bit into a rotten apple. "If that's your plan, why tell me? You brought me here so you can gloat?"

"No," Joey said. "So you can help."

DeMayne scoffed. "You expect me to help you? You *are* mad."

"There's a method to the madness. See, if I want to bring the Imagine Nation back, all I have to do is wave this wand and say something clever. That's what this wand does. It makes my imagination real. Problem is, if I use the wand to do something too big, it'll kill me, just like it killed Merlin. I don't just want to change the world. I want to live in it too."

"I see," DeMayne said, the trace of a smile forming on his lips. "You're afraid. Why don't you give that wand to someone who can handle its power?"

"Like you?" Joey laughed. "You should thank your lucky stars you never got your hands on this thing. The question isn't *if* you'd go too far with it, but how long it would take you to wipe yourself out. I don't think you'd last a single day."

DeMayne lifted his shoulders half an inch. "Let's test your theory. I'm game."

"Can't do it. I need you alive." Joey looked at Hypnova. "I need you both."

Hypnova put a hand on Joey's shoulder. She leaned in close and spoke softly so only he could hear. "Joey, you know I'll do whatever I can to help you. I want to bring the Imagine Nation back too, but I don't know how to do it if you can't use the wand. This is bigger than the Invisible Hand. We have the Secreteers to contend with as well. They're the ones who keep the Imagine Nation hidden from the world. They've done it since Merlin first created the island. I don't know how they keep it hidden, or in constant motion, floating all over the earth. That secret is known only to Oblivia, Grand Majestrix of the Clandestine Order of Secreteers. If we want to take down whatever it is that keeps the island hidden—without using the wand? We'd need to get Oblivia to tell us how to do it." She shook her head. "That's never going to happen."

"We don't need to talk to her," Joey whispered back. "Not when we can talk to someone who was there with Merlin all those years ago."

A second passed before Hypnova realized who Joey was talking about. "Him?!" she said, pointing at DeMayne.

Joey nodded. "I have another theory about our friend here," he said, raising his voice to include everyone in the conversation. "We spent the last year finding out how to break the dark magic markers, but we found out something else, too. Ledger DeMayne is the same Emperor's Hand who helped cut off the world's access to magic a thousand years ago. This is the man who stole the world, for a little while anyway. Merlin, the first Secreteer, and a handful of other heroes defeated him and took the Imagine Nation into hiding. His stolen kingdom gone, DeMayne formed the Invisible Hand to control the world's remaining magical items. He's not the group's most recent leader; he's the only one it's ever had."

"You're saying . . . he's a thousand years old?" Hypnova asked. "Even with magic, that's not possible, is it?"

"Don't let his good looks fool you," Joey said. "I'm willing to bet it's just a glamour. Who knows what he really looks like under that. Probably not very pretty."

"But glamours just disguise your appearance," Hypnova said. "They don't keep you young."

"I don't know how he does it." Joey tilted his head to the side. "I don't even know for sure if I'm right, but I've got a feeling. I got the idea when I was thinking about his name. All the names they use in the Invisible Hand . . . Mr. Black, Mr. Gray, Ms. Scarlett . . . They keep their aliases simple on purpose. It's an inside joke with them. The idea is, they can't be bothered to get creative about fooling 'the little people' because they'll fall for anything anyway." Joey turned to address DeMayne. "You like fooling people. It makes you feel powerful. Even your real name is fake. 'Legerdemain' is a word that means trickery, deceit, or deception. I looked it up. It's an old word with origins in the late Middle English time period. A thousand years ago. I started to wonder, What if the name isn't fake? What if you're where that word comes from? Last year you used the Sword of Storms on us, an Arthurian relic. It was broken when Camelot fell. I think you were there. Now, tell me I'm wrong."

DeMayne stared at Joey, a smug, superior look on his face. "That's an interesting take on my life's story, but your timeline's a bit off. If the legends are true, King Arthur lived fifteen hundred years ago, not one thousand. Doesn't quite add up, does it?"

"No, it doesn't," Joey admitted. "But legends can be true and a little bit off at the same time. Don't forget, Merlin and the Secreteers rewrote history after they defeated you, so who knows what happened when? For all we know, five hundred years of nothing happening during the Dark Ages was just them fudging their dates."

"And that's not exactly a denial," Janelle added.

"You're wasting your breath," DeMayne said. "Even if everything you're saying is true . . . even if I knew where to find this Imagine Nation, or how it stays hidden, I wouldn't tell you. I won't tell you anything."

"Not willingly," Leonora said.

"What are you going to do, torture me? You think you have what it takes to make me talk?"

"We don't need to," Hypnova said, realizing what Joey and the others had in mind. "Memory powers, remember?"

6

Head Games

Ten minutes later, it was obvious something was wrong.

"It's not working," Leanora said. "Why isn't it working?"

"Could he be resisting her somehow?" Shazad asked.

"I don't know about that," Janelle replied, doubtful. "Judging by the look on his face, he's not resisting much of anything right now."

They had moved to Hypnova's cabin in the interior of the ship. The room was filled with pictures, souvenirs, maps, and charts from her travels around the world. All of it was very interesting to everyone but DeMayne. He was seated across from Hypnova, or more accurately, precariously balanced in a handcrafted wooden chair with his feet propped up on a stool. Still tied up in Gleipnir, DeMayne was completely helpless, not to mention catatonic. His eyes were glazed over, and his jaw hung down, a thick bead of drool forming on his lower lip. Hypnova had her hand raised in his direction. Her eyes were closed, and she had a look of intense concentration on her face.

"I don't understand," Joey said. "Usually, it's just a tap on the forehead or a bit of that smoke and *boom!* That's it. What's taking so long?"

"Maybe it always takes this long and she just rewrites everyone's memory afterward to make it look easy?" Shazad suggested.

"No," Joey said, dismissing the idea out of hand. "I mean, she *could* do that, but I don't think she'd do that to us. What would be the point? I think we have a problem here."

Hypnova opened her eyes, breaking her connection with DeMayne. "We have a problem here," she confirmed.

DeMayne came around a second later. He woke with a start, sucking up his drool with a loud slurp. Joey smirked as his eyes darted left and right, checking to see if anyone noticed.

"What's wrong?" Leanora asked.

"I'll tell you what's wrong," DeMayne said with his chin in the air. "I'm too strong-willed, aren't I? You can't break me."

Hypnova cast her eyes at the ceiling. "Don't flatter yourself," she said without turning around. "You're not the problem."

"And, just so you know, you have drool all over yourself," Janelle told DeMayne. She waved her hand in a circle. "*All over you.* It looks like someone spilled a glass of water on your shirt."

DeMayne looked down at his collar. Sure enough, it was drenched. "That's not funny," he said, sulking. Everyone laughed as he tried to hide his embarrassment, but Joey was worried that DeMayne might be right about being unbreakable.

Joey leaned in close to Hypnova and spoke in a low voice. "What's wrong? Is he using something to keep his memories hidden from you?"

"We should have searched him before we tied him up," Leanora said.

"There wasn't time for that," Shazad replied.

"It wouldn't have mattered," Hypnova said. "It isn't anything he has or anything he's doing. His mind's an open book, except for the last page."

"What's stopping you, then?" Joey asked. "Why can't you read it?"

"His memories aren't hidden from me—they're hidden from him. One memory in particular. There's something in there, but I can't access it, because he can't access it. It's something even he doesn't know about. A memory he's repressed or been forced to forget. But you're right about him. His memories go way back. I looked past centuries before I started to lose my way. The memory we're after . . . it's buried deep."

"Too deep?" Janelle asked. "You can't reach it?"

"Even I have limits. If I go too far down the well, I might not make it back." Hypnova paused a moment. Her eyes lit up with a new idea. "But you could. The four of you."

Joey, Shazad, Janelle, and Leanora traded looks of confusion and disbelief. "Us?" they said in unison.

"What are you talking about?" Joey asked. "We can't do what you do."

"You can if I help you," Hypnova said. "I could join your minds. You could go in to unearth the memory, and then I could pull you back out."

"Can you really do that?" Shazad asked.

"The question is, can *we* do that?" Janelle said.

And the answer is, I don't think so, Joey thought.

He wasn't the only one who was skeptical. "If you can't reach the memory, and you were a Secreteer, how are we supposed to find it?" Leanora asked.

"You can find it," Hypnova said. "You won't have to worry about keeping one foot in the real world while you look. I can do that for you. I'll be your anchor out here, which means you can explore his mind with a freedom I never could."

"What are you saying over there?" DeMayne barked out from his chair, trying to follow the conversation. "No one's going to do any *exploring* in my mind. I won't allow it. This is a violation! It's assault!"

"QUIET!" everyone yelled at once. Hypnova raised a stern finger toward DeMayne, and he wisely stopped complaining.

"What if we get lost?" Joey asked her. "You said if you go too deep, you might not make it out. How are we going to find our way back?"

"I'll pull you out," Hypnova promised. "I know it's hard to understand, but it's different if I go in alone. If I surrender myself to the expedition, I'm operating without a net. If we do it this way, *I'm* your net. I'll join your minds, but

I'll stay here, focused on you. Tracking you, so I can extract you." She snapped her fingers. "Just like that."

"Ha! Just like that!" DeMayne laughed. "I hope you're not falling for this. 'You go in. I'll stay here,'" he said, in a mock impression of Hypnova. "Listen to what she's really saying. She's afraid. That's good. She ought to be. I wouldn't do this if I were you, children. Look out for yourselves. That's what *she's* doing."

Now it was Hypnova's turn to be quiet. Joey knew DeMayne couldn't be trusted, but he had to admit he was making sense. "I don't know about this," Shazad said, looking uneasy.

"I've done this before from both sides," Hypnova assured him. "Secreteers do it all the time."

"With other Secreteers, I bet," Shazad said. "This isn't our specialty."

"Your specialty is doing impossible, dangerous things. You wouldn't be here otherwise. Am I right?"

"Let's talk about the dangers," Leanora said. "What's it like in there?" she asked, pointing at DeMayne.

"I won't lie to you," Hypnova said. "It's ugly. His mental defenses will come after you. They'll try to kill you."

"Count on it," DeMayne said with sinister glee.

"But it'll just be the version of us that's in his mind," Joey said, hoping for some good news. "We're not really there, so it doesn't matter what happens to us. It's like a video game, right? We die in there, we get kicked out and respawn out here. No big deal. Right?"

Hypnova said nothing.

"Right?" Joey asked again.

"Yes and no," Hypnova said reluctantly. "It depends on where you are at the time. I've been back and forth across his mindscape. I can put you close to the memory we want, but past a certain point, things get murky. As long as you're conscious, I can track you anywhere, but the deeper you go, the harder it gets. If you die inside his mind, our connection will be momentarily broken. If that happens and you're somewhere I can't see you . . . I might not be able to reacquire you."

"What does that mean?" Shazad asked. "We'd be trapped in there?"

"Maybe forever," Hypnova admitted. Her words hung heavy in the air. No one liked the sound of that.

"We *do* know how to defend ourselves," Janelle said, holding up the Staff of Sorcero.

"That's the other thing," Hypnova said. "No magic weapons. Those are here in the real world. You won't have them with you in the mindscape, because you're not really there."

"This keeps getting better and better," Joey said.

"Excuse me, I have an announcement to make," DeMayne said, smiling his first genuine smile of the evening. "I've decided to have an open mind about this whole endeavor. By all means, come in. Explore."

"He wants a shot at us," Shazad said, nailing the reason for DeMayne's sudden change of heart.

"I think it's only fair. Let's even the playing field. See what happens." DeMayne's smile turned cruel. "I'm game."

Joey looked at the wand in his hand. "The alternative is, I use this to get the information we need."

"No," Leanora said instantly. "It's fine. I'll go."

"Not alone you won't," Shazad told her.

Joey, Janelle, Shazad, and Leanora looked at one another. No one said anything. Everyone already knew where they stood. Together.

"We'll all go," Janelle said.

The decision made, they dumped DeMayne out of his seat and deposited him on the floor. Joey and Shazad sat across from him, leaving the two wooden chairs for Janelle and Leanora. "How do we do this?" Joey asked.

"Nothing to it." Hypnova held up an open palm. "Just look here." Joey watched as Hypnova waved her hand across her body in a slow, sweeping motion. Purple smoke trails ran off her fingertips as she moved, and Joey's vision blurred.

"I'll see you on the other side," he told his friends. His voice sounded warped and dreamlike inside his head.

"I'm looking forward to it," DeMayne's voice returned, clear as a bell.

Joey closed his eyes, and when he reopened them, he saw nothing. Pitch-blackness. He blinked again and he was there. Inside Ledger DeMayne's mind. The effect was instantaneous, devoid of any fanfare or spectacle. One second Joey and his friends were sitting in Hypnova's cabin, and the next thing he knew, they were standing on a dreary mental plain. There was nothing around for miles but crooked, spiky mountains and barren fields. Everywhere Joey looked, he saw jagged rocks and hard earth. Geysers of flame erupted across the land in random bursts. Some came and went in seconds, and others remained, burning low like little campfires. Dry weeds poked out of the ground at the foot of blackened trees, and a gloomy, overcast sky stretched over the land like a blanket of depression.

"Isn't this lovely?" Leanora said sarcastically, surveying the dismal wasteland of DeMayne's mindscape. "I don't know if this is the ugliest place I've ever been, but it's up there."

"I'd still take it over Transylvania," Joey said. "Don't hold me to that," he added. "I might change my mind."

"DeMayne's office was way nicer," Janelle said. "I guess this is what he's like on the inside. Pretty creepy."

"Hypnova did warn us it wasn't pleasant here," Shazad reminded them.

"She also said she'd drop us near the memories we're here to find." Leanora scanned the area with dubious eyes. "I don't see anything, do you?"

"We may have—problem." Hypnova's voice came in as if it were being broadcast by a radio station with a dying signal. "Listen to me careful—don't—much time."

A gentle breeze kicked up a cloud of dust, forming an image of Hypnova that was much clearer than anything she tried to say. It was like watching a lagging video where the audio didn't match the picture. Hypnova's face kept freezing and skipping.

"What's wrong?" Joey asked her.

Hypnova's image fluttered a moment, but quickly re-formed. "DeMayne—working against me. Trying—he wants to separate us."

"I think it's working," Janelle said.

"Where is DeMayne?" Shazad asked.

"DeMayne—everywhere—ground beneath your feet. His head—world. He has the power here—makes the rules—what he wants."

"I've got a bad feeling about this," Shazad said.

"I—like it either." Hypnova's image ruptured again, but this time she wasn't able to rematerialize fully. Her sentences grew choppier and harder to understand. "Be quick . . . I— pull you out—up to you."

"Did she say she wanted to pull us out?" Leonora asked.

Hypnova's image collapsed before she could reply. This time it didn't come back.

"That can't be right," Joey said. "We just got here. We haven't learned anything yet."

"Something tells me she couldn't pull us out right now if she wanted to," Janelle said. "Hypnova?" she called out, turning around and looking up at the sky. No one answered. "I don't think she can hear us."

Everyone stared at one another in silence as their predicament became clear. They were on their own in enemy territory. For the time being, at least.

"Hypnova will come through," Joey said. "She can take DeMayne. I've seen her do it. We all have."

"What are we supposed to do in the meantime?" Shazad asked.

"We find the memory, of course," Leanora said.

"Find it where?" Shazad spread his arms out. "There's nothing here. Which way do we go?"

"I know which way I don't want to go," Janelle said, pointing off in the distance. She looked like she had seen a ghost, but the reality was much worse than that.

Joey turned to look where Janelle was pointing and saw what appeared to be a pack of orcs on patrol. They were twenty yards away on the crest of a ridge, which was way too close for comfort. The orcs were big and terrible with thick, knotted muscles, hard as chunks of rock. Their skin was a mix of gray and green, and their bodies were smeared with black grease and oil, or maybe it was the blood of their most recent kill. Joey couldn't tell from this distance, and he didn't care for a closer look. The orcs were armed with all manner of brutal weapons and wore iron-plated armor that was decorated with bones. The largest of the bunch, the pack leader, flipped up the visor on his helm and let out a guttural snarl. A low, clicking noise echoed across the rock trail. Joey's stomach dropped. The orc was looking right at him.

"RUN!" Joey shouted.

No one needed to be told twice. After a brief moment of indecision about which way to go, the group chose a direction and made a break for it. Unfortunately, the orcs did the same, and they were better at it. Joey and his friends scrambled across the trail as fast as they could, but there wasn't much of a trail to follow. As they stumbled through unfamiliar territory, dodging fiery blasts and climbing over rock formations that slowed them down, the orcs charged ahead as if they had been shot out of a cannon. They knew the terrain and were sprinting all out, covering the distance between them and their prey with ease.

"I take back what I said about Transylvania!" Joey said, feeling a newfound appreciation for Dracula's hometown. At least there were no real monsters there. Joey knew there were no "real monsters" inside DeMayne's head either, but that didn't make him any less afraid of the hideous beasts chasing him. As he hurried across an uneven path, desperate to escape, he told himself he was still on Hypnova's ship and the orcs were merely figments of DeMayne's twisted imagination. If he was captured and killed, he'd wake up in the real world without a scratch on him. That had been the plan, but there was no denying they had hit a major snag. DeMayne had cut off their connection to Hypnova from the moment they had entered his mind. Joey worried that DeMayne's will was stronger than anyone realized. What if Hypnova couldn't see them well enough to pull them back to reality? If that was the case, all bets were off and there was no safe space anywhere. Off-balance and unprepared for the chase, Joey felt like a wounded deer trying to escape a pack of hungry wolves. The orcs were gaining fast.

Tired of running, Leanora crested a hill and turned to fight. Janelle joined her, and together they began throwing rocks at their pursuers. They were decent-sized rocks, and the girls' aim was good enough to score a few direct hits, but the orcs laughed them off. It was like throwing pebbles at an oncoming train to try to slow it down. The orcs kept coming, pausing only to return fire. Everyone ducked for cover as spears whistled through the air, just missing them.

"Stop it!" Shazad said, pulling Leanora back. "You're just making them mad."

"I think they started out mad," Janelle said.

The spears hit hard enough to sink into the rocks, breaking them apart. Cracks ran out from the point of impact in a zigzag pattern, destabilizing the ground.

"Keep running!" Shazad said.

Leanora stopped throwing stones and ran, but not before doubling back to grab one of the spears and take it with her. The chase went on, but the outlook was increasingly bleak. Joey and his friends scaled a rocky crag trying to get away. Their energy was fading and their progress was slow.

"How can I be this tired in a metaphysical realm?" Janelle wondered aloud as Shazad helped her over the top. "I'm not even really here!"

"It's DeMayne," Joey huffed, coming up behind her. "We don't belong here. In his head. Puts us at a natural disadvantage." He was already winded when they started the climb. Now his strength had all but left him. The orcs looked like they could go another ten miles without breaking a sweat, but the finish line was closer than anyone thought. The

117

fissures created by the orcs' spears had never stopped growing. Soon the fault lines caught up to Joey and his friends, and the ground gave way beneath them.

"Look out!" Leanora shouted, but there was nothing anyone could do. Caught up in a rockslide, the group tumbled down a steep slope and rolled to a stop at the base of a mountain.

"Ouch," Joey said, scuffling to his feet. He and his friends got up and assessed their injuries. A few cuts and scrapes aside, they had survived the fall without incident, but they were about to enter a world of hurt. Joey looked up at the nearly vertical rock face behind them. They had slammed into a mountain wall at the bottom of the ravine. There was nowhere to go. He looked back the way they'd come. One by one, orcs appeared, lining the top of the hill. There was no way out.

The orcs brandished swords, spears, and maces that were studded with spikes. Their weapons were stained with rusty red blotches, and they laughed in a way that made Joey's skin crawl. Their mouths were full of rotten, razor-sharp teeth, and they smelled awful. It was an odd thing to worry about, but Joey wondered if their stink was the last thing he'd ever smell. The leader of the pack quieted the others and said something in orc-speak. Joey didn't understand the words, but hearing them made him cringe just the same. The way the other orcs reacted, whooping it up and gnashing their teeth, Joey got the feeling they had just been told that dinner was served.

Joey and his friends called out for Hypnova but got no response. No one was coming to help them. The group huddled together as the orcs slowly advanced on their position. Joey's heart was racing. It didn't matter if they were "really there" or not. He had to imagine it would hurt to die at the hands—or teeth—of an orc, and he couldn't be certain of what would happen after that. Still holding her spear, Leanora stepped out in front of everyone, ready to stick any orc who got too close. She was as fearless as ever, but she didn't stand a chance. None of them did. They were up against eight fully armed warriors, and they had one spear to split between the four of them. The hero in Joey wanted to step up and save the day with the wand, but he didn't even have that option. Not in this place. That was the problem. They had more than just the orcs to contend with. Everything worked against them here, which was what Hypnova had been trying to tell them earlier. DeMayne was everywhere, including the ground that had disappeared beneath their feet. Joey thought about how willing DeMayne had been to give everyone a crack at his brain. His confidence now seemed more than justified. As the orcs closed in, Joey thought about DeMayne and his great game and how well he had played them, snatching victory from the jaws of defeat.

The first orc reached the bottom of the hill. He had a sword in each hand, and he scraped them together with a menacing grin. Leanora backpedaled slightly as he approached, but before the beast could strike, a cloaked figure leaped out of nowhere and landed between them.

"Hypnova!" Joey shouted.

Only it wasn't Hypnova. It was a man. His hands gave it away. They were the only parts of the stranger visible underneath his cloak, and they were large and pasty white. His drab cloak was the wrong color too, as was his sword. A blade appeared in one of the stranger's hands, and it was not Hypnova's shiny golden saber, but a broadsword forged from dull gray steel. Before anyone had a chance to react, the sword flashed out in a blur, slicing the orc in two. The creature exploded in a puff of black smoke, shocking everyone, the remaining orcs most of all. They roared with anger and charged down the hill, expecting to overwhelm the stranger, but they were sloppy and untrained. He was quick and deadly. The orcs swarmed the stranger, coming at him from all sides. They couldn't touch him. He parried their attacks with graceful, polished movements. His cloak flew out as he spun away from the tips of their swords, giving the orcs a target to flail at. They stabbed at the stranger and hit nothing but fabric. One orc accidentally ran through another orc trying to get him. It was another bloodless death as the unlucky orc disappeared in a smoky blast. The stranger dashed through the black cloud with his sword, and a third burst of smoke appeared, followed by a fourth, and a fifth. The haze spread out, obscuring everything. Joey heard the clanging of swords inside the dark, billowing mass. It went on for a few seconds and ended with two soft puffs. When the dust settled, the stranger was the only one standing.

But the orc leader had lingered back from the fray. With his crew defeated, he came down the hill seeking revenge. The stranger had just effortlessly taken out seven blood-thirsty orcs, but the eighth and final enemy wasn't like the others. He was bigger, stronger, and much better with a blade. He cut a swath through the air and flipped his sword around, moving it from hand to hand and showing off his skills like a gunslinger twirling a pistol. He finished his routine at the bottom of the hill and roared at the stranger, challenging him to a fight—a real fight.

The stranger snatched the spear from Leanora's hands and threw it.

Poof.

Just like that, it was over. The orcs had all been reduced to a sooty black mist. The danger had passed, and the stunning reversal of fortune left everyone speechless. Joey inched forward, coming up behind the mysterious stranger. The man was looking the other way, his face still hidden by the hood. Joey didn't ask who he was. All he could think about was Indiana Jones taking out the swordsman in *Raiders of the Lost Ark*.

"That. Was. Awesome!" he gushed.

The cloaked swordsman sheathed his blade. "Follow me." He spoke in a gruff, hoarse tone as he pushed past Joey on his way to the mountain wall. It was a dead end, but not for him. He pushed on a series of stones in a special order to unlock a secret passage into the mountain. "In here."

"Even awesomer," Joey said.

Janelle looked sideways at Joey. "Awesomer? Really?"

"Let it go," Shazad told her.

"Who are you?" Leanora asked the stranger before they went any farther. "Did Hypnova send you?"

"Not exactly."

The stranger threw back his hood, revealing the absolute last face Joey expected to see. The man who had just saved his life, and the lives of all his friends, was none other than Grayson Manchester.

7

Dangerous Minds

"You!" Shazad exclaimed. "You're *alive?*"

Manchester cocked his head to the side and touched his chin. "Alive . . . I wonder. To be perfectly honest, I'm not sure. I've never given the matter much thought."

Shazad scrunched up his face, visibly thrown by Manchester's response.

"You can't be here," Janelle said, jumping in. "You got sucked into a black hole! We watched you go!"

"Did you?" Manchester's eyebrows went up. "That's new information. I'd like to hear more about that."

"What?" Shazad looked around at Joey, Janelle, and Leanora. They were all equally baffled. "I don't understand. Why are you here?"

"And why would you save us?" Joey wanted to know.

"One question at a time," Manchester said softly. His smooth British accent grated on Joey. It bothered him that Manchester sounded so intelligent and in control even though nothing he said made any sense. "First of all, I'm not here. Not in the way you think I am." Manchester stepped into the secret tunnel and motioned for everyone to join him. "I'll explain everything, but we need to keep moving. We're too exposed right now. It's not safe."

Joey planted his feet. "I'm not going in there. I'm not going anywhere with you." The idea was completely out of the question. He looked at the others, expecting unanimous agreement, but his friends didn't seem to share his opinion.

Shazad put a hand on Joey's shoulder and whispered in his ear. "I think it's all right, Joey. You said yourself he saved us."

"Did you see what he did to those orcs?" Leonora added.

"I don't care what he did," Joey said, pulling away from both of them. "We can't trust him. He's working an angle. He's got to be. It's the only explanation."

"That's no explanation," Shazad said. "What possible angle could he be—"

"I don't know!" Joey blurted out, cutting Shazad off. "But you know he's got one."

"What do you want to do?" Leanora asked. "Do you have any other ideas?"

"Did you forget what he did to us?" Joey asked, turning the question back on her. "To Redondo?"

"That wasn't me," Manchester said.

"Don't give me that," Joey shot back. "We were there!"

"I wasn't," Manchester said. "I know this is hard to believe, but I'm not Grayson Manchester." His assertion shut everyone up. It was an odd thing to say, seeing as how he was obviously Grayson Manchester, but the conviction he said it with was undeniable.

"Who are you, then? His twin brother?" Joey asked.

"No, but we are related, in a sense. I'm Ledger DeMayne's memory of Grayson Manchester."

Manchester's revelation produced a collective "Oh" from Joey and his friends.

"You look just like him," Shazad said.

"Sound like him too," Leanora added.

"Of course I do. The old man's got a memory like a steel trap, but if what you're saying is accurate, the real Grayson

126

Manchester is either dead or very far away. In either case, we don't need to worry about him. However, you're right about one thing: I do have an ulterior motive for helping you."

"Now we're getting somewhere," Joey said. "Let's hear it."

"I didn't save you from the orcs because I care about you. I did it to frustrate DeMayne. You're wondering if you can trust me? You can trust me to be what he remembers me to be, which is someone who betrayed him. He doesn't remember all the details, but he knows I came between him and the wand. I worked against him in the real world and ruined his plans. Naturally, I do the same here. Does that make sense?"

Joey thought it over and decided it actually did make sense. The mental loophole allowed him to do the impossible and accept Grayson Manchester—or this version of him—as an ally. The howling of orcs in the distance made everybody jump. "Fine, let's go," Joey said, eager to get away before the orcs found out where they were. The group hustled into the tunnel and closed the door behind them.

Manchester led the group down a narrow, torchlit passage, fielding questions along the way. "Since when are you so good with a sword?" Shazad asked him. "Not that I'm complaining, but the Grayson Manchester I remember was a magician, not a fighter."

"DeMayne controls the idea of magic here, but he doesn't control me," Manchester explained. "I draw power from another well. I'm a painful memory for DeMayne. Something that gnaws at him. His only way to defeat me in this place would be to forget me, which he could never do, because he spends so much energy trying to remember what it is I did. To be honest, I don't even know myself because he doesn't know."

"This is making my head hurt," Leanora complained.

"I think I understand," Shazad said. "DeMayne doesn't know what Manchester did, because Hypnova hid those details from him when she erased his memory of us."

"So it would seem," Manchester said. "He's starting to remember though. The memory blocks your friend Hypnova put in place are breaking down. Probably a result of you all rooting around in his brain."

"You know Hypnova?" Joey asked.

"I know everything DeMayne knows, which is limited to what happened on Hypnova's ship and the reason you're here."

"So, you don't know who we are specifically?" Joey asked hopefully. "And you don't know what happened between us and the real Manchester?" Memory or not, he wondered if Manchester would be so eager to help them if he knew they were the ones who dropped him down the black hole.

"Any history you have with him, good or bad, is between you and him," Manchester said, putting Joey's mind at ease. "We may not be friends, but you're Ledger DeMayne's enemy, and that makes us allies." They came to a room filled with swords and armor. "I say let's give the old vulture a headache."

Everyone went around the room choosing their weapons and outfitting themselves with a mix of chain mail, pauldrons, chest plates, and armguards. Joey was glad to have the added protection, and he felt much better with a sword in his hand. He chose a blade that should have been too big for him and found it surprisingly light and easy to swing. It was one of the benefits of being in DeMayne's mind versus the real world. "Normally, I wouldn't know what to do with this, but I won't have a problem stabbing any of DeMayne's henchmen knowing they'll just vanish in a cloud of smoke."

"Tell me about it," Janelle said. "I hate the sight of blood."

"You don't have to worry about spilling blood here," Manchester confirmed. "We're safe as can be. Unfortunately, you can't get what you're after by playing it safe. If you want to search DeMayne's deepest, most protected memories, you've got to go back into the wild."

He took them through a doorway that led back outside. It was much darker when they emerged from the tunnel. The sun had gone down during the short time Joey and his friends had spent inside the mountain. The sky had turned from an overcast gray to a deep inky blue, shading to black. Another dark mountain sat on the horizon, and an eerie arc of green light glimmered in the air above it like the aurora borealis. The spooky vibe the light gave off clashed with something at the peak of the mountain that didn't belong. High atop the summit was a city surrounded by a wall of white stone and marble. A soft glow illuminated an inviting, peaceful haven that stood in stark contrast to the desolate, rocky crags. In the center of the city there was a castle on a green hill, and it was not the ominous, impregnable fortress Joey expected to see. DeMayne's stronghold looked surprisingly like Camelot. It was obvious where they had to go, but the castle was a long way off. Perhaps a week or more. "How long is this going to take?" Joey asked.

"That depends on which road you choose," Manchester replied.

They followed him to the edge of a cliff for a better view of the land below. A wave of hopelessness crashed over Joey when he looked down from the precipice. A vast army of orcs waited for them at the foot of the mountain. There were tens of thousands of them. An insurmountable number. Not even Grayson Manchester's swordsmanship could protect them from this many soldiers.

Janelle hit Joey on the shoulder. "You had to mention *Lord of the Rings*. DeMayne's got Mordor on the brain, thanks to you."

"Don't blame yourselves," Manchester said.

"I wasn't," Janelle said. "I was blaming Joey."

Manchester allowed himself a slight smile. "It's not Joey's fault. This is how DeMayne sees the world. Full of chaos, madness, and mindless barbarians. This is how he justifies his selfishness with magical objects. He sees himself as the noble one, holding the line against a world that would destroy itself if given the chance. That's why he hoards his secret knowledge, and that's where he keeps it. The Memory

Palace." Manchester pointed to the castle on the hill. "If you want to learn what happened a thousand years ago . . . the nature of the magic that keeps the Imagine Nation hidden, and how to break the spell, that's where you'll find your answers. It's the only place you'll find them."

Everyone looked across the sea of enemies between them and the Memory Palace. There was no way through the horde. It was an impossible journey, even for them.

"Lucky for you, I know a shortcut."

Manchester turned on his heel and started down a mountain path that wound around the corner and out of sight. Joey and the others hurried after him. When they caught up with him, they found him standing on a narrow, natural stone bridge that ran out across a chasm between two peaks.

"What is this?" Joey asked.

"Another road." Manchester presented a wooden door built into the mountainside at the far end of the bridge.

He crossed the bridge without a care in the world, stopping at the door. As before, Joey and his friends had no choice but to follow. The teeming masses of orcs below them were oblivious to their presence, but it was a nerve-racking journey even if no one spotted them. One way or the other, falling off the bridge meant certain death, and there was nothing to guard against a fatal misstep. There was no railing to hold on to. The bridge was a simple rock formation connecting two mountain peaks, and in some places, it was no wider than a balance beam. The wind tortured Joey as he inched forward, refusing to look down and hoping the orcs wouldn't look up. He was last in line to the door, and he hesitated before using it. As much as he hated being on the bridge, he couldn't shake the feeling they were walking into a trap.

"It's perfectly safe, I assure you," Manchester said, noting his apprehension. "Just keep moving forward."

Joey didn't exactly check his suspicions at the door, but he did go through it. After all, if Manchester wanted to kill them, there were less complicated ways to do it. He passed through complete darkness. Joey called out for his friends but received no reply. There was no sound at all and no light at the end of the tunnel to tell him if the passage was two feet long or two hundred. Joey was scared, but he kept moving ahead. His faith was rewarded as he emerged from the tunnel deep inside the walled city on the far mountaintop. Looking up, he felt a rush of energy. The Memory Palace on the hill was suddenly within walking distance, and the orcs were nowhere in sight. Everyone else, however, was. Joey's friends were elated, looking around with wide eyes full of wonder.

"How did we get here so fast?" Janelle asked. "This place was miles away."

Manchester smiled as he came through the door behind Joey. "Normal rules don't apply here. Everything is just a thought away. Remember that."

Joey wandered forward as if in a dream, trying to make sense of what he saw. The city was not medieval or Tolkienesque like everything else in DeMayne's head. Instead, it looked more like Main Street USA from Disney World. Even more so because of the picturesque castle in the distance. Joey and his friends were standing in an idealized vision of a turn-of-the-century American town. The previous century, to be specific. The streets were full of Victorian buildings with ornate molding, striped awnings, and inviting storefronts. They had old-timey names like the Confectionary Sweet Shoppe, the Gentleman's Haberdashery, and the Beauty Emporium. The town was quiet, peaceful, and overflowing with nostalgia. A handful of cars parked on the street were all shiny new Model T Fords, and smiling people were out for an evening stroll dressed to the nines. The men wore suits and ties with starched collars and skimmer hats. The women wore big poufy dresses with gloves that went up to their elbows. The bright colors of everyone's clothing complemented the vibrant storefronts as if a costume designer and set designer had collaborated on the palette.

"I didn't see this coming," Leanora said.

"The soul of magic is surprise," Manchester told her. "You have to expect the unexpected at all times."

Manchester took on the role of tour guide, leading the group into town and pointing out his favorite shops along the way. People tipped their caps to him and said good evening as they passed by on the sidewalk. Manchester was very polite with everyone in return. No one seemed to notice or care that he was escorting a group of children who were dressed for battle and armed with swords. The streetlights illuminated the road ahead like a parade route, and they followed it to a charming square at the center of town. It was bordered on one side by public buildings like the city hall, a post office, and a library. The other side boasted a hotel, a restaurant, and a large theater reminiscent of the Majestic.

Beyond the square was a gated park with a pond, lush green-ery, and of course, the Memory Palace. The fairy-tale castle was incongruous with the rest of the town but somehow still seemed to belong.

"You want to talk about unexpected," Joey said. "This place is like a town from an old movie or musical. Part of me is waiting for these people to do a big song and dance number."

"Beats getting eaten by goblins," Shazad said.

Joey turned. "I thought they were orcs."

"What's the difference?" asked Janelle.

"Orcs are more . . ." Joey paused, searching for an expla-nation. "You know, I'm not really sure."

"It doesn't matter. You won't find orcs or goblins here." Manchester motioned toward the park. "Shall we?" They were about to go in when a man called out behind them.

"What are you doing?"

They turned to see a handsome young couple standing a few feet away. "You can't go in there," the man warned the group. "No one goes into the park."

"It's not safe," added the woman on his arm. She put a hand up to hide her mouth. "There's magic in there," she

136

whispered as if she were saying something scandalous.

"It's all right," Leonora told them. "We'll be fine."

"Ah, ah, ah . . ." A police officer came in to join the conversation. "We have rules in this town, young lady." He tapped a PARK CLOSED sign with his billy club. "That's for your protection. You're better off out here."

The officer was a pleasant-looking fellow with a bushy mustache and a friendly smile, but Joey smelled trouble. The way he twirled his nightstick made him uncomfortable. "What's the matter? Don't you like it here?" the policeman asked, picking up on the tension.

"Of course they do," Ledger DeMayne said, making an appearance at last. He appeared out of nowhere, wearing a bright blue suit with a white sash that read MAYOR. Somehow, he made it look good instead of ridiculous. Typical DeMayne. He always looked good. "What's not to like?" he asked. "This is a world of peace and harmony. You should know, this is what you give up when you let magic run wild."

The police officer and the young couple agreed enthusiastically.

"He's right."

"He's absolutely right."

"Couldn't be more right!"

DeMayne took a moment to say hello and shake their hands. The townspeople were thrilled to see him. DeMayne was a celebrity in his own mind, fawning all over himself. Joey thought the level of ego on display was incredible.

"Keep telling yourself that," Joey replied. "This town is you to a tee. You keep a little bit of magic locked up for your own personal use." He paused, pointing to the castle in the park. "And the rest of it you keep sealed off, outside of everyone's reach." Joey pointed to the border wall at the edge of town. "And you do it all for the *greater good*."

Joey's sarcasm was palpable. DeMayne huffed. "You may not like it, but that arrangement worked out very well for a very long time."

"For very few people," Leanora said.

"I don't see anyone here complaining." DeMayne gestured to the picture-perfect town he had created in his mind. A crowd of supporters had gathered outside the park entrance to rally around their mayor.

"You're delusional," Janelle said. "This place . . . This is a fantasy. The real world isn't like this. It's *never* been like this. Even in 'the good old days,' this kind of life didn't exist for everyone. Especially for people like me. And soon it won't exist for anyone. Today we've got climate change, wildfires, global pandemics—"

"And you think waving a magic wand can make all that go away?" DeMayne interrupted. "Oh, wait. I forgot, you're afraid to do that. Your solution is to introduce magic into all that chaos." DeMayne wagged a finger at the children. "This isn't going to work the way you think it is. You're pouring gasoline on the wildfire."

"It's already done," Shazad said. "Are we taking a risk by releasing magic back into the world? Of course. But the greater risk is to do nothing."

"We're not going to make it as a planet if things keep going the way they are," Joey agreed. "Someone's got to step up and save the world."

"And change it," Janelle added.

DeMayne sighed. "It's no use talking to you. You won't listen to reason."

"Sure they will," Manchester said. "Just not your reasons. They're not the audience you're used to seeing, Ledger. You can't trick them. They know your game, and they're going to teach everyone to play, because the chance to live in a world where anything is possible is worth fighting for. We're here to fight that battle, and I stand with them."

Manchester's blade flew out, slashing through DeMayne's torso before anyone had a chance to blink. The crowd of people gasped and turned away as he burst into a cloud of black smoke.

Unfortunately, it didn't last. The plume of smoke swirled around and quickly re-formed, consolidating itself back into the figure of Ledger DeMayne. Once he was whole again, he stared at Manchester, dressing him down with his eyes like a teacher fed up with an unruly student. "I never liked you."

Manchester stared back at him. "The feeling was mutual."

The townspeople closed ranks behind their leader. They weren't orcs, but they had all the makings of an angry mob and looked oddly threatening in their stately attire.

"I think it's time to get out of here," Joey told his friends, backing away from the crowd toward the park.

"Not so fast," DeMayne said. "You came here to fight for a better world. I'd hate to deny you that opportunity." He turned to his people with a nonchalant wave, as if he were telling his butler to clear away his dinner plate. "Kill them."

8

The Memory Palace

"Into the park! Now!" Grayson Manchester shouted.

Joey and his friends did as they were told and ran inside. Manchester threw the wrought-iron gate shut behind them with one hand and swung his sword out with the other. A series of pops erupted like a string of firecrackers, followed by the metallic clang of the gate slamming into place.

Everyone stopped when they heard it. Manchester had locked the gate with himself on the wrong side. "What about you?" Leanora called out.

"Don't worry about me!" he said. "Get to the castle."

Swinging two swords, he spun around, turning more well-dressed assailants into clouds of vapor.

"Hurry!"

Joey and the others took off running. *I owe that guy an*

apology, Joey thought to himself, looking back as the residents of DeMayne's pretty little town screamed hateful things and rattled the gate, trying to climb over it. Manchester cut them down and held the crowd back—for a time. He was one man against dozens and dozens. Smoke filled the air as he fought, and he was lost in the haze, his fate unknown.

Ledger DeMayne, on the other hand, was everywhere at once. As Joey, Janelle, Shazad, and Leanora raced through the park, they passed him several times. First he was sitting on a bench. Then they rounded a corner, and he was leaning on a tree. Wherever they went, there he was. "I'm curious what good you think running is going to do?" he asked casually. "You think you're any safer in here?"

His laughter filled the air, chasing them deeper into the park. They fled as fast as they could, fully expecting to see DeMayne again up ahead. He didn't reappear, but Joey felt his presence everywhere. They ran down a garden path, bordered by hearty flower beds, manicured shrubberies, and strong old trees. They sprinted around a tranquil pond and over an old stone bridge. It was a gorgeous evening, filled with moonlight and fireflies, but everything about the park was tainted. It was too perfect, much like the town and

DeMayne himself. Joey got the sense that if he were somehow able to peel back the artificial, attractive top layer, he'd find something horrible lurking underneath the surface. With that in mind, the scenic park was no better than the endless fields of orcs. Joey decided he didn't want to be there anymore. He called out for Hypnova, but the only reply was more laughter from DeMayne. "I'm sorry, Hypnova's not available right now. It's just us, boys and girls."

Joey whirled around, looking to see where DeMayne was this time. There was no sign of him. Nothing but a disembodied voice taunting them from somewhere beyond the trees. *We're in too deep*, Joey thought. *She can't see us.*

For the first time, he worried they were already trapped in DeMayne's mind with no chance of escape. Even if he and his friends reached the castle and found DeMayne's lost memories, how were they supposed to get back out? They couldn't go back the way they came. Grayson Manchester probably could have guided them back to safety, but he was gone, and the odds of seeing him again were not looking good.

They came to a fork in the road with two trails that led in opposite directions, each disappearing around a bend. The

Memory Palace was just beyond the trees, but they had no way of knowing which path to choose. "Which way do we go?" Janelle asked.

"You think it matters?" Joey wondered. "DeMayne controls everything here. Who's to says he's even going to let us reach the castle?"

"He's toying with us," Shazad agreed.

Ever the fighter, Leanora put a hand on the hilt of her sword. "Let's have it out, then. I'm tired of running."

A shadow moved behind the trees. Joey heard the rustling of leaves and footfalls on grass. The noise was barely audible, but it was enough to let him know someone was out there. It turned out to be several someones, as a company of elves stepped into view. They had flaxen hair and smooth, beautiful features and wore ornate armor. No one said anything. The elven warriors just looked at Joey and his friends with cold eyes and unsmiling faces.

Janelle started down the path on the right, pulling Leanora with her. "I think running is good. Let's run."

Leanora didn't like it, but she was forced to agree. She lowered her sword and went along with Janelle. Everyone bolted, with Joey and Shazad acting as the rear guard.

They covered the others with their shields as the elves fired arrows at them. The path wound around a hairpin turn that momentarily took them out of firing range, but it also led away from the palace. Everyone realized they were going the wrong way, but they couldn't double back. The way behind them was blocked with elves. Soon the trees were full of them too. They were everywhere Joey looked, and there was nowhere left to run. The trail dead-ended in a courtyard garden with a statue of DeMayne in the center. The man himself stepped out from behind it.

"You went the wrong way," he gloated as the elves surrounded them.

"Was there a right way?" Joey asked.

"Not really."

DeMayne gave a nod, and the elves advanced, ready to finish off Joey and his friends. They were nearly within striking distance when, out of nowhere, Grayson Manchester came to the rescue once again. He was scratched up and bloodied from battle, but he was as fierce as ever as he threw himself at the elves. "Not again," DeMayne groaned. He balled a fist and cast his eyes upward as Manchester spun his swords around like a tornado of death. He was completely outnumbered and the elves were gifted warriors, but they were no match for him. Manchester was like a dancer, moving to music only he could hear. "I can't get rid of this guy," DeMayne complained.

"I definitely owe him an apology," Joey said, marveling at Manchester's fighting prowess.

"I'll settle for a little help!" Manchester called out. "There's a reason I gave you those swords, you know!"

"Right!" Leanora drew her sword and ran into battle. Joey, Shazad, and Janelle were right behind her. Joey had never been in a fight like this before, but he picked it up quickly. Everyone did. He and his friends were nowhere near Grayson Manchester's skill level, but they held their own in the melee, turning the attacking elves into clouds of smoke. The sound of swords clashing and elves popping out of existence rang out as they fought back.

"Anyone else notice how good we are at this?" Shazad asked as he plunged a sword into an elf, reducing it to a misty vapor.

"That's because you're getting in his head now—figuratively," Manchester explained. "You shouldn't have lasted this long, with or without my help, but the more worried about you DeMayne becomes, the stronger you get."

"You're right!" Joey said, hacking away with his sword. "I'm not tired anymore."

"I never get tired here," Manchester said. "Look at me—I'm a fighting machine! That's not who I was in real life, but that doesn't matter. All that matters is how he sees me. I'm someone who beat him at his own game, and he can't get over it. The question is, how does he see the four of you?"

Joey looked up at DeMayne. He was watching the fight unfold from the pedestal of his statue, clearly concerned that the tide was turning against him. Just like that, Joey understood that DeMayne *didn't* have absolute power in the mindscape. He was at the mercy of his own subconscious fears just like everybody else.

"I've got it!" Joey shouted. "Follow me!"

"What? Where?" asked Janelle.

"To the castle—this way!" He sliced through a bush, opening up a path into the woods. "Come on!"

"Are you sure?" Shazad asked, eyeing the uneven terrain with trepidation. There was no clear path forward.

"Trust me," Joey said, leading the way in. "He can't catch

us! That's who we are to him. The more we believe it, the more it's true. Follow me—and keep up!"

Joey and his friends charged through the forest. Moving faster and more agilely than ever, they flew across the land. Joey felt his confidence rising with every step. He reminded the others how DeMayne had spent the last year looking for them without success. That meant in DeMayne's mind, they were elusive. They used his impression of them to their advantage, leaving the elves behind as they ran toward the Memory Palace. It was closer than it looked. Growing more comfortable with the malleable nature of the dreamscape, Joey realized it was just a thought away. He stepped out of the forest right at the castle gates with his friends alongside him. Grayson Manchester brought up the rear. "You're getting the hang of this," he said with a smile.

They weren't alone. High up in a tower window, Ledger DeMayne looked down at the group, scowling. He turned away in a huff, retreating into the palace.

"Let's get what we came for," Joey said.

Outside, the Memory Palace was a fairy-tale dream. Inside, it looked like someone's storage unit had thrown up. Everywhere Joey looked, the space was littered with mounds of junk, knickknacks, and worthless odds and ends. Clear plastic bins stuffed with random trinkets lined the walls. Cardboard boxes full of letters, receipts, and hastily drawn sketches covered the floor. It was dark, musty, and claustrophobic.

"What is all this?" Janelle asked, wrinkling her nose in disgust.

"A lifetime of memories," Manchester explained. "Nothing ever gets forgotten completely. Even the things he can't quite remember, they're all in here somewhere." He led the group into the next room, a vast chamber overflowing with old newspapers. There were rows and rows of them, stacked up on top of each other, forming the walls of a maze that took up the whole room.

Joey pulled a paper out of one of the stacks. "'The DeMayne Ledger,'" he said, reading the masthead. "Cute."

"These articles are all events from his life," Shazad observed, looking at a paper of his own. "'April 20, 1977. Woke up at 7:02 a.m., brushed teeth, had eggs for breakfast . . .' Day by day, it's all here, however mundane." He looked around, overwhelmed by the ocean of newsprint. "We have to read all this?"

"We can't. That would take forever," Leanora said. "There must be thousands of papers here. Hundreds of thousands."

"These papers are a record, not a searchable database," Manchester said. "They aren't meant to be read. Even DeMayne wouldn't be able to find anything in here without help from hypnosis or guided meditation."

"I'm guessing some things are easier to remember than others," Janelle said. She pointed up at a banner that had Grayson Manchester's face and the words MR. GRAY emblazoned upon it. Dozens more banners adorned the walls displaying a variety of colors and faces: Mr. Crimson, Ms. Magenta, Mr. Indigo, Mrs. Violet. . . . The list went on and on. It was like a hall of fame for members of the Invisible Hand going back through the ages. Joey scanned the timeline from era to era, skipping from 1950s America to Victorian England and all the way to medieval times, where people named Duke Cerulean, Lord Silver, and Lady Emerald were hung in places of honor. Most of the faces were new to Joey, but some of them were all too familiar, such as Scarlett, Ivory, and Clear. He noticed that Ivory's and Clear's banners appeared fresh and new, while the others were all faded and worn. Manchester's banner, on the other hand, looked like an angry person had gone at it with a pair of scissors.

"That's a bit extreme, isn't it?" Manchester said, noting his carved-up image on the wall. "He could have just drawn a mustache on my face or given me a black eye."

"I know these names," Leanora said, looking over the banners. "My family tells stories about some of these people."

"Mine too," Shazad said. "None of them are good."

The sound of angry voices started building outside the room, coming from back the way they'd come. The unwelcome realization that they wouldn't be alone much longer quickly set in. "We can't stay here." Joey pushed forward, knocking down the walls of the newspaper maze, hoping to find a way out before generations of Invisible Hand members came to greet them. "These aren't the memories we want, anyway. Remember what Hypnova told us. We have to dig up the stuff that's hidden—even from DeMayne." He reached the edge of the room, where a large tapestry with the symbol of the Invisible Hand hung on the wall. "We came here to find out where it all began. What's behind the Invisible Hand?" Joey tore down the tapestry, revealing a secret door that was boarded up and covered in dust. Someone gasped behind him. It was DeMayne.

"Where did that come from?" he asked, genuinely shocked by Joey's discovery.

After everything Joey had seen in the dreamscape, another sudden appearance by DeMayne didn't faze him, but he was definitely surprised when a collection of elves, orcs, towns-folk, and Invisible Hand alumni burst into the room, only to stop short when their boss held up his hand.

"Has that been here this whole time?" one of the orcs asked, squinting at the door. His voice was surprisingly dis-tinguished. He sounded like an actor who had just broken character.

DeMayne didn't favor the orc with an answer. Unable to take his eyes off the newly found door, he dismissed the eclectic gathering of minions with a careless wave. Joey breathed a sigh of relief as they shrank away, realizing their presence was no longer required.

DeMayne went to the door, which he couldn't open because of the boards that had been nailed in place over it. He tried to pry them off with his hands, but they wouldn't budge. Realizing he couldn't do it alone, he turned around with a sheepish look, silently asking Grayson Manchester to help him open it.

Manchester shook his head. "Sorry. I'm just a self-defeating extension of you, mate. *Self*-defeating. I can't beat whatever's beating you."

"We can," Leanora said, stepping forward. She swung her sword at the wooden planks blocking the door. The others joined in, chopping them to pieces and breaking the latch. The door swung out freely on its hinges to reveal a stairway winding down, but not into darkness. The undulating glow of orange light waited around the corner.

Ledger DeMayne pushed his way to the front of the group and went down the steps first. Joey and the others followed him into the depths of his blocked memories. They didn't get far before reaching another obstacle.

"The good news is we're getting warmer," Joey said.

The group came to a halt at a landing where the next set of steps descended into lava. Leanora sighed. "Not again."

The fiery orange sludge appeared to flow out of a grate at the top step that fed the river of magma. A large wheel valve on the wall presented an obvious solution, but DeMayne couldn't touch it. He tried to turn the wheel, but it turned

153

red hot, burning him badly. He jumped back, shaking his hand out. Once more, he turned to Grayson Manchester for help, but Manchester put his hands up and backed away with a "don't ask me" look. Joey and the others had to turn the valve, but for them, it was cool to the touch. Working together, they closed off the source of the lava and watched it vanish into drainage slots on the stairs.

Ledger DeMayne tapped the top step with his foot, checking it for heat. Once he was satisfied it was safe to proceed, he hurried down the steps without a word.

"You're welcome!" Janelle called out to his back.

The group hustled after DeMayne, eventually catching up with him at the bottom of the staircase. They found him in a small room with a large treasure chest. He had his back to them and was hunched over the chest, breathing heavily. As they came up alongside him, they saw him as he truly was—an ancient, withered man. His perfect, unblemished skin was spotted with age and crisscrossed by a network of deeply set wrinkles. His thick wavy blond hair was actually white and scraggly, and there was hardly any left on his head. DeMayne's back was bent, and his feeble hands were curled and useless. He looked at Joey with pathetic puppy-dog eyes.

"Please. I can't lift the lid. Help me." Joey was stunned to see him this way. It was shocking to think about how old DeMayne really was and even more shocking to hear him asking for help. *He actually said please!* Joey knew it had to be killing DeMayne to have this memory on the tip of his brain but still out of reach. He was dying to know what it was that had been hidden from him for so long.

For once, the Invisible Hand and the Order of the Majestic wanted the same thing. Joey, Janelle, Leanora, and Shazad opened the chest. A blinding light poured out.

"What's inside?" Shazad asked.

"I don't know. I can't see!" Leanora said.

A creaking mechanical noise, followed by a loud *clack*, drew Joey's attention away from the chest. The lava door at the top of the steps had made that sound when they'd closed it. A creeping orange glow in the stairwell told Joey it had just opened back up.

"What do we do?" Joey asked as lava coursed down the stairs. It was coming fast, as if some kind of volcanic dam had burst.

The image of Hypnova appeared, flashing in and out. "Inside!" she said, pointing at the chest. "Go inside!"

Everyone was so eager to escape the lava, they didn't even blink at Hypnova's surprise return. They just took her advice and ran with it. Shazad, Leanora, and Janelle climbed over the side of the chest and jumped in. Joey and Grayson Manchester helped the frail Ledger DeMayne in after them. Joey sat on the edge of the chest and reached out for Manchester as lava poured into the room.

"Come on!"

But Manchester stayed where he was. Looking at the flickering image of Hypnova, he gave a nod as the lava overtook him.

"Manchester!" Joey shouted, but it was too late. He was gone—this time, Joey knew, for good. Lava rose around the edges of the chest, and Joey dove in after his friends.

He fell through a void of light and landed softly in a green pastoral field. It was beautiful, serene, and safe—the polar opposite of the secret basement in the Memory Palace. Joey's friends were all there with him. An endless run of rolling green hills stretched out before them, and a thick wall of trees filled the space behind them. Beyond the horizon, a massive crystal mountain with a nearly vertical slope and a razor-sharp summit towered over everything. Sunlight reflected through the mountain like a prism, creating a rainbow that was one of a kind. DeMayne, who was young again, looked around in wonder. "I know this place. I've been here before. Ages ago." He was in a world of his own, ignoring Joey and the others completely.

"Where's Manchester?" asked Shazad.

Joey looked up at the clear blue sky they had just fallen out of. "He didn't make it. He didn't even try."

"You don't need him anymore," Hypnova said, appearing on the field. No longer flickering, Hypnova was every bit as solid as the rest of them. "The memory of Manchester served his purpose. You made it. We're here."

"Hypnova!" Joey said, delighted to see she was still with them. He and his friends rushed to her, taking the time for a proper reunion that they didn't have before.

"You're back!" Shazad exclaimed.

"Where've you been?" asked Leanora.

"Looking for you, of course. I was finally able to find you now that he's not keeping us apart. His mind is elsewhere." Hypnova nodded toward DeMayne, who was hiking up a nearby hill, determined to get a look at the other side.

"Where are we?" Janelle wondered as they trailed after DeMayne. "Do you recognize this place?"

"I do," Hypnova said. "We're in the Outlands. The untamed edges of the Imagine Nation."

"The Imagine Nation?" Joey repeated. "We're here?" A charge of excitement ran through him. Dream or no dream, he was getting his first look at what was arguably the most wondrous place on earth—a magic island that roamed around the world in secret, hidden even from magicians like him and Shazad's and Leonora's families. He noticed the position of the crystal mountain on the horizon had moved. Most likely, they were moving around it. He hustled after DeMayne, eager to see more, but when he crested the hill, the view disappointed him. He saw a castle in the distance, obscured by fog. Upon closer examination, he realized the castle was made of fog. The land beyond the hill was too. Everything was wavy and intangible. They could go no farther. "What is this?" he asked Hypnova.

"This is all very normal," she said, joining him on the hilltop. "His memory of this place has been unlocked, but it's still hazy. Unclear. We need to give him time. And, if he'll allow it . . . some assistance." She approached DeMayne from behind and went to put a hand on his shoulder. He regarded her with a look that was both suspicious and vulnerable, but he didn't pull away. As soon as she touched him, flashes of memory entered Joey's mind. Instantly, he knew without a shadow of a doubt that Ledger DeMayne had been there when the Imagine Nation was created. The final battle had taken place in the mad emperor's palace. Joey saw glimpses of the conflict and the aftermath.

He saw Merlin in his bright blue robes, with his long white beard. "This isn't the end. It's the beginning," the old wizard said, struggling to speak. Joey could tell he didn't have long to live. "You have to carry on without me. Keep magic alive in the world."

A woman took Merlin's hand. "I will. I swear it."

Someone else was there too—a woman in a cloak much like Hypnova's. "I'll keep it safe," she promised Merlin. "This place and what's hidden here . . . I'll make sure men like the Hand won't ever find it again."

"You're going to have to kill me," a younger version of DeMayne said. He looked angry and beaten. "I don't care if it takes the rest of my life, I'll be back. I won't forget what you've cost me today."

The woman in the cloak held out a hand to DeMayne. "Yes, you will."

There was a flash of light, and Joey knew they had reached the limit of Ledger DeMayne's knowledge. This was the moment that Merlin, his apprentice Kadabra, and the first Secreteer had rewritten history, hiding the Imagine Nation from DeMayne and the rest of the world. This memory couldn't contain the information they were seeking. What kept the Imagine Nation moving? What force had kept it hidden all these years?

Before they could probe deeper and try to learn any more, the ground shook with a tremor that knocked Joey off his feet. He snapped out of DeMayne's foggy memories as he and the others tumbled back down the hill. "What just happened?" Joey asked once they had all come to a stop. "Was that an earthquake?"

"More like a skyquake," Leanora said, pointing up.

"No way." Joey looked up to see a massive, lightning-bolt-shaped crack had split the sky in two. Lines ran out from the breach as both sides began to break apart. Soon, huge chunks of solid blue sky were falling to the ground like meteors ready to crush them.

"Not now," Hypnova said, cursing their luck as DeMayne's mindscape collapsed. "We're so close."

"What's going on?" Janelle asked. "What is this?"

Hypnova stood up and dusted herself off. "We're under attack."

9

Abandon Ship

The world shook again, blasting Joey out of DeMayne's mind. He blinked and he was back in the captain's cabin on board Hypnova's ship. He looked around, feeling disoriented and sluggish. His eyelids were heavy and his vision was warped, but his friends soon came into focus. They were rubbing their eyes and groaning, every bit as dazed as he was. DeMayne would have likely rubbed his eyes too if he could reach them. He was still tied up on the floor.

The ship rocked from side to side, making it hard for Joey to stand up. The room spun on him, and it wasn't because of vertigo. Something outside was knocking them around the sky. Joey went to the window to see what was out there. Driving rain beat against the glass, and howling winds pushed the ship along an erratic, unpredictable course. The gentle, drifting fog had been replaced by a violent storm. Lightning flashed in the distance, and Joey thought he saw something—or someone—flying through the clouds.

"What is it?" Shazad asked. "What's going on?"

"They found us," Hypnova said.

"Who did?" asked Leanora. "The Invisible Hand?"

"I'm afraid not," Hypnova said. "Those are Secreteers out there."

"Secreteers?" Joey repeated.

"HYPNOVA!" someone outside shouted. "SHOW YOURSELF!" Hypnova's eyes widened in alarm. It was obvious she recognized the voice. Hypnova looked worried, which worried Joey. He left the window and went to the door, but Hypnova got there first.

"No!" she said, blocking his path. "They haven't seen you yet. They don't know you're here. I want to keep it that way." Outside the window, smoke trails flew by and lightning zigzagged across the sky in a way that was beautiful and terrifying at the same time.

"What should we do?" Joey asked.

"Stay out of sight while I try to lose them. I'll be back."

Hypnova slipped outside, leaving Joey and the others in

the cabin. They waited in silence as the storm raged outside. Seconds later, Joey had to grab the wall to keep from falling over as the ship banked hard to port. He hoped it was Hypnova taking evasive action, as opposed to the ship falling out of the sky. A quick change in course brought relief as the ship came around, turning back the other way. Joey didn't know how Hypnova was able to steer the ship with such control, bobbing and weaving through the clouds, but he was glad to have her at the helm. He stepped over DeMayne on his way to the window to get a better look at the Secreteers. Standing alongside Janelle, Shazad, and Leanora, he watched as the ship climbed above the clouds and into clear skies. Twin trails of smoke rose from below, chasing after them. One was gray and the other was deep purple. This time Joey clearly saw cloaked figures inside the smoke. Storm clouds gathered around their pursuers as they circled the ship, flying through the air.

A third stream of smoke soared through the clouds, this one as white as snow. The vapor trail paused in the air above the ship, and Joey was able to make out a woman inside it. Her long white hair flowed in the wind, and she seemed to hold lightning in her hand. "There's nowhere left to run, traitor! This ends tonight!" It was the same voice that had spooked Hypnova moments before. Now Joey understood why. The woman's eyes were full of fury, and electricity radiated from her fist. She threw her hand forward, and lightning struck again.

Fortunately, it turned away at the last second, skidding off some kind of force field that lit up just before the bolt hit its target. Joey flinched when he saw it, simultaneously relieved that the Caliburn Shield was protecting them. The ship took many hard twists and turns, trying to escape, but they couldn't shake the Secreteers or the fierce weather they had brought with them. Many more lightning strikes followed. They failed to penetrate the shield's invisible barrier, but Joey worried how long it would last. Eventually, the ship straightened out and forged ahead, sailing into the eye of the storm.

"How are they doing this?" Shazad asked. "I thought they just had memory powers like Hypnova."

"They know the world's biggest secrets," Hypnova explained, coming back into the cabin. She had taken the Caliburn Shield down from its place above the cabin door and now had it strapped over her arm. "That includes the location of many magical objects. They're using some of them against us right now." Lightning flashed again, filling the room with a flickering light. "I believe that one's called a thunderstone."

"Shouldn't they call it a lightning stone?" Janelle asked. "After all, thunder is just the sound *caused* by lightning. The sudden increase in pressure and temperature from lightning causes a rapid expansion of the air surrounding the lightning bolt, which creates a sonic shock wave that—"

Hypnova put a hand on Janelle's shoulder. "That's . . . fascinating," she said gently. "But not now."

"Sorry. Nervous rambling," Janelle said.

"Forget about it," Joey told her. "I do that too." While Janelle was going on about the proper name for the thunderstone, his imagination had been running wild about the stone itself. He wondered if it had any connection to the firestone around his neck or the "ice stone" Mr. Clear had worn as a bracelet. He wondered how many stones were out there. It occurred to him that the hypnotic red ruby Mr. Clear had frozen and shattered could have been thought of as a "mind stone," as they had used it to control the security guard's mind. That made Joey think of Marvel comics,

Avengers movies, and infinity stones. He kept those ideas to himself, deciding the others wouldn't appreciate his random thoughts on the matter any more than they had Janelle's impromptu lesson in meteorology.

A booming thunderclap rumbled so loudly, it sounded like it was coming from inside the cabin. Everybody jumped. For a second Joey thought the Secreteers had blown a hole in the ship's hull.

"There's your thunder," Leanora said to Janelle.

"It's all right," Hypnova said, patting the Caliburn Shield. "We're safe for now. I told you, if not for this shield, I'd never know any peace." Her voice was calm and confident, but Joey couldn't help noticing how tight she was gripping the shield.

"Just out of curiosity, if you're in here, who's driving?" Shazad asked Hypnova.

"Don't worry about that. There's nothing for us to crash into this high up. That's the good news." Hypnova looked out the window at her former friends in the Clandestine Order. "The bad news is that's Oblivia out there calling me out."

"Oblivia?" Joey said. "The head Secreteer?"

Hypnova nodded. "She's in quite a state tonight. I expect her mood has to do with you all taking out the dark magic markers. She's not letting up. I can't lose them."

Outside, lightning continued to strike against the protective barrier that surrounded the ship. The Caliburn Shield twinkled with an ambient glow each time the force field lit up. As the Secreteer's relentless assault continued, Joey noticed the light was fading, both inside and out. He wasn't the only one who saw it.

"Should we be worried?" Janelle asked.

"No," Shazad said. "The shield will keep us safe. It's one of the big three Arthurian artifacts. Nothing can get past its defenses except Joey's wand."

"Nothing we know of," Janelle said as the ship rattled its way through more turbulence. Her tone didn't inspire a great deal of confidence.

Joey watched the light show outside with growing unease. The Caliburn Shield was impenetrable. That was an absolute, unassailable truth, but at the same time, he knew that magic was not an exact science. Joey thought about the Sword of Storms that Ledger DeMayne used against him and his friends outside Camelot and the Majestic Theatre.

That sword had once had another name: Excalibur. It was supposed to be unbreakable too, but it had surely broken. There was always a chance the Caliburn Shield's power would fail eventually too. What if tonight was the night?

"We've got to fight back," Joey said, drawing the wand out from his sleeve.

"No," Shazad said. "Not with that."

"Shazad's right," Hypnova agreed. "This isn't what that wand is meant for. We've got to get you out of here. It's not your fight. They're here for me."

Outside, the relentless assault continued. The ship bounced up and down like an air force bomber taking flak from enemy artillery. Oblivia's voice carried over the howling wind, delivering more threats.

"She's here to kill you," Joey said.

"She's been trying to kill me for a year now. I'm still here. Believe it or not, this is a good thing. I want her distracted. The more focused she is on me, the less attention there is on you and the Imagine Nation." Hypnova looked at DeMayne, who was squirming on the ground, trying to sit up with his back against the wall. "Untie him."

"What?" everyone said at once.

"Do it."

Shazad and Leonora unraveled Gleipnir, freeing DeMayne. He rose to his feet, massaging his wrists and eyeing Hypnova suspiciously.

"What are you up to?" he asked her.

"I believe you magicians call it misdirection?" Hypnova went to a corner of the room and found a fabric and metal contraption that resembled a folded-up kite. "This is an escape glider." She tossed it over to DeMayne. "Think you can handle it?"

DeMayne caught the glider and gave it a cursory inspection. He looked like he was being asked to try on an outfit someone had just pulled out of a sewer. "We're a thousand feet up. Where am I supposed to land?"

"On the ground, of course," Hypnova said. "You'll get there eventually. This is your chance to leave here with your memory intact. If I were you, I'd take it."

"Hang on," Joey said. "With his memory *intact*?" He didn't like the sound of that. "Can we talk about this?"

"There's no time," Hypnova said as lightning struck outside, sending another tremor through the ship. "This should be an easy decision," she told DeMayne. "What are you waiting for?"

DeMayne frowned as he flexed the frame of the glider, teaching himself how to work it. "I want to be clear: Letting me go doesn't change anything between us. What's done is done. Your offenses are unforgivable."

"I could say the same to you," Hypnova replied.

"This isn't over." DeMayne sneered. "There will be a reckoning. You can count on it," he added, fixing his eyes on Joey. Then he dashed out the door. Joey watched as Ledger DeMayne ran across the deck of the ship, flapped open the glider, and leaped from the gunwales. The Secreteers took off after him as he flew out into the night. The skies cleared as they chased after him, taking the rain and thunder with them.

"He moves pretty good for a guy his age," Janelle said as DeMayne and the Secreteers disappeared from their sight.

"Why'd you let him keep his memory?" Joey asked Hypnova.

"Trust me," Hypnova said. "We're going to need it." She pushed past Joey and opened a hatch outside the cabin door. "Quickly. Get below before the Secreteers realize that wasn't me on the glider. DeMayne won't fool them for long."

Joey didn't like this development any more than he understood it, but he knew there was nothing he could do about it now. DeMayne was long gone. The group hurried outside and down the steps to the ship's lower deck. "Where are we going?" asked Leanora.

"*You're* going to the Imagine Nation," Hypnova said. "I'm going to stay here to lead the Secreteers away from you. If I can't lose them, I'll scuttle the ship."

"What?" Joey said. "No! You can't do that."

"We're too close to stop now," Hypnova insisted. "What you saw in DeMayne's mind . . . the women with Merlin? One of them was Kadabra, founder of the Order of the Majestic. The other was the first Secreteer. The first Majestrix of the Clandestine Order. I understand now. I see it. The emperor's palace became her place of power—the Secret Citadel. I've never been there. I don't know anyone who has, or what's inside, but thanks to DeMayne we have a clue where it is. His memory showed us where to look. It's somewhere in the Outlands of the Imagine Nation."

The ship tilted sharply as the unwelcome sound of thunder rumbled outside.

"They're back," Shazad said, putting a hand on the hull of the ship to keep his balance.

"That *was* fast," Joey agreed.

172

Hypnova cursed under her breath. "No matter. I'll deal with them. You have to find the Citadel and turn off whatever it is that keeps the Imagine Nation hidden. You've already given magic back to the world. Now let's set the Imagine Nation free. I'm with you."

"But you're not with us," Leanora said. "You said you were going to crash this ship. You can't be serious."

"You'll die!" Shazad protested.

"Don't count on it." Hypnova patted the Caliburn Shield. "I'll see you again before this is over. I promise."

"I don't know," Joey said. He sensed the concern his friends had for Hypnova and felt the same way himself. "I don't like the sound of this."

"You don't have to like it—you just have to trust me," Hypnova said. "It's time for you to leave."

"How?" Janelle asked. "Because I'm not taking one of those gliders. I'd rather take my chances on the ship."

Hypnova smiled. "That won't be necessary." She led the group deeper into the hold of the ship and pulled the tarp off a mystery item that had been gathering dust in the corner. Joey instantly recognized the object as a magic mirror.

"Ever use one of these?"

10

Mirror, Mirror

Out of the four of them, Janelle was the only one who had never traveled by way of magic mirror. She reached out and touched the glass. The surface rippled as if the elaborate baroque gold frame contained a vertical plane of silvery water. Thunder boomed in the distance, and the ship rolled to the side. Janelle pulled her hand back.

"How does it work?" she asked as the ripples in the glass steadied.

"Nothing to it," Joey said once the ship had stabilized. "We just go through it."

He had used a magic mirror only two times in his life, once to enter the mirror world and once to leave it, but it was like riding a bike. He plunged his hand forward. It sank into the mirror as if the glass were not glass at all, but a thick, lustrous gel. He retracted his hand and nodded to Janelle.

"You try."

Janelle poked at the glass tentatively. It remained solid for her.

"Just relax," Shazad told her. "The mirror is just like any other magical object. It has all the power you need. You just have to believe." He inserted his hand just as Joey had done, then stepped away to give Janelle another chance.

"I don't know if I can do this." She tried again with no success.

"What's wrong?" Hypnova asked. "You started to do it a moment ago. What happened?"

Janelle prodded the solid glass a few more times. "Nothing happened. It's just . . . hard to believe." She checked behind the mirror, as if she might find a secret compartment of some kind back there. "There's no scientific rationale for how this works."

"You don't need a scientific rationale," Joey said. "I've watched you spin the Staff of Sorcero from small to large and back again a hundred times. There's nothing scientific about it, but you manage that just fine."

"Actually, I think about the molecular structure of malleable metals when I do that," Janelle said.

"The what structure?" Shazad said.

"Of the what?" Leanora added.

Janelle sighed. "On a molecular level, atoms of malleable metals can roll over each other into new positions without breaking their metallic bond. It's why gold and silver can be pressed into new shapes so easily. Granted, it's not just malleability you have to think about in that case. It's ductility, too. That's the property that allows metals to stretch without—"

"You're rambling again," Joey cut in before Janelle really got going. "And what you're saying doesn't make any sense. The staff isn't even made out of metal. It's wood!"

"I didn't say it was an apples-to-apples comparison. It's just a scientific concept I keep in the back of my brain that lets me do this." Janelle was about to spin the staff around when a peal of thunder shook the room and rattled her nerves. She tensed up, nearly fumbling the staff to the floor.

"Also, there's pressure," she continued. "I usually like to sit with any new magical items a while before I use them. It's the analytic side of my brain. I study things. I take my time." Janelle took a step back. "You guys go first. Show me again."

"You need to go first," Leanora said. "I don't want to risk splitting us up. We all go through or none of us go through."

"We have to hurry," Hypnova warned.

"That's not helping," Janelle replied.

Once again, Joey thought about using the wand. He could have used it to whisk everyone away without spending too much energy, but he didn't bring it up as an option. For one thing, his friends had already shot down that suggestion, and for another, they had a perfectly good escape route right in front of them—provided they could all use it. He remembered being in Janelle's shoes, trying to use Redondo's magic mirror for the first time. The trick was that it wasn't the mirror he'd had to get past, but himself.

"So what if you don't understand how it works?" Joey told Janelle. "Who cares? It's just science we don't understand yet, right? You don't have to know how it works. You just have to know that it does. What if this mirror is some kind of wormhole? A hole in space-time connecting one place to another."

"Wormholes don't look like that," Janelle said, gesturing at the mirror.

"Says who? Do you know what every wormhole in the universe looks like?" Joey countered. "Don't overthink it. Just do it. You've got this."

Janelle took a deep breath and let it out slowly. "I'll try."

Joey resisted the urge to quote a little green Jedi master on the value of "trying" versus "doing." He and the others waited patiently as Janelle flexed her fingers and reached out with both hands. They went into the mirror as if it were made of metallic syrup. Silvery droplets fell to the floor and pooled up like mercury at her feet. She smiled at Joey and kept moving forward. Lifting her foot, she stepped into the mirror and proceeded to walk through it. Shazad and Leanora went in after her.

"For the record, I never doubted her for a second," Joey told Hypnova once they were alone.

"That's good because you're going to need each other," Hypnova said. "The road only gets harder from here." She touched a hand to her temple and reached out toward Joey. The image of another magic mirror appeared in his mind. She was showing him where to go next.

"I understand." Joey stepped halfway into the mirror. He felt guilty leaving Hypnova behind. "Are you sure you're going to be all right?"

"I'll be right behind you. Just make sure you keep going, because Oblivia will be right behind me. I'll buy you as much time as I can."

"Thank you, Hypnova."

"Don't thank me yet. This is a long way from over." She took Joey's hand by the wrist and examined the power gauge drawn on his arm. "Make this last. You're going to need all of it."

"I'll be careful," Joey promised. Hypnova gave him a skeptical look, prompting him to add, "I mean it. I will!"

"Good luck."

Thunder boomed outside the ship, louder than before. "To both of us."

He stepped the rest of the way through the mirror and set his foot down on soft, powdery sand. As Joey emerged from the portal, the mirror slipped off his body like liquid metal and re-formed into glass behind him. Not so much as a droplet clung to his clothes. Shazad was waiting for him on the other side.

"There you are. I was beginning to worry. What took so long?"

"Just saying our goodbyes. Everything okay over here?"

"Looks that way. It's better weather, at least."

Joey took a moment to get his bearings. The mirror world was every bit as strange and beautiful as he remembered it. The magical land was calm and peaceful, a white sand beach under a pale, violet sky. The shoreline stretched out for miles with no one in sight. There was nothing but sand, water, and mirrors everywhere Joey looked. Hundreds of magic mirrors were stuck in the ground, running up and down the beach. They came in every imaginable shape, size, and design. The mirror behind him, which he had just walked through, was an exact match for the mirror on Hypnova's ship. Janelle and Leanora were down by the water, where crystal-clear waves lapped gently against the shore, glowing with a bright, phosphorescent light.

"Are you kidding me?" Janelle said to Joey when she saw him by the mirror. "This place is amazing!"

"It is pretty cool," he said.

"Where are we? Is this another dimension?"

"It's the mirror world," Shazad said. "Every magic mirror back in our world comes out on this beach. You can go through one mirror on your way in and use a different mirror on your way out. It's like a magic transportation hub."

"We can pick any mirror? Go anywhere?" Janelle asked.

"Oh no," Leanora said. "You don't ever go through a mirror in this place unless you're absolutely certain where it leads. There's no telling where you might end up."

Janelle looked around at the rows and rows of mirrors, flabbergasted. "You knew about this place?" she asked Joey.

"I've been here before," he admitted.

"You've been holding out on me."

"I didn't want to blow your mind," Joey said. "Besides, I was only here the one time, and it's not a good memory. I ran into Grayson Manchester on this beach, and not as friends. It was pretty much the exact opposite of what happened in DeMayne's head."

"Joey's right," Leanora said. "As beautiful as this place is, we can't stay. We've got to go."

"Why?" Janelle asked. "What's wrong?"

"It's like Shazad said. These mirrors link back to their counterparts in our world. The Invisible Hand controls most of the known magic mirrors, which puts us in a very vulnerable position."

"Can they see us?" Janelle asked, suddenly wary of the mirrors surrounding her.

"They can if they happen to be looking through their mirrors right now," Shazad answered.

"We should assume they are," Joey said. "You know they're going to be looking for DeMayne. Which means we have to be on the lookout for Mr. Ivory and Mr. Clear."

"Ivory and Clear," Shazad said. "From the banners in the Memory Palace?"

"We met them in DeMayne's office." Janelle spun the Staff of Sorcero out to its full length, putting her guard up. "I'm not in any rush to see them again. What about you guys? Did you run into anyone from the Invisible Hand on your missions?"

Shazad and Leanora both said they had not, which Joey found interesting.

"What's the plan?" asked Janelle. "There have to be a thousand mirrors here. Which one do we take?"

"I can find my family's mirror," Shazad said. "We'll escape to Jorako and regroup."

"No." Joey shook his head. "Hypnova showed me where to go. Somewhere on this beach, there's a mirror that leads to the Imagine Nation. That's the one we want."

"You know where to find it?" Shazad asked.

Joey held out a finger. He looked around the beach, trying to feel out which way to go. As he scanned the collection of mirrors, he pictured the mirror Hypnova had shown him before they parted company. Joey closed his eyes and saw it clearly in his mind—a rectangular full-length mirror with a patchwork frame made up of six different design patterns, none of which went together. Part of the frame was ornate and extravagant, like a mirror from a medieval castle. Part of it was plain white stone with no markings whatsoever. The other elements of the frame were equally distinct. One portion was made of red wood with a decorative golden line that formed an endless knot in the corner, and there were three vastly different high-tech sections of the frame. Hypnova had implanted the image of the mirror very clearly in his brain. It would be hard to miss. But where was it? Had Hypnova also told Joey its location on the beach? He wasn't sure, but eventually he settled on a direction that felt right.

"This way."

Joey struck off down the beach, trusting to instinct. He was going with his gut, but it felt like something more as well. He was following a deep-seated feeling, hoping that it had been placed there by Hypnova and that it would lead them to the Imagine Nation.

As they passed mirror after mirror, searching the beach, Joey grew increasingly uncomfortable. He kept spotting people in random mirrors. At least, he thought he did. Every time he double-checked a mirror to catch a glimpse of the person inside it, he saw nothing but his own reflection.

"How much farther is it?" Leanora asked. Her burned-up boots were coming apart at the seams.

"I don't know." Joey looked ahead, hoping to see the mirror he was searching for nearby. The beach seemed to go on forever.

"Are you sure we're going the right way?" Shazad asked him.

"I think so," Joey hedged. He didn't want to admit it, but he was starting to wonder that himself.

"Anyone else get the feeling we're being watched?" Janelle said.

"No doubt about it," Joey said.

He described the mirror to his friends, telling them what to look for, and picked up his pace, trying to hide his concern. He knew the mirror was on this beach, and he was fairly confident he would find it if he kept going in this direction, but he had no way of knowing if the mirror was ten feet ahead or ten miles away. A blurry figure appeared in a nearby mirror and quickly vanished. Joey felt a knot tighten in his stomach. It had been a long time since the Invisible Hand had known about him and his friends. He didn't like having them back in his life. He also remembered the last time he had felt like they were watching him. One of their agents, Ms. Scarlett, had tagged him with a magic paintbrush that allowed her to track and follow him everywhere. She was gone now, but he kept looking over his shoulder for Mr. Ivory or Mr. Clear. What if it had been them in the mirror?

Fortunately, he didn't see them anywhere. What he did see was a mirror with a strange, multicolored, and multi-styled frame planted firmly in a nearby dune. "There!" he said, pointing. Joey and his friends ran to the mirror. Sure enough, it was a perfect match for the image Hypnova had placed in his mind—their ticket to the Imagine Nation.

"Let's get out of here before we have company," Leonora said.

One by one, they went through the mirror, this time without any difficulty.

They came out the other side in an empty room crafted entirely from white wood. It was sparsely decorated, but cozy, like a rustic hotel room. There was a bed, a night table, and a comfortable-looking chair. Outside, the room opened up onto a terrace. A gentle breeze came in through flowing white curtains that separated the bedroom from the balcony. There were unlit lanterns on the floor and what looked like a string of lights hanging down from the ceiling. Little jars filled with white crystals dangled over Joey's head. The crystals in the jars had a soft glow in the darker corners of the room, but outside the sun was coming up. Joey had been the last one to enter the room. Shazad, Leonora, and Janelle were already outside admiring the view. He joined them on the balcony and saw they were high up in a tree overlooking a forest. A winding staircase with a sturdy railing led down to another room below them, but it was hard for Joey to see. The exterior of the lower level was covered with mirrored shingles that reflected the dense thicket of trees around it so perfectly as to make it nearly invisible. The upper level was built the same way. It was a treehouse hideout. The best Joey had ever seen.

He went to the other side of the balcony. His friends' eyes were firmly fixed in the opposite direction. Squeezing between them, he saw it. The massive crystal mountain from the long-lost memory buried deep in DeMayne's mind. It was even bigger and more awe-inspiring in person. The peak was impossibly tall and knifelike. It was as if the whole mountain was a pointed shard that had been cleaved from a diamond the size of the moon. The mountain sat above the horizon, hovering in midair. High up near the summit, crystalline fragments floated around, orbiting the apex. The sun was rising behind the mountain, and the dawn's first light bent out in a halo of rainbows. The sight took Joey's breath away. It was the most wondrous and beautiful thing he had ever seen, and that was saying something.

"This is it," he whispered with stunned reverence. "The Imagine Nation."

11

Wild Imagination

"We made it," Leanora said. "We're actually here."

"I don't even know what to say anymore." Janelle held her hands out toward the crystal mountain, astonished. "I thought the mirror world was amazing, but this . . . *Look at this!*"

"What's that over there?" Shazad asked, pointing in a new direction. As he spoke, the wind pushed away a fine white mist that coated the forest treetops. High atop a far-away hill, a city came into view. It was unlike anything Joey had ever seen and beyond anything he had ever imagined, which was fitting given where they were.

"What the . . . ?" Joey's voice trailed off in stunned disbelief.

For almost a full minute no one spoke. There were no

words that could possibly do the moment justice. The city on the hill defied explanation. It was like a mash-up of several different cities that had somehow been crammed into one space. Joey counted six distinct, fantastical boroughs within it. One section of town was made up of gothic castles and medieval villages. Three separate sections of the city looked like something out of a sci-fi movie, but the sci-fi elements didn't conform to any one particular style. One of them was a next-generation metropolis with impossibly tall, flashy skyscrapers. Another one had clean, high-tech towers with minimal design, and yet another had an otherworldly, alien quality to its architecture. The final two boroughs of the city were equally diverse. One of them appeared to be constructed from a blend of futuristic buildings and ancient temples, and the final unique section of the city was an assemblage of interlocking white stone buildings that fit together like puzzle pieces. Ships filled the air above the city with an inexplicable mix of sporty flying cars and dirigible airships that resembled Hypnova's airship. The city was miles away, but it was clearly alive and full of people. Joey wondered who they were and what their lives were like.

Most of all, he wondered what they had been doing for the last thousand years.

"What is this place?" Shazad asked, breaking the silence. "I thought it was supposed to be a refuge for magic."

"It is," Joey said with his eyes full of wonder. "Magic and more. Redondo told me that—in a dream," he added, trying to explain. "He said this place was home to all the spectacular and unbelievable things the world has to offer. I didn't understand what he was talking about. I didn't think it would be anything like this."

"I thought it was going to look like a lost kingdom from the past," Leanora said. "This place looks like the future."

"It's both," Janelle said, thoroughly entranced. "Look at the skyline. It's like the mirror."

Joey turned around to look back inside the room at the mirror they had used to enter the Imagine Nation. "The mirror," he repeated, wondering how he had managed to miss that. Janelle was right. Each varied piece of the mirror's frame matched up with a specific section of the city on the hill. Joey grabbed the mirror by the frame and pushed it over.

"Wait!" shouted Shazad, reaching out for the mirror.

It was too late. Joey stepped back as the mirror fell. It landed hard on the floor, shattering the glass in the frame.

Janelle was baffled. "What are you doing? Why did you—"

"Watch out." Joey stepped in front of Janelle and turned her around. Knowing what to expect, Shazad and Leanora covered up before the mirror exploded outward. Shards of glass shot up and filled the air as the magic energy that was trapped inside the mirror escaped.

When the dust settled, Shazad was at a loss. "What is it with you and magic mirrors? Why did you do that? *Again?*" he asked, referring to when Joey had smashed one of Redondo's magic mirrors after escaping the mirror world a year ago.

"I had to," Joey said. "We can't have anyone following us."

"What about Hypnova?" Shazad asked. "How is she going to catch up with us if we break her mirror?"

"Hypnova told me Oblivia would be right behind her. She said she'd buy us as much time as she could."

"Did she say to leave her stranded in the mirror world?" Shazad asked. "She's going to run her ship into the ground. If it comes to that, she might need the mirror on her ship to get away, and this one to join us. She could end up trapped there with no way out now."

Joey paused for a moment. "I didn't think about that." He hoped that he had not acted too rashly. "She wanted us to keep going. She didn't tell me to hold the door for her."

"She probably didn't think she had to," Leanora said quietly. "How was she supposed to know you were going to smash her only escape route?"

"Oh no." Joey put his hands to his head. His friends had a point. "Guys, I'm sorry. I wasn't thinking. I just acted. I . . ." He trailed off, looking at the broken pieces of glass on the floor. The person he really needed to apologize to wasn't there. He felt horrible.

"Leanora, look over here," Janelle said suddenly. She held up a pair of sandals she found near the door. "These have your name on them."

Janelle was right. The sandals she held had a note tucked into one of them with Leanora's name written in what, Joey realized, was most likely Hypnova's handwriting. "What is this?" Leanora asked as she took the sandals and sized them up against her feet. They were a perfect match. Just the thing to replace her ruined boots before they completely fell apart.

"How did she know to leave these here? How did she know I'd need them?"

"Hypnova always knows more than she lets on," Joey said hopefully. "She said we'd see her again. This mirror can't be her only way of getting here, can it?"

"Let's hope you're right," Shazad said. "For her sake as well as ours. We're going to need help to get past the Secreteers and the Invisible Hand."

"You think the Invisible Hand will show up here?" Joey asked.

"DeMayne said there would be a reckoning," Leanora said. "He was looking right at you when he said it."

Joey groaned. "Don't remind me."

"Don't worry. He's not coming for us," Shazad said. "Not yet, anyway. Did you see the look on his face when we unlocked his memories? Whatever threats he made on board Hypnova's ship, his first priority won't be revenge. It'll be this place—the Imagine Nation. This island makes Camelot look like a sandcastle. It's the biggest magical arti-fact of all time. He's going to want a piece of it. He's proba-bly already on his way."

"You think he'll be able to find it?" Joey asked. "He

193

doesn't have the map in his head like we do."

"No, but he's been here before," Shazad replied. "DeMayne has a connection to this place he's only just beginning to understand. My guess is he's going to want to find out everything he forgot about it. Everything the Secreteers *made* him forget. There's only one place he can do that."

"The Secret Citadel," Joey said.

"DeMayne's going the same place we are," Shazad confirmed. "We have to get there first."

Joey grimaced, coming to terms with the reality of the situation. He had hoped to avoid another confrontation with Ledger DeMayne, but he realized now that wasn't an option. If Joey and his friends wanted to change the world, they would have to go through the Invisible Hand to do it. There was no getting around that—especially now that DeMayne had his memory back.

"We better get moving," Shazad said. "Any idea which way?"

"That way," Janelle said, pointing deep into the woods. "As much as I want to go explore every inch of that city, there's obviously nothing secret about it. Not to the people who live here, anyway. Also, DeMayne had no memory of the place. In the vision we saw, these woods were behind us. We have to go through them."

"Into the Outlands of the Imagine Nation," Joey said. "That's where Hypnova told us to look."

"What are we waiting for?" Leanora asked. "Let's go."

The group started down the steps to the lower level of the treehouse. Janelle tapped Joey on the shoulder and nodded back toward the city. "Look at that place. It's magic and science together at the same time—just like I'm always talking about! You and I are going back there the first chance we get."

Joey put on a thin smile as they descended the staircase. "It's a date," he said, hoping he would be able to keep it.

The journey down from the treetops took a long time. The platform below them had steps that led to another platform below it. There were more platforms after that, followed by a network of rope bridges and ladders. Together, they created a winding path that led down to the ground, but the mist that covered the forest canopy was thicker inside the trees. The deeper Joey and the others descended into the forest, the harder it became to see and the slower they had to go.

Joey tried to wave away the murky haze, but it was no use.

The greenish-white vapor was heavy in the air and seemed to grow denser with each passing minute. The fog had a creepy supernatural quality that seemed to amplify every random noise in the forest, causing Joey to wonder what kind of creatures were in there with them. He hoped that any animals they encountered would be furry and cute, but judging by their habitat, it didn't seem likely. If any predators were living in the trees, Joey knew he and his friends would have no warning against them. He could hardly see two feet in front of his face. Everyone had multiple missteps that nearly sent them tumbling down through the branches. The fog was so thick they couldn't see the ground, and no one had any idea how high up they were or how far they had to fall. The uncertainty of it all made the group move even slower despite their desire for haste. After an hour, Joey was sweaty, tired, and very much over Hypnova's treehouse. He would have liked to use Houdini's wand and whisk them all away—not just down to the ground, but out of the forest altogether. However, he couldn't do that and no one asked him to. Everyone knew he was saving the wand to be ready for whatever they found in the Secret Citadel, including Oblivia, the head Secreteer, and Ledger DeMayne if he made it there before them.

Joey reached a rope ladder at the end of a wood plank in between two branches. He started climbing down, but the misty air was full of moisture and his palms were sweaty, which caused him to lose his grip as he went. His hand slipped from one of the rungs of the ladder and he fell. Joey screamed on the way down, but he quickly saved himself, grabbing hold of a tree branch.

"Joey!" Leanora called out. "What happened? Are you okay?"

Joey let out a painful cough. Landing on the branch had knocked the wind out of him. "It's all right!" he croaked, trying to talk. "I slipped, but I'm o—"

The branch he was holding on to snapped. He cried out for help and flailed around, falling through the air, but this time there was nothing to grab on to. Instead, he broke more branches on the way down. He banged his head on one of the branches, and suddenly his thoughts were as hazy as the air around him, but one thought was clear—he was going to die. Then he hit the ground.

"Unh!" Joey grunted as his back slammed down on soft, muddy earth. He didn't bother trying to get up. Everything hurt too much. He looked up at a blur of fog and tree branches as his friends called his name with increasing desperation.

"Joey!"

"Where are you?"

"Answer us!"

He tried to spot his friends in the trees, but he couldn't see anyone. Their voices seemed so far away.

"Mmmokay," Joey called back in a groggy, wavering voice. "I'm okay. I fell . . . 'issnot that far. I only fell . . ." Joey tried to gauge out how far he had fallen, but he couldn't seem to focus. His head was throbbing, and his whole body ached. Meanwhile, the damp earth felt like a soft bed. He decided to lie there a moment and rest his eyes while his friends finished climbing out of the trees. They'd find him soon enough. All they had to do was go down.

Joey had no way of knowing how long he was out, but it was clearly longer than he would have liked. When he came to, he had vines growing over his body. He was tied down like a giant, but it was easy enough to break free. He sat up, snapping the vines around his chest and arms. He pulled on the vines that covered his legs, uprooting them all except for one. A thick root had wrapped itself around his ankle, and it didn't want to let go. The more he struggled with it, the tighter its grip became. The root seemed to be pulling his foot down into the mud.

"What is this? How long have I been here?"

Joey scanned the area, trying to get his bearings. The fog was just as thick at the ground level of the forest as it was up in the trees. It had an eerie, spectral shimmer that made him wish he wasn't alone, but he saw the outlines of his friends nearby. "Over here!" he called out to them. "Am I glad to see you guys. Don't worry. I'm all right. I just have a major headache. And I need help getting my foot out of this root."

"GNNAAAAGHHHGH," the silhouettes in the mist groaned.

Joey froze. "What?"

The figures in the mist lurched toward him. As they came closer, it became very clear they were not his friends. First of all, they were too big. Second, they weren't human. They were creatures made up of stones, moss, and dirt. Some of them had vines for arms, and some had hands made of soil and clay. None of them had eyes. They just had deep pockets burrowed into the dirt where their eyes should have been. "Okay, you're definitely not furry and cute," Joey said as the earth monsters advanced on him. Each of them was at least six feet tall and weighed several hundred pounds. Joey counted three of them, but the roots and rocks bursting up from the earth all around him told him there were more on the way. They weren't subterranean creatures pulling themselves up from the underground—they were the ground itself. The forest had come to life, and it was coming after him! The creatures stalked toward Joey, shuffling like zombies. He pulled on the root around his ankle, trying to free himself. It wouldn't budge. Another vine shot out of the ground and coiled around his wrists, binding him to the spot. "No!" Joey tried to pull his hands free, but he had no leverage. He panicked as the eco-zombies closed in.

"Help! Shazad! Lea! Janelle! HELP!"

Joey was trapped and alone. No one would have blamed him for using the wand to save himself, but he couldn't pull it out of his sleeve. He couldn't even move his hands. The monsters took him by the shoulders and started pushing him down into the earth. "No! Why are you doing this? Please! Stop!" They responded with more wailing and wheezing. There was no reasoning with them, Joey realized. They were sentient creatures, but they were mindless. They were about to bury him alive, when out of nowhere a high-pitched tone filled the air, assaulting his ears.

Joey winced when he heard it, but then he quickly got used to the sound. For him, it was a minor discomfort. But it was agony for the eco-zombies attacking him. They backed away and stumbled around, writhing in pain. Then they started to break apart. Some of them dissolved into piles of dirt, while others blew up in violent explosions that splattered mud and pebbles everywhere. Once they were all gone and Joey was covered in muck, the vines that were holding him let go and slithered back into the ground. He staggered to his feet and looked around in confusion.

There was a young boy about his age in the forest with him. He tapped at something on his wrist, and the high-pitched tone stopped ringing.

"What the heck just happened here?" Joey asked. "Who are you?"

"My name's Jack," the boy said. "Jack Blank. Who are you?"

12

Drastic Measures

The boy named Jack was still shrouded in the luminescent haze. He moved in closer, and Joey got a better look at him. He had messy hair and a large birthmark on his face. It circled his right eye and ran diagonally down his cheek. Joey felt himself staring and made a conscious effort not to do so. Jack looked to be about the same age as he was. Maybe a year older. He was dressed the same too, wearing a T-shirt and jeans, but he looked far more at home in this place than Joey felt.

"What were those things?" Joey asked, wiping mud off himself. "Why were they after me?"

"You never heard of the Gravens?" Jack asked him.

"No." Joey nudged one of the nearby dirt piles with his foot. The earth churned slightly in response, trying to regain its shape. Joey backed away, but the dirt mound fell apart before it re-formed into anything resembling a person.

"This forest is Gravenmurk Glen," Jack explained. "It belongs to them. Or, should I say, it *is* them. Parts of it anyway. The Gravens take every snapped twig as a personal attack. I'm guessing you came through here a little rough?"

"You could say that," Joey said, rubbing a sore spot on the back of his head. "I fell out of a tree and broke some branches on the way down. Does that count?"

"That would do it. These things are touchy. A friend of mine once made the mistake of cutting away some branches to get a better view from the treetops. We had a similar run-in with the Gravens. It wasn't fun."

"What did you do to them?"

Jack tapped a sleek watch on his wrist. "Sonic disruptor. Don't worry. I didn't kill them. I designed this to keep them under control. I've got it running at a low volume right now so they won't come back. We're good here now."

"You made that?" Joey asked.

"Sure." Jack shrugged. "No big deal."

"You sound like a friend of mine." Joey offered his hand. "I'm Joey. Thanks for saving my butt."

"Anytime." Jack gave Joey's hand a hearty shake. "You need help getting out of here? What are you doing in these woods anyway? No one ever comes out here."

"Why were you here?" Joey asked, turning the question back around on Jack. "Do you live here?"

Jack squinted at Joey, clearly finding the question to be an odd one. "Not here in Gravenmurk Glen, no. I came here looking for someone. I was hoping you might be her."

Joey looked back up at the trees and thought for a second. "Hypnova?" he guessed.

Jack's eyebrows shot up. "You know her?"

"Yes, I know her. She sent us here! We just left her."

"You're kidding! That's amazing. Where is she?" Jack caught himself, realizing he had sped past an important detail. "Wait a minute, who's *we*?"

"Me and my friends."

Jack put a finger to his ear, touching a miniature earbud communicator. He paused a second, listening. "I think *my* friends just found them."

Soon after that, a group of people appeared in the mist walking toward Joey and Jack. This time, the silhouettes turned out to be exactly who Joey hoped they were. When

Shazad, Leanora, and Janelle arrived on the scene, they were joined by two new faces. One of them was a boy with shoulder-length black hair. He was dressed like he had just come from a renaissance fair and carried two swords on his back. The other person was a girl with shiny silver skin and hair. She looked like she was made of liquid metal. Joey assumed Janelle had already gotten over the initial shock of seeing her and had completely exhausted the subject of malleability and ductility, because she was more interested in him than anything else. Joey's friends embraced him, relieved that he was all right.

"I'm fine," Joey assured them. "Thanks to Jack," he added, introducing Jack to his friends.

"Looks like someone had a run-in with the Gravens," the boy with the swords said, noting Joey's mud-covered clothes.

"The what?" Shazad asked.

"Don't ask," Joey said. "Just watch where you step. Don't break any branches in here if you can help it."

"They told us," Leanora said. "I guess you found out why. Joey, I want you to meet Skerren and Allegra."

"Allegra's an alien," Janelle whispered in Joey's ear.

"What?" Joey whispered back, trying not to stare at the

shiny silver girl. "It's . . . nice to meet you both."

"They know Hypnova," Jack told Skerren and Allegra.

"WHAT?" Skerren and Allegra blurted out in unison.

"Exactly," Jack said, sharing their amazement. "Joey told me she sent them here."

"What are the odds of that?" Skerren wondered, speaking with an English accent.

"Sent you here to do what?" Allegra asked. "Where did you come from? Who are you?"

"We're the Order of the Majestic," Leanora said.

Jack, Skerren, and Allegra looked at each other, checking to see if that name meant anything to anyone in their party. It didn't.

"I've never heard of you," Skerren said.

"Are you a superhero team?" Jack asked.

"A superhero team?" Joey replied. "You mean, like in comic books?" It was an odd thing to be asked. Magic was real, but there was no such thing as superheroes. Then again, there was no such thing as a lot of things in Joey's life. "I guess it depends on how you look at it. We do have archenemies. And we are trying to save the world."

"We're not superheroes," Shazad said. "We're magicians."

"And scientists," Janelle chimed in.

"We're here to break the spell over this place so everyone can see it," Joey said. "We're bringing magic and imagination back to the world, which means we have to bring the Imagine Nation back to the world."

Jack, Skerren, and Allegra were visibly shocked.

"Are you serious?" Jack said eventually.

"You can do that?" Allegra asked. "The four of you?"

"Of course they can't do that," Skerren said. "It's impossible."

"Nothing's impossible," Leanora replied.

Jack shook his head, struggling to process what he was hearing. "For you to just come out and tell us that . . . You obviously don't know how most people here would react to what you want to do. Is Hypnova part of this?"

"Of course," Joey said. "I told you, she's the one who sent us. We've been planning this for a year."

"Really. That's . . . surprising," Jack said. He sounded conflicted. "Don't take this the wrong way, but we just met you guys. I'm happy to help you out of a jam here in the woods, but this is different. I need to talk to Hypnova about this. Where is she?"

"She's coming," Joey said.

"We hope," Shazad muttered.

"She'll be here," Joey said, his voice a little firmer.

Jack looked at Skerren and Allegra. "What do you guys think?"

Allegra gave a tiny shrug. "I think I'm less surprised than you are. Hypnova did get kicked out of the Order of Secreteers."

"That was because of us," Skerren said. "I didn't think she was capable of this. The laws of secrecy and intervention are the Imagine Nation's oldest laws."

"What laws?" Joey asked, suddenly wishing he had been less forthcoming about his plans.

"The law here states that we're only allowed to get involved in the outside world to try to help it," Allegra explained. "But everything we do has to be a secret. We can't leave behind direct proof of the Imagine Nation's existence."

"Why not?" Janelle asked.

"That's just the way things are," Skerren said. "It's the way they've always been."

"So?" Janelle said. "That's not a reason. What if the whole world kept doing things the way 'they've always been

208

done'? We'd never make any progress on anything. We'd still be using horse-drawn carriages to get around. I saw flying cars in that city out there!"

"Actually, some of us still use horse-drawn carriages," Skerren said. "They work fine. I prefer them."

"I'm serious!" Janelle said, getting worked up. "The second I got here, I could tell this island is full of things that can change the world for the better. How are you going to do that and keep this place a secret?"

"It's not that simple," Jack said.

"Sure it is," Leanora argued. "Don't tell me you never thought of trying this yourselves. Didn't you ever want to share this place with the world?"

"We can't," Skerren said. "Not only because of the rules. The outside world's not ready for the kind of things we have here."

"How do you know what the world is ready for?" Janelle asked. "Who decides?"

Jack, Skerren, and Allegra traded sheepish looks. No one seemed to have a good answer for that.

"I used to think the way you do," Shazad said. "In fact, my whole family did. I was raised to keep magical items out of the wrong hands. For a long time, I thought that was enough. It's not. The world needs magic. It needs this place. Didn't you ever question the system here?"

"To be perfectly honest, we haven't had a ton of time to think about things like that," Jack said. "You would have no way of knowing this, but for the last ... I don't know ... year and a half? We've been going from crisis to crisis, saving the world over and over."

"Saving the world from what?" Joey asked.

"Ever hear of the Nightlander Horde?" Jack asked. "The Iconoclasts? The King of Pain? The Singularity?" Joey and his friends squinted at Jack Blank as he rattled off names. "Right. From the looks on your faces, I'm guessing you haven't. We're the reason why not. You're welcome."

"We saved the world from *both* singularities," Skerren added proudly.

Allegra pinched the bridge of her nose. "Skerren, we talked about this. There was only one Singularity. That's why it was called the *Singularity*. You're thinking of the Multiversal Convergence."

"How about the Rüstov invasion?" Skerren went on, refusing to acknowledge his error. "We didn't just save the world that time. We saved the universe. I had to fight my parents. Jack had to fight a future version of *himself*. It came back in time and tried to kill him."

"That's messed up," Joey admitted.

"It was," Jack agreed. "It was a lot to deal with, but that's life in the Imagine Nation. We've always got something to deal with. Everybody here does. The world never stays saved for long."

"Don't get me wrong, saving the world is cool—and we appreciate it—but what about changing the world?" Janelle asked. "Does that ever enter the equation?"

"If it had, we wouldn't be here," Leonora said. "Ever hear of the Invisible Hand?" she asked Jack, Skerren, and Allegra.

"The Invisible Who?" Skerren asked.

Leonora nodded. "That's what I thought."

"They control the world's supply of magic," Joey explained. "For the last thousand years, they've been hoarding magical objects. They got their start right here in the Imagine Nation. We want to stop them, but they're not some invading alien fleet you can just blow up or put behind bars. They're more subtle than that, manipulating people and events from behind the scenes. We have to take away their power."

"They're the ones who benefit from keeping this place a secret," Shazad said. "You might think you're protecting 'normal people' from forces they don't understand. The truth is, your laws of intervention and secrecy protect the Invisible Hand's monopoly on magic more than anything else."

"Meanwhile, the world is a house on fire, and no one is bothering to put it out," Janelle added.

"I just told you, we put out fires every day," Jack said.

"But the temperature is literally rising constantly," Janelle said. "We've got climate change, water shortages, wildfires, school shootings, global pandemics. . . . The planet is falling apart. We can't go on this way. We won't make it. Someone has to open the world up to new possibilities. That's why we're here. We can make a difference. You could help us."

"You want to make a difference," Jack repeated. "I get that." He chewed on his lower lip, thinking it over. "You sound like a friend of *mine*. We could help you, but—"

"We can't reveal the Imagine Nation to the world," Allegra cut in. "We can't. That's not our call to make. We'd have to talk to people first. Important people. The Inner Circle."

"The Inner Who?" Joey asked.

"The people who run the Imagine Nation, including my king," Skerren said.

"You want us to clear our plans with the king?" Janelle asked.

"The king of Varagog Village," Jack clarified. "There are other people who would have to weigh in too. Varagog's just one part of Empire City. That's where we live. What you're talking about doing . . . It's complicated. This is over our heads."

"Way over," Allegra said.

"I don't think it is," Janelle replied. "If you're talking about the same people who let the Secreteers keep this place hidden for a millennium, we're not looking to have that conversation. I'm pretty sure I know what those people would say, and we don't have time to waste hearing it. The world's messed up, the future looks bleak, and we're doing something about it. Period. It's not up for debate."

"You just got here," Jack said. "You really should talk to more people before you do something drastic like this. The Inner Circle are good people—most of them," he added quickly. "We can take you to see them. We can talk about it."

"Thanks but no thanks," Joey said. "This is part of the problem. Most people don't think they have the power to change the world, and the people who do have the power don't think they have the permission. We'll talk later. Right now the world needs something drastic. Otherwise, the bad guys stay in charge, living it up with a stranglehold on something that should belong to everyone. I don't know the last time you left this island, but it's getting worse out there, not better. Ledger DeMayne and the Invisible Hand have been stealing our future since before we were born. Enough is enough. We're taking back what's ours. We're taking back tomorrow."

"When you put it like that, it's hard to argue," Jack said.

"This has been a long time coming," Joey said. "It's what we were put here to do."

"There's no way we can talk you out of this?" Allegra asked.

"I don't think you understand," Shazad said. "We're halfway done. More than halfway. Right now magic is already flowing back into the world. Ancient doors that got slammed shut centuries ago are open again. We did that part before we came here. This place is the final piece of the puzzle. If you're not with us, that's fine. It was nice meeting you, but we've got a job to do."

"I don't think *you* understand." Skerren drew his swords. "So do we."

13

Comic Book Connections

The children in each group sized each other up and paired off, choosing their opponents. Allegra morphed her hands into large, shiny silver hammers. Skerren adopted an intimidating stance, scraping his swords together. Janelle responded by spinning the Staff of Sorcero out to its full length, preparing to strike.

Leanora held out her hand to Joey. "Can I have my fire-stone back please?"

"What are we doing here?" Joey said. "Let's take it down a notch. Not everything has to be a fight, remember, Lea?"

"Joey. The firestone," Leanora insisted.

Joey sighed. Asking Leanora not to fight was like asking a fish not to swim. He placed the stone in her palm. She gripped it tight and wrapped the string around her hand like a boxer taping up her fists. A second later, her right hand smoldered with fiery red-orange energy. She was ready to throw down.

Shazad pulled his transfiguration cape off his shoulders and shook it out like a matador ready to face a charging bull. He was less eager to fight than Leanora, but Joey knew if push came to shove, he'd be there to back her up. With that cape, Shazad had the power to turn anyone who came at him into a slug, a snail, or worse.

Across from them, Jack Blank stood with his hands at his sides. "This doesn't have to happen. I don't want to fight you guys."

"You really don't," Leanora said. "We have you outnumbered. Just walk away."

Joey was relieved Leanora didn't feel the need to add the words "while you still can" to make her point, but he still didn't like the direction things were going. It was true the Order of the Majestic had Jack and his friends outnumbered four to three, but that slight edge was no guarantee of victory. While fighting outside of Camelot and the Imaginary Vortex, Joey had learned that the battleground itself was sometimes the difference between winning and losing. As

Joey watched, Jack Blank turned off the sonic disruptor on his wrist, which would make the Gravens return. It was obvious Jack had learned that lesson too.

"You only have us outnumbered if we play nice," Jack said as the moaning, zombielike earth monsters rose up, surrounding Joey and his friends. The Gravens inched forward, reaching out with grubby paws. Jack slid the disruptor's volume back up as the creatures moved in, causing them to crumble into pieces once more. "I'd still rather settle this with a conversation."

"You want to talk? Fine, let's talk," Joey said. "But not here. Not with these things creeping all over us." He pulled the wand out of his sleeve. "Sky high."

There was a flash of light, and suddenly everyone was suspended in midair, high above the trees of Gravenmurk Glen. Once again, a view of the massive crystal mountain dominated the horizon, and the diverse metropolis Joey now knew as Empire City was visible far in the distance. It was a spectacular sight, but even better was the look on Jack's, Skerren's, and Allegra's faces. They hovered in the air at a safe distance, shocked at how quickly Joey had turned the tables on them.

"What is this?" Jack asked. "What did you do?"

Joey's friends had the same question. "What are you doing?" Shazad demanded.

"I'd say he's doing magic," Skerren said. He sheathed his swords, no doubt realizing they wouldn't be much use to him at the moment. "Very powerful magic."

"Don't worry. It's not that powerful. Look." Joey pulled up his sleeve to show his friends the power bar on his arm. The green mark lit up with a magical glow as Joey's energy level fell into the high 80, low 90 percent range.

"This is a waste," Shazad said.

"Let's hope not," Joey replied.

"Put us down," Jack ordered. "Now."

"First things first," Joey said. "I want to explain something to you. My friends and I all have magical objects—things that got enchanted centuries ago—but this wand here . . . the thing I used just now? It's special. This wand channels *pure* magic energy. I could use it to do anything I want. *Anything.* It never runs out of power, but eventually I will. If I wanted, I could use it to send you a million miles away. I could use it to bring the Imagine Nation back to the world right now. I could do it with one word, but I wouldn't live to see it. This

219

wand's got more power than the human body can handle, and using it too much is a death sentence."

Joey tapped his arm, showing off the green mark. "This lets me know how much power I've got to work with. I have to be careful not to overdo it, because every time I use the wand, it drains me, and here's the kicker: I never know how much of a toll it will take before I do it. I have to guess."

"So, you're risking your life right now . . . just to make a point?" Allegra asked.

"I had to show you. I could put a stop to this right here, but I don't want to fight you. Shazad's right. This is a waste of energy I can't afford. I want to use the wand to change the world for the better. Before today, I hadn't used the wand in a year, because I've been saving it for whatever we find in this place. If I have to fight you, the Secreteers, the Invisible Hand, and the Inner Circle, or whoever else is in that city out there, I won't have anything left for the island. I might not even make it to the Secret Citadel. You want that on your conscience? You want to fight us to keep the messed-up status quo?"

"Hang on," Jack said. "What's the Secret Citadel?"

"It's the Secreteers' base of operations," Shazad said. "Their headquarters."

"You're going to the Secreteers' stronghold?"

"Yes!" Joey replied. "That's the key to all of this. There's something in there that keeps this island moving and keeps it hidden at the same time. If we can turn it off or destroy it, I won't have to use the wand."

Jack, Skerren, and Allegra looked at each other, silently debating their options. The mention of the Secreteers' stronghold had clearly had an effect on them. Shazad noticed too and seized on that. "If you know Hypnova, then you know she used to be a Secreteer. She sent us here! If she can change her mind about your laws, others can too. Maybe together we can convince the other Secreteers."

"Not likely," Skerren said.

"What about changing your minds?" Shazad asked. "We've got a better chance at success if we work together. I don't think Hypnova would want us fighting each other."

"No, probably not," Allegra agreed. As she spoke, she relaxed her hammer hands back into regular hands.

"You came here looking for Hypnova," Joey said,

remembering what Jack had told him earlier. "What did you want with her?"

Jack took a moment before answering. Allegra stretched her liquid metal arm out to take his hand, offering her support. Jack swallowed hard and spoke.

"I wanted to ask her about my mother."

"Your mother?" Joey said, taken by surprise.

Jack nodded. "She was a Secreteer too. I never knew her—not because she was a Secreteer," he added quickly. "It's because she died when I was just a baby. I wanted Hypnova to tell me more about her. I thought there might be something of hers she could give me or help me find. Even just a picture would be something. There are no pictures of my mom, but Hypnova could lend me a memory. She could do that." Jack's eyes were welling up. "Hypnova's a friend, but we haven't seen her in a while."

"She's been on the run," Leanora explained. "The other Secreteers want to kill her because she told us the truth about the Imagine Nation."

"That sounds about right," Jack said. "I found Hypnova's hideout here in Gravenmurk Glen last year and rigged a sensor to let me know if she came back. That's why I came out

222

here. You triggered the alarm. I was hoping it was her."

"Why don't we stick together until she shows up?" Janelle suggested. "Maybe we can help each other."

"Do you know where the Secret Citadel is?" Allegra asked.

"Hypnova said it was somewhere in the Outlands," Shazad replied.

"Where?" Skerren looked skeptical. "I've been to the Outlands. There's nothing there to find."

"Looks can be deceiving," Leanora said. "That's the first rule of magic. We've been all around the world finding places that don't exist. Places you can only get to if you believe in them. Maybe you weren't looking the right way."

"The Imagine Nation is one of those places," Jack said. "You can't just stumble across it. If you want to find the Imagine Nation, you have to go looking for it specifically. You have to believe in it to get here." He seemed to be talking to himself as much as anyone else. Joey got the sense they were getting through to him.

"You asked if we were superheroes before," he said. "Where I come from, superhero movies are more popular than ever. Personally, I think it's because the special effects are good enough now to make everything look real, so people finally get it. They get that these are great stories with great characters and real meaning. Not just kid stuff."

"Joey." Janelle motioned with her hands, telling Joey to get to the point.

"Right," Joey said. "The point is, people *are* ready for this place. They're buying in. They want to believe incredible things are real and impossible things are possible. We can show them that they are. You three seem like you're 'the good guys.' Help us out."

"We are the good guys," Jack said.

"So are we," Joey replied. "Back home, I still read comic books all the time. In the comics, whenever one set of superheroes meets another, they always have to fight before they become friends. Good guys versus good guys. It's idiotic. There's no point except to settle fan arguments about who's tougher, and you don't even get that because it's always a stalemate. Can't we just skip that part and go straight to the team-up?"

Jack cracked a smile. "I used to read comic books too. I forgot, that *is* what always happened. Every crossover had some overly complex misunderstanding and a fight that nobody won, because halfway through it, the heroes all realized they were on the same side."

"Exactly," Joey said. "And when they do finally decide to work together, it's always for the most ridiculous reasons, like their mothers are both named Martha, or they're both from New Jersey."

Jack grinned and nodded along, but he stopped himself, and a curious expression came over his face. "Hang on, are you from New Jersey?"

Joey paused. "Yeah," he said, wondering if he had said too much.

Even up in the sky, Jack was floored. "Get out of here. I'm from Jersey!"

"What?" Joey exclaimed. "No way!"

"It's true! I grew up in an orphanage near the Meadowlands."

"The Meadowlands?" Janelle repeated. "We live in Hoboken! That's, like, twenty minutes away."

"We're practically neighbors," Joey said. "How'd you end up here?"

"It's complicated." Jack looked around, taking in the bird's-eye view of the Imagine Nation. He kicked at the layer of mist that coated the forest canopy below his feet. "Why don't you put us down? I'll tell you all about it."

14
Magic Powers

"Let's start over," Jack said after Joey had used the wand to lower everyone back down to earth. "Put that wand away. Don't hurt yourself. We'll help you."

"We will?" Skerren asked.

"I will," Jack clarified. "It's my best shot at finding out about my mom. Maybe my only shot. Are you with me?"

"I'm always with you," the young swordsman replied, but his tone indicated he was on the fence.

"But . . . ?" Jack pressed.

"What about *their* plans? Revealing the Imagine Nation to the outside world?"

"Maybe it's time." Jack shrugged. "I don't know. Maybe it's not such a bad idea after all."

Skerren blinked at Jack in disbelief. He was clearly reluctant, but Joey could tell he wasn't going to leave his friend hanging. "We're going to have a lot of explaining to do when this is over."

"What else is new? Better to beg forgiveness than ask permission," Jack said. He turned to Allegra. "What do you think, Allegra?"

She gave him a semi-playful punch on the shoulder. "Like you even have to ask."

Jack rubbed his shoulder, a pained smile on his face. "I guess that settles it. We're in."

"Really?" Joey asked. "We're teaming up? Just like that?" He was shocked by the Jersey connection that he and Janelle shared with Jack, but he was even more surprised by how quickly it had helped them all find common ground. "I guess the comic books aren't so ridiculous after all."

"I've never been so happy to be from Hoboken in all my life," Janelle agreed.

"It's not just that," Jack said. "I'm not a big fan of secrets. In my experience, they're more trouble than they're worth. I've got a feeling you guys are doing the right thing. If we're picking sides, that's the side I want to be on."

"Speaking of sides, I'd like to know what we're up against,"

Allegra said. "What can you tell us about your enemies in the Invisible Hand?"

"Plenty," Shazad replied. "Think you can tell us how to get out of this forest?"

"That's easy." Jack tapped at his wrist and cued up a holographic compass. "Just follow me."

As they hiked through the forest, carefully watching where they stepped, Joey and the others shared what they knew about the Invisible Hand and its role in the origin of the Imagine Nation. Jack, Skerren, and Allegra were surprised to learn the island had once been part of a continent the size of Texas. They also had no idea that it had been the seat of power from which Ledger DeMayne, the founder and ancient leader of the Invisible Hand, had once ruled the world from the shadows. If not for Merlin, the first Secreteer, and a handful of other brave magicians and heroes, history would have been very different. Had they not cut DeMayne's rule short ages ago, he might still be in power today.

"And you're sure it's the same guy?" Jack asked. "He's been hoarding magical objects for a thousand years?"

"It's definitely him," Leanora said. "We saw how old he

is inside, the way he should be. I don't know what he's using to extend his life and preserve his youth. Most glamours fade over time. His is the best I've ever seen. He looks like a movie star."

"What's a glamour?" Allegra asked.

"It's a disguise," Skerren explained. "A magical way of changing your appearance to look better."

"Sometimes worse," Leonora said.

"I suppose," Skerren said. "But, unless I'm mistaken, it's just on the surface. Does he fight like he's a thousand years old?"

"No," Joey, Shazad, and Leonora all said at once.

"He must use something else to stay young for real," Joey said. "I don't know what. There's a lot we don't know."

"Who else knows about this?" Jack asked. "The Imagine Nation's history with DeMayne?"

"No one except the Secreteers," Joey said. "After Merlin broke the island loose and set it adrift, the first Secreteer rewrote memories on a global scale so that no one would remember any of this—including DeMayne. She erased his memory and let him go. The Secreteers have kept this place hidden ever since. They created a safe place for magic to exist in the world, but they made it such a small part of the world. If you ask me, they're not much better than the Invisible Hand. No offense to your mom."

"None taken," Jack said. "The Secreteers and my family . . . we have a complicated history. The Clandestine Order didn't approve of my father. That's partly how I ended up in New Jersey."

Jack went on to explain how the Order didn't like the idea of his parents getting together back in the day. Secreteers weren't allowed to have relationships outside the Order, and Oblivia, the head Secreteer, wouldn't let Jack's mom quit. They were grooming her for leadership and didn't want to lose her, so they got rid of Jack's father instead.

"Got rid of him how?" Shazad asked.

"They rewrote his memory and made him forget my mom."

"They did what?" Leanora said, appalled.

"It gets worse," Allegra said. "They also made him forget who *he* really was and sent him off into space."

"Into *space*?" Janelle repeated.

"Secreteers don't mess around," Jack said. "I only just met my dad last year. I didn't know any of this until I came here. My mother died during the first Rüstov invasion. The Rüstov are alien parasites that turn people into cyborg zombies and use them like puppets until they die." He said the last sentence as if he were talking about something mundane like a new brand of toothpaste he had recently purchased.

Joey stared at Jack with his mouth open, trying to wrap his head around what Jack was telling him.

"Whatever you're picturing in your mind right now, trust me, the reality is worse," Skerren said. "The Rüstov make the Gravens look downright cuddly."

"I'm just trying to keep it all straight," Joey said. "You said the Rüstov invasion was when a future version of Jack came back in time to kill him, right? Like in *The Terminator*?"

"The what?" Skerren asked.

"It's a movie," Jack told Skerren. "And it was sort of like that. Only it wasn't a future version of me. It was more like an alternate-timeline version. He came back on a suicide mission to prevent a future where I—or we, depending on how you look at it—helped the Rüstov take over the world. Fortunately, we found a more creative solution. One that didn't involve me dying."

Jack tapped at the mark around his eye, but he didn't elaborate further.

"That's a whole other story. The point is, my mom died saving me when the Rüstov attacked fifteen years ago. My dad was already gone, so the people here hid me away in Jersey until it was safe to come back. For most of my life, I didn't have any family. That's as much the Secreteers' fault as it is the Rüstovs', but they never had to answer for it. No one ever questions the Secreteers because of what they can do to you. People are afraid of them. Even my mom was afraid of them. The more I think about it, the more I like the idea of putting them out of business."

"And we're absolutely sure that's the right thing to do?" Skerren asked again. "Don't get me wrong, I'm no fan of the Secreteers either, but are we sure people out in the Real World can handle all this? You keep talking about magic. There is magic here, but it's mostly in Varagog Village, where I live. It's just a small part of this place. Our powers don't come from magic."

"Where do they come from?" Leanora asked.

"From us." Skerren took out his swords and spun them around, putting on a show. "From years of training and practice. I've been studying with the sword ever since I was old enough to hold one. These blades are a part of me. I can cut through anything with them as long as my heart's in it. I could cut a mountain down to size if I wanted to."

"It's true," Allegra said. "I've seen him chop through a three-foot wall made of pure Invincium. That's a super-strong metal alloy my people use to build spaceships."

"Interesting," Leanora said. "What happens if your heart's not in it?"

"Nothing," Skerren said with a shrug. "If I don't believe I can cut something, I can't cut it. It all depends on me and what I think. A stick of warm butter would be too much to slice through if I didn't believe in myself. Fortunately, I don't suffer from a lack of confidence. Never have."

"I'm picking up on that," Shazad said with a smile. "I hate to burst your bubble, Skerren, but it sounds like your powers are one hundred percent dependent on magic."

Skerren abruptly stopped flipping his swords around. "What?"

"You just described exactly how magical objects work," Shazad said. "If you want to harness their power, you've got to believe in them. Those swords are magical objects."

"No," Skerren said. "I believe in me. The power isn't in the swords. It's in me."

"There's one way to find out," Shazad said. "Let me try them. We'll see if the swords work for anyone else."

"No, that's not possible." Skerren put both swords away. "It's not safe to cut anything in this forest. You'll wake the Gravens."

"Later, then?" Shazad asked. "When we're out of the forest?"

"I'll think about it," Skerren said, sulking a bit.

There was an awkward beat of silence, and it became clear that Skerren was a bit put off by the idea of his powers being tied to some external object rather than himself.

"I think the point Skerren was trying to make is that the Imagine Nation is bigger than magic," Allegra said finally. "It's bigger than just this world. Take me, for example. All the women from my planet can change their shape like I can." She stretched an arm up to shake a tree branch that was twenty feet above their heads. Water that had pooled up on the leaves came down like raindrops, but Allegra flattened out her other hand to form a makeshift umbrella that kept everyone dry. "The farther I stretch, the less solid

I become. It also depends on my state of mind," she admitted. "I have to choose courage over fear and believe in myself to maintain stability, but there's obviously no magic object involved. It's just me."

"True, but who's to say your people aren't tapping into some form of magic to do that?" Janelle asked. "There's no reason to think magic is limited to this world, or that different alien races would use it the same way humans do. By the way, I know I should be more amazed to meet someone from another planet, but we went through another dimension to get here today. We used magic energy to do it. More and more, I'm realizing that's all magic is. Belief-based energy. It's just as strong as the person using it."

"What about Jack?" Allegra asked. "His power isn't like that. He can talk to machines and make them do what he wants. He deals with computers and technology. Isn't that the opposite of magic?"

"That depends," Shazad said. "How does it work? Any machine, anytime? No limitations?"

"We've all got limitations," Jack replied. "My powers are tied to knowledge and science. I ask machines to do what I want. If they won't cooperate, I can take control of them, but only if I know how they work."

"There you have it," Leanora countered. "To know something is to believe it."

"No, I have to learn it," Jack argued. "I can't just *believe* I know the ins and outs of a complex machine like a warp engine. I have to hit the books, tinker in my lab, and build things. It's a lot of work. Sometimes I feel like I'm going to have homework for the rest of my life."

"I know the feeling," Janelle said. "I have had to unlearn and rethink everything I know about science to get the hang of magic, but learning magic is the same as learning anything else. You just have to believe in yourself and stick with it until you know it backward and forward. Magic and science are flip sides of the same coin. It's not an either-or choice. If we can reveal this place to the world, everyone will see that."

"Janelle has a point," Joey said. "Why is Skerren able to use magic swords like a pro even though he was never trained in magic? Because he grew up in a place where people believe in the impossible. We're going to give everyone that chance. It's not a question of whether or not they're ready. They'll learn."

"Who's going to teach them?" Allegra asked. "You've got to be around if you want to be a part of that. What's your plan? How are you going to unveil the Imagine Nation without using the wand too much?"

"That's the tricky part," Joey said. "I'm still trying to figure that out."

"You don't have a plan?" Skerren asked.

"A great magician once told us, 'We don't go onstage because we're ready. We go on because it's showtime,'" Leanora said.

"It's showtime?" Jack repeated. "That's it?"

"We have no way of knowing what's inside the Secret Citadel," Joey said. "There has to be something there that can help us. This wand chose me for a reason. I don't think it was to die."

"You make it sound like it's your destiny to do this," Jack said.

"It feels that way sometimes," Joey admitted.

"I wouldn't buy into that if I were you," Jack said. "A great man once told me, 'Character is destiny.'"

"That's Heraclitus," Janelle said.

Jack looked confused. "Who?"

"Heraclitus," Janelle said again. "The ancient Greek philosopher. He's the one who said that. Character is destiny."

"Oh, Hera-*clitus*," Jack said. "Of course," he added, pretending to know the name, but in a funny way. "I never actually met *him*, but the guy who told me that line might have. He's pretty ancient himself, and he's always quoting people. The point is, there's no such thing as destiny. We make our own destiny."

"I don't know about destiny," Joey said, unwilling to dismiss the idea entirely. "But I do know about responsibility. We have to do this because no one else can. We didn't start it, but we have to finish it. It's our job."

"Our sentiments exactly," a raspy voice hissed, coming out of nowhere.

"Whoa!" Joey spun around with startled urgency. It sounded like someone was speaking right in his ear, but there was no one behind him. They were in an open clearing, surrounded by nothing but trees. "Did you guys hear that?"

Jack had an uncomfortable look on his face. "I heard it."

Janelle looked even more uncomfortable. She dug a finger into her ear as if a bug had climbed inside and she was trying to get it out. "Who said that?"

Skerren drew out his swords and stood in a fighting stance. "It's the Secreteers." He turned slowly, scanning the trees for threats. "They're here."

15

Hostile Environment

Joey's eyes swept the clearing, but still he saw nothing. Thinking fast, he produced the wand and whispered the words "steel trap." He did it just in time. A second later, he saw two Secreteers standing in the forest, blocking the way forward. They wore hooded cloaks like Hypnova, with masks that covered their faces from the nose down. One of them was clad in deep indigo, and the other was dressed in dark gray. Joey glimpsed them for only a moment before he got dizzy.

"Nnngh." Joey swayed, trying to keep his balance.

"Are you all right?" Skerren asked him.

"I'm fine. I just . . ." Joey had to stop talking. He dropped to a knee, unable to stay on his feet. The forest spun around on him. He closed his eyes, but somehow that made it worse.

He felt a tingling sensation in his arm and forced himself to look at his magic power gauge tattoo. Joey's stomach tightened as he watched the green bar shrink, dropping to almost 50 percent.

Before anyone could say anything, the Secreteers flapped their cloaks and transformed into swirling streams of smoke.

Twin trails of blackish-gray and blue-violet rocketed around the clearing. The smoke quickly expanded to fill every inch of the air.

"What's going on?" Janelle shouted.

"It's the Secreteers from the ship!" Leanora called back.

Hopefully not all of them, Joey thought. If the thunder and lightning started up again, it was going to get ugly. They didn't have the Caliburn Shield to protect them anymore, and Joey wasn't ready to cast another spell. Not by a long shot.

A violent wind picked up, and everything went dark. Joey covered his eyes and peeked through his fingers to try to see what was going on. He called out to his friends and heard them calling back, but they sounded miles away. He couldn't see them. He couldn't see anything. The wind roared like a massive turbine engine and whirled around the clearing like a tornado. Joey gritted his teeth as tiny projectiles made of pebbles and dirt pelted his body. The smoke was so thick, Joey could barely open his eyes. He made the mistake of breathing some of it in. The next thing he knew, he was coughing so much, he couldn't breathe at all. Just when Joey thought he couldn't take any more, everything stopped. One long last gust of wind blew hard enough to force Joey down to one knee. Then it vanished, along with all the smoke. The air was calm and clear.

Joey was coughing so hard, his eyes were tearing up, which helped wash the dust and dirt out of them. As he worked to get his breathing under control, he saw all of his friends were in the same boat. Shazad, in particular, sounded like a cat hacking up a hair ball. "That was unpleasant," he eventually managed to say. "Let's please not do that again."

"What happened?" Skerren asked. "We're still here?"

"Why wouldn't we be?" Leanora replied.

"We've been through this before," Allegra said. "If I had to guess, that smoke was supposed to wipe our memories and get rid of us."

"You shouldn't have come back to yourselves until you returned to your homes," the Secreteer in gray confirmed.

"How is it you're unaffected?" asked the other Secreteer. They were both dumbfounded.

"I can answer that," Joey croaked. He held up the wand. "I cast a quick spell. It was the only way," he added, looking at his friends. "As of thirty seconds ago, we all have memories like steel traps. Their memory powers won't work on us. Our minds are untouchable." Joey locked eyes with the Secreteers. "You're not getting rid of us that easy."

"Is that why you fell over?" Leanora asked.

Janelle grabbed Joey's wrist to check the mark on his arm. "Oh my God!" she exclaimed when she saw how much the green bar had gone down. "Joey, no!"

"It's all right," Joey said, pulling his arm back. "I'm okay."

"No, you're not," Shazad said. "You can't even stand up."

"I can stand." Joey got back up. "I'm just not very good at it right now." Shazad was more right than he realized. Joey didn't feel okay at all. The physical weakness was already passing, but he felt scared. Using the wand had never affected him like this before. Obviously, guarding against the Secreteers' powers had been a heavier magical lift than he had expected. "It was a onetime thing. I won't have to do it again."

"You'd better not," Shazad warned.

"Look at it this way," Jack said. "If he didn't do it, our walk in the woods would be over. It probably wouldn't even be a memory. This is a nice change of pace." He looked to the Secreteers. "Maybe now that your biggest weapon against us has been disarmed, you'll be willing to talk."

"We have nothing to say to you," the indigo Secreteer replied. "We know why you're here. What your goal is. You won't be allowed to continue."

"That's fine," Jack said. "We don't want to talk to you. This conversation is above your pay grade. We want to talk to Oblivia."

"The majestrix is dealing with the traitor Hypnova," said the Secreteer in gray. "We're dealing with you. Out of respect for your past heroics, we had hoped to make it quick and painless and send you on your way with a simple memory adjustment. However, if you insist on doing things the hard way, we can do that, too."

"I'm curious how you intend to stop us," Jack said. "You mentioned our past heroics. You know what we're capable of."

"We're pretty capable ourselves," Leanora said, ready for

a fight as always. "When Oblivia attacked us on Hypnova's ship, she had a thunderstone to back her up. I don't see any magical weapons on you."

"Then you haven't been paying attention," the indigo Secreteer replied. "You're surrounded by magical weapons."

Machete blades appeared in the hands of both Secreteers, but they didn't use them against Joey and the others. Instead, they attacked the forest, hacking off branches and chopping away at tree trunks.

"What are they doing?" Leanora asked.

"They're calling in reinforcements," Skerren said as the floor of the forest began to rumble and churn.

"This again?" Leanora asked as the Gravens emerged from the earth once more. "What the heck are these things?"

"They're the reason I'm so muddy," Joey said, backing away from the rising wave of monsters.

"I don't understand," Allegra told the Secreteers. "Aren't they going to attack the two of you now?"

"They would if we let them," the Secreteer in gray replied. "The Gravens go after anyone who disturbs or dis-respects this forest, but they're simple creatures with simple minds." As he spoke, his partner took out a small pouch and cast a cloud of blue-violet dust over the Gravens. It had a disturbing effect on them. Joey watched as the Gravens grew increasingly agitated, growling in anger and climbing out of the earth in greater numbers. "Your memories might be untouchable, but theirs aren't. Right now they think you're responsible for this." The Secreteer motioned to the carved-up trees and broken branches. "In fact, they're under the impression you've done a great deal worse. They're not happy with you lot at all."

"That's a neat trick," Joey said. "Too bad for you we don't have to worry about the Gravens. Not as long as we've got Jack's sonic disru—"

Joey broke off midsentence as Jack cleared his throat and held up his wrist. The screen on his smartwatch was shattered. "They took it out during the dust storm."

"Oh." Joey gulped as an army of Gravens formed a circle around him and his friends, leaving them nowhere to go and no choice but to fight. "I guess we're doing this."

"We gave you a chance to leave," the indigo Secreteer said. "You should have taken it."

The Secreteer and his partner retreated into the forest as the Gravens trudged forward. They were bigger than before—more menacing and more disgusting. The ground was wet in this area of the forest, and the Gravens contained a higher percentage of muddy brown goop and sludge. Earthworms and other creepy crawlies moved in and out of their eyes and mouths, a sight that made Joey want to throw up. His friends seemed equally nauseated, but Jack, Skerren, and Allegra didn't react except to prepare for battle. Skerren stood ready to take the Gravens on with his magic swords. Allegra morphed one hand into a blade and the other into a shield. Jack went into his pocket and took out a pair of black gloves lined with golden circuitry.

"We haven't had to fight these things in a while," Skerren said.

"Eh," Jack replied, unconcerned. "It's like riding a bike."

"I don't suppose you could just wave them away with your magic wand?" Allegra asked Joey.

"No. He's used it too much already," Shazad said, answering for him.

"I know I shouldn't," Joey agreed. "But I might have to."

"No, we're fine," Jack said. "We got this." He strapped on the gloves and bumped his knuckles together, causing them to light up and crackle with energy. "I've been looking for an excuse to try these out."

Janelle raised an eyebrow. "What are those?"

"These are one of my favorite inventions," Jack said with pride. "Nuclear Knuckles. Don't worry. They're safe to be around. There's no harmful radiation. I just call them 'nuclear' because they're powered by atomic energy. Each glove is made from artificial atoms with discrete energy states that I control. The science behind them is actually quite fascinating."

Skerren rolled his eyes. "Here we go."

"Right now every atom in each glove is absorbing photons and making hundreds of successive quantum jumps," Jack went on, ignoring Skerren. "That means—"

"That means millions of electrons are entering an energetically excited state," Janelle said, following Jack's logic without difficulty.

"Exactly," Jack said, smiling. "See? She gets it." He waved his hands around. They were enveloped by halos of white light so intense Joey had to squint to look at them. "Pretty cool, right? These used to be way clunkier. The Mark-1 design used big metal gauntlets and looked like some kind of a steampunk contraption. For this one I used synthetic fibers in the gloves to re-create the reaction at one-quarter of the size. After all, why do the gloves have to be big when the atoms are so small?"

"That's what I said!" Janelle said. "I built a mini super-collider in my school basement based on the same exact theory."

"Really?" Jack said, clearly impressed. "That's amazing. Did it work?"

Janelle made a face. "Well . . . it did, and it didn't."

"I hate to interrupt, but can you two talk shop later?" Allegra asked Jack in a sharp tone as the Gravens closed in. "Right now, hit something!"

"I like her," Leanora said, getting ready to charge her fire-stone.

"Sorry. I get carried away talking about this stuff." Jack swung his fist around like a comet. It connected with a Graven and knocked its upper body clean off its lower body. An abandoned pair of legs stood upright for a brief second before collapsing in a muddy mess.

"That's more like it," Skerren cheered. "Actions speak louder than words, I say." Skerren let his blades do the talking for him. He stood his ground, never moving more than a few steps in either direction, slicing away as he spoke. Skerren didn't chase his targets. He let the Gravens come to him. When they got too close, he cut them to pieces. Whirling, slashing, and stabbing in constant motion, he made it look easy.

Allegra did the same, stretching her right arm to strike at oncoming attackers while shielding herself and her friends with her left. Allegra's elastic body enabled her to cover lots of ground, and her blade arm ran through Gravens like a farmer culling a field. As aggressive as she was on offense, she was every bit as effective on defense, guarding the others against attacks. Joey noticed she seemed especially protective of Jack.

Working together, they formed a loose perimeter around Joey, Shazad, Leanora, and Janelle. They were polished fighters, and it was obvious they had been in situations like this before. Maybe even worse situations. None of them seemed the least bit overwhelmed by the moment. They were professionals doing a job, and they made short work of any Graven that came near them. For a second it looked to Joey as if they could take on the whole army themselves, but for every Graven they took out, three more climbed out of the ground. Joey looked deep into the trees in every direction. An endless army of zombies made of soil and stone was marching on their position. As impressive as Jack, Skerren, and Allegra were, it was too much even for them.

"We'd better do our part if we want to get out of this," Shazad said, pulling off his cape.

Leanora didn't need anyone to tell her that. She had already stepped up to join the fray. Swinging a fist of fire to match Jack's Nuclear Knuckles, she blasted a Graven apart and moved forward to fill a gap in the perimeter. Standing in between Skerren and Jack, she shouted at Joey and the others. "What are you waiting for? Don't just stand there! Fight!"

"Coming!" Shazad called back. "Just give me a second to get changed." He handed his cape to Joey. "A little help?"

"I got you." Joey took the cape and shook it out. Suddenly, it was the size of a picnic blanket.

"Take good care of that," Shazad told him. "I'm going to need you to change me back when this is over."

"Let's just make sure we're still aboveground when this is over," Joey replied. "Any requests?"

"Yes. Don't use the wand again."

"I mean requests with this," Joey said, holding up the cape.

Shazad shook his head. "Surprise me."

Joey threw the cape over Shazad, covering him completely. When he pulled the cape away, Shazad was gone. In his place was a twelve-hundred-pound grizzly bear. He reared up on two legs, standing ten feet tall, and roared loud enough to grind everything to a halt. Even the Gravens paused to take notice.

"Brurggh?" an approaching Graven sputtered just before Shazad brought his full weight down on top of it, turning the creature back into a pile of muck. After that, he was off and running. Shazad charged into the horde of Gravens, mauling them with the ferocity of a wild animal and the tenacity of a soldier looking out for his brothers-in-arms.

"There's something you don't see every day," Jack said, watching him go.

"You've been away from Jersey too long," Janelle said, whipping the Staff of Sorcero around. "*All* of this is something you don't see every day." She moved like a martial arts master with a bo staff. Joey watched her cut a Graven at the knees, then jab the end of the staff into its forehead, causing it to explode in a muddy mess. The Graven slid apart, and she was on to her next target in seconds, sweeping the staff around through several more Gravens, taking them out.

"Not bad," Skerren complimented her.

"You think these things would go easier on us if I told them I'm a committed environmentalist?" Janelle asked.

"You could try," Skerren said, stomping at a Graven that was crawling toward his feet. "But I don't think they care."

Joey stood in the center of the circle, the only one not directly involved in the fight. As the Gravens continued to rise like zombies and pour in by the dozen, it was getting harder and harder for him not to use the wand. He knew he couldn't risk it after using such a massive expenditure of magic energy with the Secreteer spell, but he felt helpless and useless. If only he hadn't lost that bag of tricks outside DeMayne's office, he would have been able to do his part. Jack spotted Joey out of the corner of his eye and noticed he was late to the party. He quickly put two and two together.

"You don't have anything besides the wand to fight with?" Joey shook his head no. Jack peeled the glove off his right hand and tossed it to Joey. "Take this!"

Joey caught the glove. Jack had just cut his own ability to defend himself in half. He had done it without a moment's hesitation. "You sure?"

"Totally sure. I'm a lefty!"

He went back to the fight without another word. As before, there was no time for talking it over. There was only time for action. Joey tucked the wand away and put the glove on. The Nuclear Knuckles hummed with energy, and a warm, buzzing sensation ran up Joey's arm past his elbow.

"How does it feel?" Leanora asked, checking up on Joey.

"Like the firestone," Joey said. As he spoke, he saw a Graven appear behind Leanora while her back was briefly turned. Joey lunged forward to deliver an atomic punch and splatter it across the battlefield. "Whoa," he said, looking down at his fist afterward. "A *lot* like the firestone."

"Nice of you to join us!" Skerren shouted. "It's about time. I can't do this all by myself, you know." Joey didn't even get a chance to respond to Skerren's snark before he turned around and went back to the fight. "Well, I *could*, but it would take much longer." Skerren swung his swords wild and free, nearly giving Joey a haircut.

"Ignore him." Allegra pushed back a throng of Gravens

with two hands shaped like large crowd control barriers. "There, that's your ground," she said, clearing a space for Joey to fight and defend. "We all fight back-to-back. Nothing gets past you. Nothing gets past any of us. Got it?"

"Got it!"

Joey filled in the gap in the perimeter, completing a tight circle of defenders. With Shazad rampaging around the group in the form of a grizzly bear, they mounted a strong defense against the Gravens. Every now and then a hand would claw its way out of the ground and clutch at their ankles, but they were quickly kicked free and swatted away with a power glove or stabbed with the business end of a sword. Finding their rhythm as a team, they took down anything that got too close, but it was like shoveling sand against the tide. No matter how many Gravens they defeated, there were always more behind them, ready to take their place.

"They just keep coming!" Leonora said. "When do they stop?"

"I don't think they do stop," Allegra said. "We ran the first time we faced these things. After that, we've always had Jack's sonic weapon."

"Can you fix it?" Janelle asked Jack.

"Not without my tools," Jack said. "I think we might be in trouble."

"Trouble?" Joey said. "I thought you said we were fine!"

"I know what I said! But does this look fine to you?"

"So we run," Janelle suggested. "I'm fine with that."

"Run where?" Skerren asked. "Do you have any idea how big this forest is? There's nowhere to go!" He had started this fight as a blur of blades, but he was slowing down. They all were. Meanwhile, the Gravens were everywhere. The children were outnumbered, surrounded, and if Joey didn't do something, they would soon be overrun. "We tried doing it the old-fashioned way. It's not working," Joey told the others. "I'm going to use the wand."

"Don't you dare!" Leanora said. "We can take them!"

"For how long?" Joey asked. "We can't keep this up forever. There's too many of them!" He went to pull the wand out of his sleeve. It was not an action he took lightly. Joey was more concerned than anyone about how much he had used the wand in the last few hours, but he saw no other way out of the Secreteer's death trap. Then he saw his breath appear as a white cloud in front of his face and felt the temperature in the forest drop rapidly. Joey looked at the ground as a layer of frost ran over it like a wave running into the shore. It reached the Gravens' feet and quickly traveled up their legs, freezing them in place. They looked like mutant snowmen.

No sooner had they stopped moving than an oversize wolfman came bounding into the clearing to tear them apart. Frozen chunks of earth flew through the air as the snarling creature pounced, swiping at defenseless Gravens. Unlike before, no fresh Gravens emerged to replace the fallen. The ground was frozen solid.

"What's going on?" Leanora asked. "Where'd this ice come from?"

"Where did he come from?" Allegra asked, nodding toward the wolfman.

"Who cares?" Skerren replied. "We're saved."

"No we're not." Joey noticed the wolfman was very well dressed. Or at least, he had been. His clothes were torn at the seams by his bulging muscles, no doubt the result of his transformation into wolf form. Joey had seen it before. He had seen that outfit before too. The wolfman was wearing a white dress shirt and vest. He had a small pouch at his waist, attached to a gold chain.

"Perhaps we can be of assistance?" Ledger DeMayne

said, stepping into sight. Wielding the Sword of Storms, he decimated any frozen Gravens that were still standing. Hurricane-force winds poured out of the broken sword once known as Excalibur. DeMayne struggled to hold and control it, gripping the hilt with both hands to direct the raging winds that obliterated the Gravens, reducing them to particles of frozen granules. He didn't stop until the field was clear of hostiles. Only then, and only with great effort, did he "turn off" the storm and lower his sword.

After the winds died down, the werewolf calmed down and reached into his own mouth to pull out a fang and regain his natural form. As Mr. Ivory once again lamented the ruined state of his clothes, his friend Mr. Clear came in shivering and rubbing his arms for warmth. He looked just as cold and sickly as ever, but Joey and his friends were about to be colder. Mr. Clear raised a shaky hand, and the crystal on the bracelet he wore lit up. The children all cried out in shock as a miniature iceberg formed behind them in the center of their circle. Its edges grew to encase their feet and hands, trapping them. Shazad, who was still in bear form, had been frozen from head to toe.

"What the—" Jack said, struggling to free himself. The

light in his left hand flickered on and off. The same thing was happening with Joey's right hand. Evidently, the Nuclear Knuckles didn't respond well to extreme cold. "Who are these guys all of a sudden?"

"These are the people we told you about," Joey said. "Ledger DeMayne and the Invisible Hand."

DeMayne took a bow. "Guilty as charged." He walked up to Joey with a smug smile on his face, thoroughly enjoying the moment. "Hello, Joey. Wonderful to see you again."

16

Let's Make a Deal

Jack's malfunctioning glove lit up and stayed lit up. There was a loud crack as his hand busted loose. He swung his fist around to pound the block of ice behind him, freeing himself and Skerren. Allegra slithered out of her bonds, ready to fight. It would take more than ice to hold her liquid metal form. Joey tried again to get his power glove working, but nothing happened. He was about to ask Jack to use his powers to fix it when he felt something sharp jab him in the neck.

"Hold it right there," Ledger DeMayne told Jack, Skerren, and Allegra. "Stop or I'll blow his head off—literally." He held the Sword of Storms at Joey's jugular. "Of course, I don't even need to use magic to end you, do I?" Joey held his breath as the jagged edge of the broken blade poked at his throat.

"Nobody move," Janelle said. "Don't do anything."

"That's good advice," DeMayne said, his eyes darting around to keep tabs on everyone. "Believe it or not, we aren't here for you. Not the way you think. We could waste a lot of time fighting each other, but what would that accomplish? Mr. Clear freezes you. You break free. He does it again, you break free again. Mr. Ivory changes into something exciting to match blows with your grizzly friend over there. . . . I'm forced to make an example out of young Kopecky here. . . ." DeMayne pressed the blade into the soft, meaty part of Joey's neck, but not hard enough to break the skin. Just hard enough to scare him. DeMayne twisted his lips, showing his distaste for the scenario he described. "It's all very messy, and worse than that, it gains us nothing. Meanwhile, the true enemy roams this forest, waiting to pick us apart and keep us from achieving our common goal."

"What common goal is that?" Leanora asked, sounding very suspicious.

DeMayne lowered his hand, taking the blade away from Joey's neck. "Let's talk about that. Are you willing to talk? Can I trust you to behave?"

DeMayne motioned with the Sword of Storms as he

spoke. Joey's eyes followed the pointy end of the broken blade, still within striking distance. Still deadly. He knew Ledger DeMayne was up to something. It was in the man's nature. Things couldn't be otherwise. But Joey decided he would rather hear about DeMayne's scheme without a weapon mere inches away from his neck. "All right. Let's talk."

A short while later, Joey and the others had been released from the ice, and Shazad was back in human form. The ground was still frozen so the Gravens could not renew their attack, and everyone stood around shivering, waiting for DeMayne to make his pitch. Oddly enough, Mr. Clear seemed more bothered by the cold than anyone else.

"Make it colder," DeMayne said, ignoring his discomfort. "I don't want these things waking up." Mr. Clear gave a weary nod, and the temperature dropped another ten degrees. When he was finished, he put on a winter hat and gloves, but he still looked like he was freezing. "What I'm about to say will no doubt surprise you," Ledger DeMayne continued, turning to Joey. "I propose we form an alliance."

Joey scrunched up his face. "An alliance? What?"

"How could *we* have an alliance?" Leonora asked.

"I seem to remember you promising to kill us," Shazad said.

"You said you'd kill us twice," Janelle added.

"I was upset," DeMayne replied. "Justifiably so, in my opinion."

"But now we're all good?" Joey asked. "Whatever. This is just another trick to get your hands on the wand."

"I don't need to trick you to get the wand. I need to kill you, remember? The wand only has one master at a time, but fortunately for you, that's not my focus at the moment. You're a smart boy, Joey. Think it through. I had you at my mercy a moment ago. I could have opened up your throat and taken the wand just like that." DeMayne snapped his fingers. "I didn't do it. I restrained myself."

Joey thought about what DeMayne was saying. It was all true enough, but that only meant he had an angle Joey didn't see. "Why is that?"

"Why indeed?" DeMayne asked. "I'm not going to pretend I didn't think about it. You certainly deserve it. Had I gotten my hands on you an hour ago, I would have throttled you without hesitation." He made a choking motion with his hands, seeming to relish the thought of wringing Joey's neck. "I've calmed down since then. I do try not to act rashly. 'Don't react. Respond.' That's what I say. I would have killed you already if that were what I came here to do. The easiest thing would have been to do nothing. I could have let *them* kill you." He gave the nearest Graven a push. It toppled to the ground and broke apart like a tower of blocks. "I chose instead to focus on that which is most important to me."

Now we're getting to it, Joey thought. However much Ledger DeMayne would have liked to see him dead, Joey knew DeMayne's primary objective was not to kill him. It wasn't Joey's death he truly cared about, but rather, what Joey's death bought him. It was about the wand. It was always about the wand with him. But DeMayne had a chance to take it a moment ago. Why didn't he go for it? Why wasn't he going for it right now?

"I give up," Joey said. "What's more important to you than the wand?"

"After everything I've been through?" DeMayne asked. "Revenge. I need your help to get it. And you need mine. We're after the same thing, you and I."

"We're not looking for revenge," Joey said.

"But you are looking for something. And you're lost. You don't have a prayer. Not unless you use that wonderful wand to find what you're searching for, and we both know that's something you're desperately trying to avoid. Tell me, what's your plan? Do you have any idea where you're going? Where to look? Where even to begin? Of course you don't." DeMayne grinned like a Cheshire cat. "Only I do."

Joey's eyebrows went up, suddenly understanding DeMayne's position. He saw the same look of recognition in the eyes of his friends. The conversation just got interesting.

DeMayne tapped at his temple. "I'm starting to remember things. Lots of things. You jogged my memory, and now all sorts of interesting pieces are falling into place. You want to find the Secret Citadel? You need me to lead the way."

"And you'd do that for us," Shazad said with heavy skepticism.

"No, I'd do that for me. Aren't you paying attention? My own self-interest comes first, obviously. That doesn't mean we can't be of use to each other. I know where to go, but I can't get there. You can get there, but you don't know where to go. You see what I'm getting at."

"You need protection," Leonora said.

"Memory protection," DeMayne confirmed. "The Secreteers have tampered with my mind more than I'll ever know, but I can tell you this much—it's never going to happen again. Not ever. They've abused their power for the last time. I'm going to see to that."

Joey smirked, appreciating the irony of DeMayne's anger. He couldn't help himself. DeMayne noticed, and he did not appreciate Joey's insolence. "Did I say something funny?" he asked in a hard voice.

"Actually, you did," Joey said defiantly. "You complaining about other people abusing their power is very funny to me."

DeMayne sighed and cast his eyes upward. "You really are insufferable. Spare me your lectures. Your pointless idealism. I'm not interested in your opinion of me. You certainly don't care to hear what I think of you. We disagree with and despise each other. We know that. We understand that. It doesn't matter. All that matters is what we can accomplish together. People have tried to uncover the Secreteers' secrets for a thousand years. No one has ever had a chance of success until now. Until me. I know where to find them, and you can guarantee us safe passage. It's an alliance of convenience. I'm offering you a truce." He extended his hand. "Do we have a deal?"

Joey stared at Ledger DeMayne's hand. The hand of the man who had threatened to kill his parents a year ago. Who had threatened his life and the lives of his friends earlier that day. He made no move to shake it. "I need to talk it over with my friends first."

DeMayne stared at Joey. The hate in his eyes was palpable, but he took a breath and kept his temper in check. "Talk fast. I don't like being made to wait."

Joey and the others huddled together away from DeMayne and his men.

"What do you think?" Joey asked the group.

"I think that man wants to kill you," Allegra replied. "And he's going to try to kill you before this is over."

"One hundred percent," Jack agreed. "You can't trust him. He's a bad guy."

"I know we can't trust him," Joey said. "The question is, do we need him?"

"Can we find the Secret Citadel on our own?" Shazad asked.

All eyes turned to Jack, Skerren, and Allegra.

"Don't look at us," Jack said. "We're following you."

"You said you knew where to find it," Allegra said.

"I never said that," Leanora replied. "I said we've discovered long-lost, hard-to-find places before."

"What kind of places?" Skerren asked, displaying a clear lack of confidence in the group's quest. "How hard to find are we talking about here?"

"Ever hear of Camelot?" Shazad asked.

Skerren's eyes widened. "That was you?" Shazad nodded, and Skerren softened his tone. "All right, that's impressive."

"Even here, that was big news," Jack said.

"We had a map for Camelot," Joey said. "For this, we're only going off glimpses we saw inside DeMayne's head."

"I know it isn't much, but it's something," Shazad told the group. "We saw a castle in the fog beyond the edge of this forest. Or a castle made of fog. We can't really be sure. Might have just been foggy because his memory wasn't clear."

"Does any of this sound familiar to you?" Janelle asked Jack, Skerren, and Allegra. "If we keep going in this direction, are we going to find a castle once we get outside the forest?"

"There's nothing outside the forest," Allegra said. "Nothing but open country."

"Ninety percent of the island is undeveloped," Jack added. "It's like a big national park."

"It's got to be there," Janelle said. "It's just hidden. We can find it. We don't need DeMayne and his henchmen. You found Hypnova's hideout, didn't you?"

"That was luck," Jack said. "Maybe not even. For all I know, Hypnova planted the seeds for that in our heads to let us know how to find her if we ever had a need."

"Or maybe Hypnova wanted us to meet each other," Joey suggested. "Maybe she wanted you guys here to back us up if she couldn't be here to guide us herself."

"It's possible," Jack said. "But I don't know why we'd be the best choice for that. I've never gone looking for the Secreteers' headquarters. I never even thought to try."

"I have," Skerren said. "On a dare. It's something people do in the village. Teenagers mostly. We challenge each other to find the Secreteer's stronghold, but no one ever makes it. If anyone gets close, the Secreteers turn them around and make them forget what they're looking for. They come back in a daze, and that's the end of it. People say if you keep trying, they make you forget who you are. The Gravens must be another one of their deterrents. I'm only just now realizing that. My point is, the Secret Citadel is surely close by, but I couldn't tell you how to find it. None of us could."

"Maybe it's not that hard to find," Janelle speculated. "It sounds like the Secreteers themselves are the line of defense no one can get past. But we can, thanks to Joey. What if the castle is right there outside the forest?"

"What if it's not?" Joey asked. "DeMayne's been there. He knows for sure. I hate to say it, but we have to protect him. He has information we need. If the Secreteers catch him and wipe his memory again, we'll lose the best lead we've got. Maybe forever."

"All this talk about memories, I think maybe you're forgetting something," Shazad said. "Look at your arm. The protection spell took a lot out of you. Maybe too much."

"I know, but there's fewer of them," Joey argued. "Casting a spell on three people instead of six has to use less power."

"You said it was a onetime thing," Shazad said.

"I guess I was wrong."

"I don't like it," Shazad said. "If you do this, it's going to take you down to what? Twenty-five percent? That's getting into the danger zone."

"But not over the edge," Joey argued. "What else can we

do? The other option is I use the wand to help us find the Citadel, and there's no telling what that will take out of me. At least if I do this, we know what to expect."

"If we don't work with them, we're going to have to fight them," Leanora said. "We're probably going to fight them either way."

"You're probably right, but then what?" Joey asked. "We can't wander around this forest forever. Unless you guys want to give up, I don't see another way. We have to do this."

"You're sure you haven't done enough already?" Skerren asked. "What you told us about the dark magic markers . . . breaking down the barriers that hide magic and hold it back. That's not enough to change the world?"

"No," Joey said firmly. "I thought that after Camelot. We have to finish this or they'll find a way to undo it. We can't let that happen. Not again."

Everyone was quiet. Nobody liked it, but everyone seemed to agree there was only one way forward.

"Time's up," Ledger DeMayne announced. "Have we reached a decision?"

"I think we've been forced into one," Joey muttered. He looked at his friends, old and new. A silent vote was taken.

One by one, everyone nodded their assent. Some nods were more reluctant than others, but there were no objections. Joey turned around to face DeMayne, wand in hand. He was going to use the same "steel trap" spell he had used before, but at the last minute, he had another idea.

"Stuck with each other."

A blue flash of light ran out from where Joey was standing, illuminating every human being in the area. The ice-covered Gravens were untouched by the wand's magic.

When it was over, the world tilted on Joey, and he nearly fell over again. The effect was much worse the second time around. Feeling nauseous, Joey staggered over to lean on a frozen Graven. He hunched over, breathing heavily and trying to steady himself.

"Joey, are you all right?" Janelle asked.

"Talk to us," Shazad said. "What's going on?"

Joey put up a hand. "I just need a . . . just need a minute." He gulped and made a queasy face. "Ugh. I just threw up in my mouth."

"Is it done?" Mr. Ivory asked. He tapped his chest and studied his hands, checking to see if Joey had done anything unpleasant to him. "I don't feel any different."

I do, Joey thought. He forced himself to straighten up and stand without assistance. He took it slow after he let go of the Graven he was using as a crutch. Joey didn't want to worry anyone, but he still felt dizzy. As he looked around, his field of vision kept darkening around the edges, as if the sun was passing in and out of heavy cloud cover. His eyelids drooped, and he leaned back on the Graven, unable to abandon its support. "I feel like someone just hit me with a tranquilizer dart."

"Let me see your arm," Shazad said, taking Joey's hand by the wrist and turning it over. The power gauge on Joey's arm lit up to reveal the extent of the damage he had just done to himself. Everyone gasped as they watched the green bar fall below 50 percent, sink down to 25 percent, and keep going. When it finally stopped, it was at the 10 percent mark.

"I don't understand," Shazad said. "Why did it take so much?"

Joey took his arm back and pulled down his sleeve. "I threw in a little something extra."

"Why would you do that?" Janelle asked.

"An extra what?" DeMayne wanted to know.

"Call it an insurance policy," Joey said, finding his voice.

The feeling of weakness lingered, but his head was starting to clear. "I extended the memory shields we have to the three of you, but there's a catch. Any protection you get depends on us staying alive and unharmed. I may not be a thousand years old, but I wasn't born yesterday. I know you're planning some kind of double-cross. It's who you are. We'll be watching you, but now you need to watch out for us. You have to protect us from the Secreteers and anything else we run into out here."

DeMayne frowned. "All of you?"

"Think of it as extra incentive not to betray us," Joey replied. "Anything bad happens to us, and poof, you're defenseless again. It doesn't do you any good to know the way to the Secret Citadel if they can wipe your memory as soon as you reach the front door. Even one Secreteer is too many for you to get past."

"I'm aware of that," DeMayne said, clearly annoyed that Joey had been smart enough to put conditions on their deal. "I understand why you want to take precautions with me, but this was a waste of your magic, tying us together like this. I don't like you, Joey, but I *hate* the Secreteers. They need to pay for what they did to me a thousand years ago. Making me forget what happened here. What they cost me. I'm going to destroy their order, and you're going to help me do it. Our fates are already intertwined. Neither one of us can get what he wants without the other. That makes us allies."

"What about after?" Joey asked. "I suppose we can go back to fighting each other then? I know you have no interest in bringing the Imagine Nation back to the world. I'm not going to let you stop us."

"You misunderstand me," DeMayne said. "There's no hidden agenda here. My motives are plain. I have no intention of stopping you from 'bringing magic back.' In fact, had I remembered this place before now, I might have tried it myself a long time ago. But since you're so eager, I'll leave it to you to do the grunt work. You want to reverse what Merlin did all those years ago? Be my guest. Hiding the Imagine Nation killed him. Bringing it back will do the same to you."

"We're not going to let that happen," Shazad said.

"I'd like to know how you plan to stop it," DeMayne replied. "Maybe you could avoid that fate. You strike me as a very levelheaded young man, but not this one." He jerked a thumb in Joey's direction. "He's got his head in the clouds. He wants so badly to be the hero. He always has. When push comes to shove, he'll tell himself he didn't have a choice. He'll finish himself off—for the greater good, of course. And the wand will still be here after he's gone. If a new age of magic is coming, so be it. As long as I end up with the world's most powerful magic object, I'll have no complaints."

"Is that the plan?" Mr. Ivory asked DeMayne. "Bringing magic back?"

"The plan is you do what I tell you to do," DeMayne replied without turning around. "That's the only plan you need to worry about."

Mr. Ivory buttoned his lip, but he didn't seem happy about it. Mr. Clear also looked uncomfortable, but for different reasons. He was chilled to the bone. Leanora caught him staring at her firestone pendant and tucked it inside her shirt.

Meanwhile, Joey's confidence took a hit as he considered the possibility that he might succeed in changing the world only to serve it up to Ledger DeMayne on a silver platter. He had been proud of himself for thinking two steps ahead of DeMayne, but there was always a chance he was playing right into a pair of invisible hands.

"Maybe you're right about me," Joey told DeMayne. "Or

maybe I'll find another way to do this. You never know. I might surprise you. It wouldn't be the first time."

Joey was trying to project strength. When you couldn't be brave, pretending to be was the next best thing. But DeMayne saw through Joey's bluster. "I suppose we're both taking a gamble, but I like my chances." He smiled like a con man who'd just closed a billion-dollar deal. "I always do."

"We're wasting time," Jack cut in, fed up with DeMayne's posturing. "We need to move. The Secreteers are going to notice something happened to the Gravens. They're going to come back here and find us."

"Not if we find them first." DeMayne turned around and headed into the forest. "Follow me."

17

The Fellowship of
the Wand

The group came upon a gate in the forest. They had been
walking for a while, and everyone was eager to get out of the
woods, Joey most of all. The nausea and dizziness he had
felt from using the wand had passed, but his endurance had
taken a hit, and he was struggling to keep up with the group.
Joey didn't want to say anything, but he was going to need
a break soon. He kept his eyes peeled for Secreteers and any
hint of a path to their castle, but he didn't give the gate a
second look. It was attached to nothing. There were no remnants of a fence or wall of any kind. The gate stood alone,
positioned between two ancient trees. Its wrought-iron bars
were bent with age and brittle with rust. There was no obvious reason to walk through the gate. It was easy enough to
simply go around it, which was what the group was doing

when DeMayne called out for everyone to stop. The look on his face told them he either remembered the gate or was trying to place it. The hinges screeched as DeMayne pushed the doors open. The sound echoed through the forest like a shrieking owl, giving away their position.

Skerren winced at the sound. "The Secreteers are going to hear that."

"Good," DeMayne said, clearly eager to see them again. His eyes swept the land beyond the gate for threats. No one was there. Just more of the same trees that filled the rest of the forest. "It's this way," he said, redirecting everyone through the gate.

"Why?" Jack asked. "There's nothing through there."

DeMayne disagreed.

One by one, they all went through the gate. Nothing dramatic happened as a result of their passage. The group wasn't transported anywhere, and there was no magical transformation of the forest. Gravenmurk Glen remained exactly as it was. At least, on the surface.

"Now what?" asked Allegra.

"Now we keep going," DeMayne replied.

Jack, Skerren, and Allegra didn't see it, but something

had changed. It was a subtle shift, but the air felt different to Joey. As they hiked deeper into the woods, the fog lifted and the sun came out. Not just any sun either. The light felt alive and pleasant in a way that was hard for him to describe. Joey felt like he was viewing the world through a camera filter that made everything more attractive.

"You feel it too?" Leanora asked, noting his reaction.

Joey nodded as Jack fiddled with his broken smart watch, getting it to project a small holographic map in the air around his wrist. The map view drifted as the GPS tracker tried, and failed, to locate them. According to Jack's busted instruments, the forest was suddenly way bigger than it was supposed to be. He chalked it up to malfunctioning equipment. Joey and his fellow magicians knew better.

"That's not it," Leanora told him. "We unlocked something here. We're still in the Imagine Nation, but we're somewhere else at the same time. A magical pocket in the forest. Trust me, we've done this before. Last time we used a map to do it. This time it was the gate."

"How did we all do it, though?" Janelle looked around at the forest, which seemed to grow brighter with each step they took. "What about belief? Jack had doubts. He said so."

"Maybe the bar is lower now," Shazad said. "We took out the artifacts that were holding magic back. Old doors opening up all over the world. The gate's probably one of them."

Mr. Ivory frowned. It was obvious the idea of "magic doors opening up all over the world" didn't sit well with him. He looked like he was about to say something when DeMayne called the group to attention.

"Everyone, on your guard," he ordered. "We're in their territory now. We should expect to encounter some resistance."

"There were two of them before," Joey said.

DeMayne scanned the trees, searching for the Secreteers. "The question is, where are they now?" There was no trace of fear or paranoia in his eyes. He was itching for a fight. "Ivory, we need the rat."

Mr. Ivory reluctantly fished a fresh tooth out of his bag. At this point in the journey, no one batted an eye when he stuck it in his mouth and transformed into a large, golden-haired rodent that walked like a man.

"Why a rat?" Joey asked as Ivory sniffed the air, trying to pick up the scent of the Secreteers. "Why not a bloodhound?"

"African pouched rats actually have a better sense of smell than dogs," Janelle explained. "They use them to sniff out land mines in Mozambique, Angola, Tanzania, and Cambodia."

"That may be," Mr. Ivory said. "But the fact is, I don't have a bloodhound tooth. I have a rat tooth. We work with what we've got." He stalked off into the forest and disappeared into the trees.

"I thought the rat was cute," Janelle said after he was gone. "Like a prairie dog with a longer face."

"It was definitely better than the crocodile," Joey agreed.

A short while later, Mr. Ivory returned dragging the gray Secreteer behind him.

"He's not dead, is he?" DeMayne asked.

Ivory shook his head. "Just unconscious. He tried to fend me off with a handful of dust. It didn't do much besides make me sneeze."

DeMayne gave Joey a nod, pleased to see that his memory protection had worked as advertised.

"The boy said there were two of them," Mr. Clear said. "Where's the other one?"

Mr. Ivory sniffed the air and pointed. The indigo

Secreteer burst out from behind a large tree wielding his two machetes, but he didn't get a chance to use them. Mr. Clear raised his hand, and before the Secreteer took a single step, his entire body was encased in a block of ice. Mr. Clear shuddered and rubbed his hands together, trying to warm them up. He didn't look good.

"Are you all right?" Shazad asked him.

"He's fine," DeMayne said, answering before Mr. Clear could get a word out. "Let's get our friend here up and around. I want to talk to him."

Mr. Ivory propped the unconscious Secreteer up against a tree and slapped his face a few times. "Come on. Wakey wakey . . ."

The Secreteer's eyes blinked open. He saw the frozen state of his comrade and instantly realized the position he was in.

"There you are," DeMayne said, crouching down to the Secreteer's eye level. "I've been looking forward to this." He pulled down the piece of cloth covering the Secreteer's nose and mouth, exposing his face.

The captive Secreteer scowled and looked up with defiant eyes. "You're wasting your time. It doesn't matter what you do to me. I won't tell you anything."

"Don't be so sure," DeMayne replied. "If I want you to talk, believe me, you're going to talk."

"No," Skerren said. He put a hand on the hilt of one of his swords and drew it out an inch. "I don't care what his people did to you. I draw the line at torture. I won't allow it."

"You won't allow it?" DeMayne repeated, amused. "I'm going to pretend I didn't hear that. Not to worry, young man. I'm not a fan of torture either."

"Since when?" Joey said. "You didn't have any problem torturing me outside of Camelot last year."

"I didn't say I was above torture," DeMayne clarified. "But it's a lot of work, and not always the best way to obtain information." As he spoke, he slid a black ring onto the pinkie finger of his right hand. Joey recognized it. The Ring of Ranguul was a magic artifact that allowed DeMayne to control the minds of anyone he shook hands with. Joey had seen him use it before, turning innocent people into puppets on a string. Mr. Ivory forced the Secreteer to take DeMayne's hand. He grabbed DeMayne's shirt, trying to resist, but it was no use. His eyes went black, and his body went limp. After that, the interrogation began.

It was more of an interview, really. An easy conversation with a hypnotized subject that yielded several valuable pieces of information. One fact that everyone was surprised to learn was that the two Secreteers Mr. Ivory and Mr. Clear had captured were the only ones patrolling the forest. It seemed the Secreteers had grown complacent about their defenses. Two guardians had always been enough to keep people out of Gravenmurk Glen in the past, and despite their failure to turn back Joey and the others, reinforcements were unlikely to arrive. There were many other Secreteers in the Clandestine Order who could have come, but they were busy. Apparently, the past twenty-four hours had seen an unprecedented outbreak in magical phenomena all around the world, including the reappearance of several ancient doors that led back to the Imagine Nation and other magical realms. The Secreteers preferred that such things stayed lost and forgotten. They were working hard to prevent their discovery, but they were fighting a losing battle.

"How do you like that?" Shazad said with a smile. "Sounds like what we did to set magic free helped clear a path to our destination."

"When we tell this story later, let's pretend that was the

285

plan all along," Joey said. "Speaking of our destination . . . where is it?"

Unfortunately, the entranced Secreteer couldn't tell them which way to go next. He didn't know the answer himself.

"He's lying," Jack Blank said. "The Secreteers all share each other's secrets. That's how they work. That's how they know everything."

"Not this secret," the gray Secreteer said in a dazed monotone. "Only the grand majestrix of our Order knows the location of the ancient temple. Only she is permitted to enter."

"He's not lying," DeMayne said, twisting the Ring of Ranguul on his finger. "He can't lie. Not to me. And it's not a temple. It's a castle," he added to the Secreteer. "He really doesn't know." DeMayne chewed on the inside of his cheek, weighing his options. "I don't suppose your majestrix would grant us access if we promised to spare your life?"

"Never," the gray Secreteer replied. "The Order comes first. My life is nothing."

"Less than nothing," DeMayne said. "Not to worry. It's almost over."

"What?" Joey shook as DeMayne took out the Tempest

Blade and raised it toward the Secreteer's throat. "No!"

"Stop!" Jack exclaimed at the same time. He and Joey were standing the closest to DeMayne. They both went at him, knocking him off-balance before Mr. Ivory or Mr. Clear could move to protect their leader.

DeMayne fell backward from his crouched position, landing on his rear end. "Have you gone mad?" he asked, indignant.

"We could ask you the same thing," Jack said. "What are you doing?"

DeMayne stood up and dusted himself off. "What do you think I'm doing? We're done here. This man has out-lived his usefulness."

"So?" Jack shot back. "You're just going to kill him?"

"Don't be so squeamish," DeMayne said. "This should come as no surprise. I told you I was going to destroy the Secreteers."

"You do that by destroying their life's work!" Joey said. "By defeating them. Not by killing them!"

DeMayne frowned. "That was never a condition of our deal."

"Then I'm changing the deal," Joey said. "I'm updating

287

it. No killing. Unless you want to lose my protection, that's part of it now. No killing."

"Stop it. We both know you're not going to waste a spell like that."

"Something tells me it'll take a lot less magic to remove those protections than it did to put them in place. Want to find out?"

Joey's ultimatum created a staring contest between him and DeMayne.

"I don't respond well to threats," DeMayne said. His voice was calm and even but all the more menacing for his complete lack of emotion. "Maybe I don't need your protection anymore. Have you considered that? We already know there won't be any more guards from this point on."

"There's still one more Secreteer waiting in the castle," Joey warned DeMayne. "We've seen Oblivia in action. I don't care how many magical artifacts you've got hidden on your body. You won't last five minutes against her without this." Joey held up the wand.

DeMayne's eyes narrowed.

"Speaking of hidden magical objects, what does that one do? I've never seen that stone before." Leanora pointed out a black stone pendant that hung around DeMayne's neck. It was like her firestone, only darker, and it had strange markings carved into its sides. The pendant had been exposed after the Secreteer clawed at DeMayne, popping buttons on his shirt. DeMayne ignored Leanora's question and tucked the stone out of sight. "Fine. We'll do it your way," he grumbled. "No killing. But if you ever touch me again, that will change, starting with the lot of you."

Jack Blank leaned back, making a hands-off gesture, but the expression on his face said, *Bring it*. Joey got the sense that he was used to having his life threatened by people like DeMayne.

"We'll keep our hands to ourselves. You do the same," Joey said, trying to match Jack's casual toughness.

"Mr. Clear," DeMayne called out while removing the Ring of Ranguul from his finger. "The ring's effects will wear off when we leave here. I don't want this man following us. Put him on ice."

Mr. Clear nodded, still shivering. "I just need a few minutes to warm up."

"Now," DeMayne ordered. "I want to keep moving. We're close. I can feel it."

Clear sighed and raised his hand toward the gray Secreteer.

Once the opposition had been turned into ice cubes, the Fellowship of the Wand continued. It turned out that "close" was a relative term. The forest went on longer than anyone expected, continuing out over a body of water.

Joey didn't realize until he stepped in it. The water was completely still, and a thick layer of pollen coated its surface. Oaks and evergreens went on as far as the eye could see, creating an optical illusion. What looked like solid ground was actually a strange sort of bayou. For all anyone knew, it was the size of Lake Michigan.

"We're going to need a raft," Skerren said, testing the water's depth with a sword. Even at the edge it was deep. He looked around at the forest. "Plenty of material to work with here, but . . ."

"We can't chop down these trees," Allegra said, finishing his thought. "The Gravens might come back."

DeMayne put up a hand. "Never mind the trees. We don't need them." He took out a thin metal case that looked like a business card holder. It contained several thin sheets of colored paper. He gave one to Joey and kept another for himself. "Take this and follow my instructions carefully."

"What is this?" Joey asked.

"Origami paper," DeMayne explained. "Special origami paper. I took it away from someone in Japan many years ago. I don't remember who they were. It doesn't matter. What matters is that you do exactly what I do."

Joey listened as DeMayne guided him through a series of folds, telling him how to make a paper boat. It was a relatively simple process, but the result was extraordinary. When Joey and DeMayne reached the final step and unfolded their boats into their finished form, the paper expanded rapidly, growing too big and heavy to hold. Everyone jumped back as two full-size boats splashed down in the water, ready to be boarded.

"Are you kidding me?" Jack said. "I don't believe this."

"That's why I had him do it," DeMayne replied, nodding to Joey. "Magic requires belief."

"But I don't understand. They're just paper!" Jack said, inspecting the boats. "Won't they get soggy and sink?"

DeMayne nodded. "Yes, which means there's no time to waste."

Everyone stepped forward to get in the boats. Janelle

tapped Jack's shoulder as she passed him. "It's best not to think about it too much. Just go with it."

In a move that surprised no one, but annoyed everyone, DeMayne took one boat for himself and forced the rest of the group to cram into the other. "Typical," Mr. Ivory muttered as they squeezed into place and shoved off. Using fallen branches as oars, they rowed out, floating between the trees and following DeMayne's lead. It appeared that the farther they went, the more he remembered. That worried Joey, but as much as he didn't trust DeMayne, there was no denying they needed him. There was a reason no one had ever gotten this close to the Secret Citadel before. Between DeMayne's memories and Joey's protection, they were the perfect team, even if they weren't really on the same side. Turn by turn through the bayou, DeMayne called back to the group, telling them which way to go. Joey wondered what he wasn't telling them. In their boat, Mr. Ivory had a few questions of his own.

"What did you mean before?" he asked Shazad. "When you said that you already set magic free? Set it free how?"

Shazad stopped rowing. The question took him by surprise. "Doesn't your boss tell you anything?"

Mr. Ivory looked back over his shoulder toward the lead boat. DeMayne was out of earshot, but he lowered his voice just the same. "He's never been one for sharing."

Shazad nodded. "Fair enough." Speaking quietly, he and Leonora explained how they broke the dark magic markers that had held magic back for centuries, releasing its energy back into the world.

Mr. Ivory couldn't believe his ears. "You did what? Are you out of your mind?"

Shazad and Leonora made no apologies. "The world needs magic," Leonora said. "Maybe you noticed?"

"Magic is dangerous," Mr. Ivory retorted. "Maybe *you* noticed? The world needs protecting from magic. If anyone knows that, I do."

Joey rolled his eyes, following the conversation. "This guy really drank the Kool-Aid, huh?"

"What do you mean?" Jack asked him.

"Protecting the world from magic," Joey explained. "DeMayne acts like he's doing the world a favor. He says magic isn't for everyone and he keeps dangerous power away from people who might abuse it. It's all a front. He just wants it for himself."

"I'm aware of that," Mr. Ivory rasped, speaking to Joey out of the side of his mouth. "I'm not a fool. I know the Invisible Hand wasn't formed out of any desire for public service, but we do keep magic out of other people's hands where it might be a danger to them. I told you about my introduction to magic. How many kids you think that old witch ate before I stole her bag of teeth?" Mr. Ivory looked disgusted. He didn't like to think about it. "How about Mr. Clear over there?" he asked, nodding to his frosty comrade. "He's flat-out cursed by that bracelet on his wrist. Sure, he's got incredible power, but he's always cold. He can't get warm. It gets worse when he uses his power, but he can't take it off. It's bound to him. There isn't a day that goes by that he doesn't wish he could just get rid of that thing."

Leanora looked at Mr. Clear, who was shivering next to Skerren and Allegra. "Did DeMayne ever try to help you?" she asked him.

Mr. Clear looked at her like she was hopelessly naive.

Mr. Ivory scoffed. "Please. Do you even hear yourself?"

"That's the difference between us," Leanora said. "We would have helped. Our families would have helped too. You just met the wrong people. Made the wrong friends."

"No one ever said life was fair," Mr. Ivory said bitterly. "Would have been nice if I ran into your folks back in the day instead of that old witch, but I can't turn back time, can I? Mark my words, other kids are going to end up like I did because of what you did. Bringing magic back out into the open isn't going to solve the world's problems. It's just going to create a whole bunch of new ones."

"If it does, we'll deal with them," Shazad said. "Out in the open. No more secrets. People are going to know about it. If you really care about trying to keep people safe from magic, you should be working with us. That's what our families are going to do when this is over. That's what *we're* going to do—keep the wrong kind of magic out of the wrong people's hands and help the world use magic for good."

Mr. Ivory let out a mirthless laugh, as if the conversation was ridiculous. "If I were you, I wouldn't make any big plans for 'after this.' You don't know DeMayne like I do."

"I know him well enough," Joey said. "He's no better than that old witch who tried to eat you. By the way, what do you think is going to happen when he destroys the Order of Secreteers? You're helping us break down the biggest magic barrier there is. Belief. Once this place goes public, everyone's going to believe. If you don't want everyone to have magic, you might want to have a conversation with our tour guide up there."

"Ledger DeMayne doesn't have conversations. He tells you how it is."

"He's a bully," Jack said, understanding perfectly. "I don't like bullies."

Mr. Ivory shrugged. "The Secreteers are just as bad. They deserve to go down. Messing with people's memories? That's a violation. They're scum lower than the lowest—"

"His mom was a Secreteer," Janelle cut in, pointing to Jack.

"Oh." Mr. Ivory clammed up. "No offense."

"None taken," Jack said.

"What are you talking about back there?" DeMayne shouted back, growing suspicious of all the chatter in the boat behind him.

"Nothing important," Mr. Ivory called ahead. "I was just insulting the boy's mother."

DeMayne looked puzzled for a second, but he found the answer acceptable and went back to rowing his boat. "In that case, carry on."

"Do you *have* to work for him?" Joey asked Mr. Ivory in a hushed whisper.

Mr. Ivory grimaced. "If anyone should be rethinking their deal with him, it's you. The big man's been at this game a long time. I wouldn't bet against him."

Joey looked at Ledger DeMayne alone in his boat. Mr. Ivory was right, and he knew it. DeMayne almost certainly remembered more than he was telling the group. That was who he was and how he operated. He always had an ace hidden up his sleeve. Joey had a bad feeling he was going to find out what it was before this trip was over. Would he somehow force Joey's hand and put him in a position where he had no choice but to use the wand? Redondo did tell him he would have to die before this was over.

"You okay?" Jack asked Joey. When Joey didn't answer, Jack tapped him on the shoulder. "Hey. Don't listen to these guys, telling you what's going to happen to you. I used to have a future that everyone 'knew' I couldn't avoid. It never ended up happening. It came close, but I didn't want that future, so I made my own."

"You're talking about the evil version of yourself that came back in time to kill you," Joey said.

"Everyone here thought I was gonna grow up to be that guy," Jack said. "And back in Jersey? Forget about it. They thought even less of me. I had to take this placement test at school to find out what my ideal job would be." Jack snorted. "The answer didn't come back superhero, I can tell you that."

"You're talking about the PMAP!" Janelle said. "We took that test. Mine said I was going to be a rocket scientist."

"Mine said I could do whatever I put my mind to," Joey said. "What did yours say?"

Jack stared at Joey and Janelle for a few seconds. "It's not important. That test didn't mean anything. The point is, no one knows what's going to happen. You decide your future. No one else."

Jack gave Joey's shoulder a shake and looked across the water to see what lay ahead. Joey nodded along, but when no one was watching, he stole another glance at Redondo's old deck of cards. He drew three from the top. Once again, they were three blanks. In his dream, Joey had thought the empty cards meant he had no future, but now he wondered if they meant he was supposed to meet Jack Blank. And now that he had, who could say what might happen next.

18

The Right Kind
of Nothing

The group met no resistance on the water. It was smooth sailing all the way to the edge of the woods. They hit land and came out of the forest in a meadow identical to the one from DeMayne's blocked memories.

"This is it," DeMayne said. "We're here."

"What are you talking about?" Jack asked. "There's nothing here."

DeMayne smiled. "Exactly."

"I don't understand," Leonora said. "Nothing is good?"

"It can be," Joey said. Redondo's words echoed in his ears:

Even nothing can be something if you look at it the right way. Nothing now represents the possibility of something later.

"This is the place," DeMayne said, sounding sure of

himself. "The castle is here, but it's hidden. We have to bring it out."

"How do we do that?" Shazad asked.

A crease appeared in DeMayne's forehead. He looked around at the empty meadow. There was nothing for miles. Just a lone tree that sat on a green hill in the distance. "I don't know."

"You don't know?" Shazad repeated. "What do you mean, you don't know?"

"I don't remember," DeMayne admitted.

Shazad frowned. "I thought you had your memories back."

"I remember some things, not all. I know the castle is here. I don't remember how to unveil it."

Everyone scanned the horizon, hoping some kind of clue might present itself. There was nothing there. It was a wonderful place to have a picnic, but that was about it.

"I'm confused," Leanora said. "Isn't 'remembering stuff' your job in all this? Isn't that why we let you come with us?"

DeMayne eyed Leanora with a scowl. "Let's get one thing straight. You didn't *let* me do anything. I agreed not to kill you in return for protection from the Secreteers. You wouldn't even be here without me."

"You mean here, in the middle of nowhere, with no idea what to do next?" Leonora shot back. "Thank you. This is really helpful. I'm so glad we had you to guide us to nothing."

DeMayne aimed a stern finger in her direction. "Don't test me."

"Or what?" Leonora asked. "Right now, it seems you need us a lot more than we need you. Joey held up our end of the bargain and got us past the Secreteers. If you can't help us find the castle—"

"We did find it," DeMayne cut in. "It's here."

"I can see that. It's very impressive," she said, her voice dripping with sarcasm.

"Why don't you use the wand to find it?" Mr. Clear asked. He had finally stopped shivering.

DeMayne raised an eyebrow. "There's an idea. Good thinking, Mr. Clear. I knew we brought you along for a reason. How about it, Joey? Why not use the wand?"

"You know why not," Shazad said. "I see what you're doing."

"What am I doing?" DeMayne asked in a slimy voice.

"You want Joey to use the wand as much as possible on the way to the castle, so maybe he's too weak to do anything when we get there. Or worse. You don't want to help us. You're just scheming to get your hands on the wand."

"I'm doing nothing of the sort," DeMayne said. "I never told you I share your cause. I *don't* want to help you. I simply find myself temporarily in need of your services, just as you find yourself in need of mine. Whatever you might think of me, there's no scheming on my part. I don't have to manipulate the situation to usher Joey into his grave. He's been chasing it just fine without my help." DeMayne turned to address Joey and motioned to the empty meadow. "I told you I'd take you to the castle. I have delivered. Now do what you came here to do."

"He didn't come here to die," Shazad said.

"That depends on how strong he is," DeMayne replied.

"Don't even think about it," Shazad told Joey. "There's got to be another way."

Joey looked around, wondering what that could be. He knew he couldn't use the wand to unveil the castle and survive. He still felt a little weak from the spell he had cast to

302

shield DeMayne and his cronies from the Secreteers. There was no telling how strong the magic protections around the Secret Citadel were, but the Secreteers had managed to keep the place hidden for a thousand years, so Joey was guessing they were pretty strong. Breaking down their defenses would almost certainly push him over the edge. Maybe Shazad was right and that had been DeMayne's plan all along.

"You realize if I die using this wand, you lose whatever protection I gave you," Joey told DeMayne.

"I'm willing to take that chance," DeMayne replied.

"Right," Shazad said. "You're willing to risk *his* life. I don't think so. We don't even know if this is the right place. All we have is your word on that."

Joey considered the possibility that DeMayne was lying. He didn't trust the man at all, but Joey did believe him when he said this was the place. He recognized it from DeMayne's memories. Unfortunately, the meadow was just as empty in real life as it had been in DeMayne's head. There was no magical door to open or puzzle to solve, nothing but an empty horizon. Joey knew in his heart they were standing on the doorstep of the Secret Citadel, but they might as well have been a million miles away.

He didn't know what to do. He and his friends had been through so much and fought so hard to reach this point. He couldn't let their journey end here, but he didn't want *his* journey to end at all. Sacrificing himself wasn't part of the plan.

Joey pulled the wand out of his sleeve. "Anyone have any good ideas?"

"Besides waving that wand and hoping for the best?" Shazad asked. "It's not an option."

"What else is there?" Joey asked.

"Nothing," DeMayne answered. "You have to do this. It's why you have the wand. It's your responsibility, isn't it?"

"No." Jack Blank put a hand on Joey's wrist, pushing the wand down. "Don't do it. I've got something."

"What have you got?" Joey asked, full of hope.

"Everybody quiet!" Jack shouted. "There's something here." Leanora and DeMayne stopped barking at each other as Jack put a hand to his ear. "There it is again."

Everyone paused to listen. The forest was dead quiet.

"I don't hear anything," Mr. Ivory said.

"That's because they're not talking to you," Jack replied. "Not that it matters. You couldn't hear them if they were. None of you could, but I can."

"Who?" Allegra asked Jack. "Who's talking to you?"

"Not who, what. And they're not talking to me. Or us. They're talking to each other about us." Jack paused, listening closely to what sounded to Joey and everyone else like nothing. "It's just whispering now. They know I'm onto them."

"Who?" Skerren asked.

"The machines. This place is full of them."

"Machines?" Shazad said. "Where? Next to the castle?" he added with a sarcastic gesture at the tree on the hill. "That doesn't make any sense."

"It definitely doesn't, but I'm telling you, they're here. They're everywhere. Their voices are . . . old and strange. It's something I've never heard before, but I'm positive it's mechanical." Jack wandered around the meadow, investigating. "Where *are* you?" he wondered aloud. Suddenly he stopped short and spun around to face the forest with wide eyes. "No way."

"What?" Joey asked, dying to know what was going on. "What is it?"

"I don't believe this," Jack said. "It's the trees."

Jack walked back to the edge of the forest and put his

hands on the nearest tree. Again, he seemed to be listening to it. "Amazing," he whispered. "Can you show me?"

"What's he doing?" DeMayne asked, still confused.

"He's having a conversation," Allegra said. "Relax. This is what he does."

Jack rejoined the group a few minutes later, clearly floored by what he had discovered. "This is incredible."

"What is?" Joey asked.

"Watch."

"Enough of this," DeMayne said, fed up with waiting. "If you know something, spit it out. I don't like being kept in the dark."

Jack smirked. "Well, since you asked so nicely . . ."

With that, the trees "turned on," sparkling as if they were decorated with Christmas lights. There were no strings of colorful bulbs draped across their branches or wrapped around their trunks. The light came from the trees themselves. It wasn't all of them. Only the trees that lined the meadow lit up, but they went on as far as the eye could see. Twilight was setting in, and the light show was a wonder to behold. Leaves twinkled, and a soft glow emanated from between the ridges and bumps of tree bark. Jack tugged on a branch to examine a leaf and told the others to do the same, but carefully.

Joey looked and saw the veins that covered the face of the leaf were lines of glittering circuits. He was holding an organic microchip in his hand. Joey let go of the leaf and approached a tree with a large knothole in its trunk. He stuck his head inside. The interior of the tree was lit up like a mainframe computer. It was as advanced as anything Joey had ever seen, even at his school.

"That's new," he said when he pulled his head back out.

"More like that's old," Jack corrected him. "A thousand years old, but I know what you mean. I've never seen anything like this. I've never even heard of anything like it. A living machine, growing, evolving, and learning all this time. Who could have built this?"

"Dwarves," Leanora said. Everyone looked at her, wondering how she could possibly know that. "Maybe," she added, hedging a bit. "There's an old story from Norse mythology. Two dwarves, Brokk and Eitri, the ones who made Thor's hammer, had a bet with Loki. If he lost, the dwarves got to take his head. They wanted to use his brain to make a thinking machine. Who knows if it's true or not, but that combination of magic and machinery . . . It's kind of like what Janelle is always talking about."

Jack shrugged. "I can't say if dwarves built them or grew them or whatever, but these trees are what's hiding the castle. They power some kind of reality distortion wave between us and it. That's the best way I can describe what's happening here."

"Can you turn the trees off?" Janelle asked Jack.

"*I* can turn them off," DeMayne said. He pulled the Sword of Storms from his belt and aimed it at the forest, planning to summon its hurricane winds and uproot the trees.

"I wouldn't do that if I were you," Jack warned him.

"Quiet," DeMayne barked. "You don't tell me what to do. I tell you. Understand?"

The broken sword hummed with power and a mighty storm brewed, but before the swirling winds could even bend a branch, the trees gave DeMayne the shock of his life. Bright blue bolts of light shot out from every glowing twig and stem to zap him with magic energy. He went sailing backward and tumbled across the grass. When he eventually skidded to a halt, his tailored suit was ruptured and burned.

His perfect hair was singed and frazzled. His handsome face was flushed red, and his body smoked like a cartoon character who had just been electrocuted.

"I understand." Jack smiled.

Janelle stepped over DeMayne's sizzling body to join Jack near the trees. "If they're machines, can you control them? Do you understand how they work?"

"Not even a little," Jack said. "This is a mixture of magic and science. Organic living circuitry powered by magic. It's probably more in your wheelhouse than mine. You want to take a look?"

Janelle took a peek inside the tree that Joey had looked in earlier.

"What do you think?" Joey asked her.

Janelle came out shaking her head. "If you gave me a year to study all this, maybe I could come up with something. Right now I wouldn't even know where to begin."

"Same," Jack said. "Except I might need a little longer."

"So what do we do?" Joey asked. They were running out of options. It was looking like he might have to use the wand after all.

"There is one thing I can try," Jack said. He closed his

eyes and reached out a hand to the trees. At first nothing happened, but soon lights began to fade throughout the forest. As the trees powered down, a strange tremor ran across the meadow like a pulse signal being sent out into the world. Joey watched the air ripple as if it were a body of water, and the world began to bend, distort, and reshape itself. The peaceful meadow was a false reality. As the illusion crumbled and fell away, the ground fell away with it. Joey and the others jumped back as the earth beneath their feet turned to ash and dropped down to form the edge of a cliff. The hill in front of them came apart in the shape of a castle. It was more of a tower, really. An incredibly tall spire that ran straight up, perched on a natural stone column. They had found it. The Secret Citadel.

Mr. Ivory's mouth fell open. "How did you do that?"

Jack played it off like it was no big thing. "Simple really. I asked."

"You asked," Mr. Ivory repeated.

Jack nodded. "Sometimes you have to think small to think big."

"That's it?" Mr. Ivory said. "You asked? And the trees turned themselves off just like that? Magic trees that stood guard here for a thousand years?" He pointed at his boss, who was still dazed and sizzling. "They fried him like a strip of bacon!"

Jack looked down at DeMayne. "He didn't say the magic word."

"What's the magic word?"

"Please."

19

Back Where It All Began

Ledger DeMayne was furious with Jack for letting him get zapped when he had the ability to turn off the trees all along. Jack tried to tell him he didn't actually "turn off" anything, and also, he had no way of knowing if the trees would do what he asked, but DeMayne wouldn't have it. "That's it," he snapped at Jack. "You're on my list too."

"I thought I was on your team," Jack countered with a touch of snark.

"For now," DeMayne growled.

"It's your own fault," Allegra told DeMayne. "Jack warned you not to threaten the trees."

"I can't help it if they like me better than you," Jack added. "They said they feel like they know me."

"Bah!" DeMayne turned his back on the conversation and stalked off.

"Just ignore him," Shazad told Jack. "No one else is complaining. If you ask me, that couldn't have gone any better."

Everyone gathered at the edge of the newly formed cliff. A hole in the earth the size of the Grand Canyon stretched out before them. Careful not to get too close, Joey looked down into the chasm. A foggy mist drifted through the air below the ledge, hiding the ground from view.

"Remind you of anything?" he asked, nudging Janelle with his elbow. The foggy, bottomless pit was similar to the strange hallway in DeMayne's office building, but there was no bridge here. The tower was inaccessible.

It was the latest in a long list of unbelievable sights. The tower was like a medieval skyscraper. It was a hundred feet tall and precariously balanced on a small patch of land that sat on top of an ancient stone column. The tower's slender foundation looked dangerously unstable. It was less than half the width of the structure it supported and was built like a child's Lego tower. A narrow column of blocks rose out of the mist, stacked one on top of the other, all the way up to the base of the Secret Citadel. The whole thing looked

313

like a gentle breeze could knock it over, but it stood firm, as it had for a millennium and counting. At the edge of the land in front of the tower was a wooden dock that extended out into the open air. An airship was tied to it.

"That's Hypnova's ship," Allegra said.

"Where's Hypnova?" Leanora asked.

"Inside," Shazad said. "I hope."

DeMayne cleared his throat. "Mr. Clear. We need a way across."

"Really?" Mr. Clear complained. "I just warmed up."

DeMayne gave his pale henchman a hard look, and that was that. Mr. Clear abandoned his protest and reached out a hand. The blue crystal on his wrist lit up, and an ice bridge formed between his feet and the entrance to the tower. It was an instant glacier the length and width of ten football fields that anchored the shaky tower to the cliff.

DeMayne didn't say "thank you," or "good job," or anything like that. He just stepped out onto the ice, leading the way across the frozen plain. Joey and the others followed, with Mr. Clear shuffling along behind them, his collar turned up against a chill he couldn't escape. They walked a long mile across the ice, occasionally slipping and falling on the slick, glassy surface. When they finally reached the tower, they faced a new challenge. There was no way in. The tower's great iron doors were not doors at all. They were painted on. The entrance was all bricked up.

"How do we get in?" Skerren asked.

"Something tells me 'please' isn't going to cut it this time," Mr. Ivory said.

Joey wished he hadn't lost the Hand of Glory back at DeMayne's office. Ms. Scarlett's magic paintbrushes might have come in handy too. He could have painted a new scene with open doors over the bricks. Shazad encouraged Leanora to try to break the wall down with a firestone punch. She was about to give it a try when DeMayne told everyone to step aside. He reached into his collar to retrieve a necklace and take it off his neck. It wasn't the black stone pendant they had seen before. Instead, a thin metal rod made of gray steel dangled at the end of the string. Everyone moved out of the way as he struck it against the "door" like a tuning fork. A clear note rang out. It started out sounding pleasant, but the tone grew in volume and pitch until it became unbearable. Joey winced. It was downright painful to listen to, but it had an effect that was worth the momentary discomfort. The bricks began to loosen and move. Everyone covered their ears as stones inside the painted doorway dislodged from their mooring. They swung out as if on hinges, granting access to the tower. Once they were open, DeMayne grasped the metal rod tight, silencing it. When he let go, it cracked and disintegrated into dust.

"What was that?" Joey asked.

"A Chime of Opening," DeMayne said. "It can open any door, but it can only be used ten times. This was the last use. I was saving it. I didn't know what for, but it seems I was saving it for this." He let go of the empty string that once held the chime. The wind carried it off across the canyon. "There's a reason I stayed alive all this time. I was always going to end up back here. This is fate."

Joey stared into the darkness beyond the doors, wondering what his own fate would be. He steeled his courage and gave a nod to his friends. "Let's do this."

Inside the tower, the entrance hall was as grand as it was empty. The floor was made up of large marble flagstones arranged in a black-and-white checkerboard pattern. In the center of the room, an ornate compass rose had been crafted out of gold, white, and black marble and seamlessly laid into place. Doric columns lined the walls, bracing a mezzanine, and beautiful stained-glass windows circled the room, letting in a rainbow of light. There was a large fireplace on the far wall, centered across from the door. A fire roared to life with a whoosh, illuminating the base of the tower. Joey spotted a staircase that led up to the mezzanine and wound its way up the interior walls in a spiral pattern. There were no floors above them, just open air all the way to the top.

"I thought this was supposed to be a castle," Skerren said. "There's nothing here."

Joey looked up, tracking the stairs around and around until they disappeared into shadow. There had to be something up there. He figured they would have to climb all those stairs before they found anything or anyone, but that wasn't the case.

A wisp of smoke entered the room, and a voice echoed through the chamber.

"You shouldn't be here."

Joey recognized the voice. It was Oblivia, Grand Majestrix of the Clandestine Order of Secreteers.

He froze as white smoke ran around the edges of the room. It covered the walls, rising almost up to the windows.

The group moved toward the center of the room to get away from it. Joey felt like he was standing in the eye of a storm as the snow-white smoke revolved around him, obscuring everything. Everyone drew their weapons, ready for anything that might come out of the mist. There was no telling what dangers were hidden in this place. Only the orange glow of the fireplace was strong enough to penetrate the swirling fog, and even that, just barely. Joey's eyes focused on the flickering amber light and then just above it as Oblivia appeared on the mezzanine.

Joey had glimpsed her only between flashes of lightning during the attack on Hypnova's ship, but he knew it was her. Fear knotted his stomach when he saw Oblivia dressed all in white. She was an older woman who was fit and formidable. She had long white hair that was voluminous and shiny, and her face was creased with wrinkles. Oblivia had a natural beauty about her that was muted not by age, but rather by her hard eyes and scornful expression. She came off as cold and unforgiving, and her words matched her demeanor.

"You've gone too far." Oblivia gripped the railing of the mezzanine, full of righteous indignation. "Too far. This is an atrocity. I cannot tolerate your presence in this place or

forgive your intrusion. There will be a price to pay for tres-
passing here."

Her words hung in the air like the sentence of an angry
judge. DeMayne was not intimidated. "I could say the same
to you. I haven't been back this way in a long while, but the
fact remains, I was here first. You're the one who doesn't
belong."

Oblivia squinted at DeMayne, no doubt confused by his
claim and his swagger. She pointed a finger in his direction,
probing for answers. Nothing happened. She was left staring
at her empty hand as if it were a weapon she had forgotten
to load.

DeMayne smiled. "Trying to read my memories? Find
out what I'm talking about? Sorry. You people aren't getting
in my head again. I've got protection."

Oblivia's eyes fell on Joey. Her jaw tightened as she made
the connection. "I see. The wand. I hope you haven't been
overexerting yourself, Joey. That kind of recklessness has
only one possible outcome."

"Don't worry about me," Joey said. "I've been careful."

"Not from where I'm standing. Believe it or not, I'm trying to help you. You and your friends are playing with fire.

You're going to get burned, and for what? Look around. I know you were hoping to find some ancient relic like the dark magic markers you destroyed earlier, but there's nothing for you here. Nothing but me."

Joey turned around inside the tower, trying to get a sense of his surroundings. He couldn't see past the smoke, but he saw right through Oblivia.

If there's nothing here, what's she hiding behind all this?

"You're right," Joey said. "I don't believe you."

"You shouldn't," Jack said. "She's incapable of telling the truth. It's against her religion."

"Hello, Jack," Oblivia said. "I didn't expect to see you again. This day is full of surprises."

"You two know each other?" DeMayne asked Jack.

"Our families know each other," Jack replied. "We're not friends."

"That much is true," Oblivia confirmed. "Your mother and I weren't friends either. We were sisters."

"She's your aunt?" Mr. Ivory asked.

"No," Jack said. "She just means they were both Secreteers."

"That may not be something you ever understand, but it means something," Oblivia declared. "Even now, it means something. Everything I ever did to your family, I did to protect the Clandestine Order and its mission. I make no apologies for it. I have a duty to something bigger than myself. What I do, I do for—"

"Let me guess," DeMayne cut in. "The greater good?" He let out a derisive laugh. "I've been saying that for years. You don't actually believe it, do you?"

"I know what *you* believe, Ledger DeMayne," Oblivia scolded. "You only see the greater good when you look in the mirror. That's what's held you back all these years. You think small."

DeMayne's eyebrows went up. "I think small?" He touched a shocked hand to his chest. "Me?"

"That's right," Oblivia said. "You lack imagination."

DeMayne gritted his teeth. "I'll show you imagination."

He took a big step forward with his hand on the hilt of the Tempest Blade, but he didn't get far. His nose flattened against some kind of force field. DeMayne cursed and stomped his feet like a bratty child.

Oblivia cocked her head to the side, taunting DeMayne. "I'm sorry, did I forget to mention the invisible wall between us?"

As DeMayne clutched his nose in pain, Jack, Skerren, and Allegra put their hands out to feel the unseen barrier that separated them from Oblivia. Joey, Shazad, Leanora, and Janelle did the same and reached right through it.

"What the?" Allegra said as Joey and the others kept moving forward, immune to Oblivia's defenses. "How come they got through?"

"Wait a minute," Shazad said, turning around to "look" at the invisible wall. "I know what this is."

"You should," Oblivia said. "You've seen it before. My memory powers may be useless on you because of the wand, but I still have cards to play."

The smoke around Oblivia cleared, revealing a body at her feet.

"Hypnova!" Joey shouted.

20

The Forgotten Memories of Ledger DeMayne

"What have you done to her?" Shazad demanded.

Hypnova was lying on her side, seemingly unconscious.

Please, let her just be unconscious, Joey thought.

"Are you all right?" Janelle called out. "Hypnova, talk to us!"

"She's fine," Oblivia said. "For now. Whether or not she stays that way is up to you."

"How did you capture her?" Leanora asked. "How did you get past the shield?"

"You mean this shield?" Oblivia lifted the Caliburn Shield up off the mezzanine floor and put it on her arm. "This item frustrated us to no end as we pursued Hypnova this past year. Unfortunately for her, she set it down while she was trapped in the mirror world, looking for a way out—and I was ready."

Joey's stomach dropped. Leanora punched him in the shoulder. "I told you not to break that mirror!"

A golden blur flashed out from underneath the folds of Oblivia's white robe. "Let's talk." She had the tip of a blade mere inches from Hypnova's neck. Joey recognized it as Hypnova's own saber.

"Please. Don't hurt her," Joey said. "What do you want?"

"What I want doesn't matter," Oblivia spat. "I *want* to see you all punished for what you've done. Unleashing magic. Defying our Order. Desecrating this sacred space. This isn't about what I want. It's about my responsibility and what I am willing to offer, which is more than you deserve—a chance to walk away."

"You can't be serious," Leanora said. "We've come too far to walk away. We're not leaving without a fight."

"You don't want this fight. This is the end of your journey. It's time to be realistic about your options. This tower is empty. It's over. Will Hypnova have to die before you admit defeat? Don't think I won't kill her. She betrayed her vows to the Order, revealing ancient secrets. Her life is forfeit, but she has reason to hope, and you . . . you have a choice. Surrender the wand to me. Abandon this foolish crusade. *Go home.* I know this isn't what you hoped for, but your quest was doomed from the start. Ending it will be easier than you think. All you have to do is let me into your minds. I can send you on your way without an ounce of regret. The Clandestine Order will undo the damage you've done to the world, and everything will be just as it was."

"That's your offer?" Joey said. "Really?"

"We haven't done any damage to the world!" Janelle protested.

"You've introduced chaos in the form of unrestrained magic. The results are completely unpredictable."

"So why are you acting like you know what's going to happen?" Shazad asked.

"Because I do know," Oblivia countered. "You've made our job infinitely more difficult, but the Secreteers will work tirelessly to hide away any trace of new magic and set the world back to normal. That's what's going to happen, and you're going to accept it. You're going to forget about all this and go back to the lives you had before. That's my offer. I'll even be so gracious as to extend the offer to you, Ledger

DeMayne. You can go back to thinking you're king of the world if you like. I won't stop you. There are worse fates."

"I'll pass," DeMayne said. "If you know anything about me, you know I'm not going to put this woman's life ahead of my own interests. Especially not after what she did to me." He fluttered his fingers at Hypnova in a dismissive wave. "Go ahead. Dispose of her. You'll save me the trouble of doing it myself."

"No!" Joey blurted out. "Please, listen to us. Can't you see you're on the wrong side of this? The world needs magic, and you're doing everything you can to suppress it. Your intentions might be different from the Invisible Hand's. You might actually care about the greater good, but the result is the same. The world is sick and dying. You can help us change it."

"You're wasting your breath," Oblivia said, disregarding Joey. "I won't be a party to your misguided endeavors no matter what you say." She prodded Hypnova's shoulder with the golden saber. "And if you try to compel my actions with the wand—"

"You'll what?" Jack cut in. "Kill an innocent person?"

"Hypnova is hardly innocent. She betrayed the Clandestine

Order's sacred mission—a mission I have dedicated my entire life to."

"Can't you for once think for yourself and just do the right thing?" Jack shouted. "You care so much about your mission. You never stop to think about how it affects people's lives. I never knew my mom because of you and your mission!"

Jack's eyes welled with tears, and Oblivia's stern facade faded slightly. It was only for a moment, but it was the first thing anyone had said that had gotten through to her. She seemed to have genuine sympathy for Jack and the pain he felt.

"I am sorry for that, Jack. Believe me, I wish your mother were here instead of me. Your loss was my loss too. I'm old. I shouldn't be doing this anymore. Your mother showed such promise. I wanted her to lead the Order one day."

"She wouldn't have done it," Jack said. "My mother tried to leave the Order. You wouldn't let her go."

"It's true," Oblivia said, her voice heavy with regret. "She had incredible potential, but she lost her faith. I'm sorry she's gone, but I didn't take her from you. The Rüstov did. We lost her in the battle of Empire City. She died defending you."

"Maybe she would have lived if she'd had my father there to fight with her," Jack shot back. "Ever think of that?"

Oblivia shook her head. "I don't second-guess myself wondering 'what if.' I stay focused on 'what *is*.' I can't help you because I believe in something bigger than myself. Unlike your mother, I will always hold the sacred tenets of our Order, handed down from the first Secreteer. I've spent my life protecting this place. Keeping its secrets. Keeping it safe. Ensuring that there will always be a refuge for magic—a hiding place for the fantastic, unbelievable, and strange. Even if it's just a tiny corner of the world, it's better than nothing. If the world knew about this place, it would never be the same."

"That's the whole idea," Leanora said. "The world needs this. We need more than just a tiny corner of magic."

"The world is not ready for this," Oblivia said.

"You don't go onstage because you're ready," Joey said. "You go on because it's showtime."

"If that's how you truly feel, what are you waiting for?" Oblivia asked Joey. "You have the wand. You have the power. You can change this world with a flick of your wrist, but only if you believe in your mission as much as I believe in mine. I don't think you do."

Joey reached for the wand again. This time Oblivia didn't tell him to stop. "You're saying I should use the wand to bring the island back."

"She's practically daring you to do it," DeMayne told Joey, speaking out of the side of his mouth.

"I'm simply pointing out the truth," Oblivia said. "He *won't* do it. If he was going to, he would have done it already from the comfort of his living room couch. You could have avoided all of this, Joey. Why didn't you?"

"You know why," Joey said. "That would've killed me."

"And?" Oblivia paused, waiting for a more valid explanation. "What's one life weighed against the fate of the world? If you truly had the courage of your convictions, you wouldn't have hesitated. But you did hesitate. You spent a whole year plotting and scheming, desperate to escape this most difficult decision. The ultimate test of your beliefs— your life in exchange for an undisputable new age of magic. You didn't do it because you aren't sure if it's worth it. You aren't ready to pay the price."

"None of us are ready for that," Shazad said, incredulous. "We came here to change the world, but not that way. Not at the cost of Joey's life."

"What if there is no other way?" Joey asked. He stared at the wand in his hand, wondering if his fate had been sealed the moment he first picked it up.

"There's always another way," Jack told Joey. "You choose your fate. It doesn't choose you. Believe me, I know."

Joey didn't know what to believe. Or what to do. If Oblivia was telling the truth and the tower was empty, where did that leave him? He had hoped to find something here he could use . . . some final dark marker he and his friends could break in order to reveal the Imagine Nation, but there was nothing. That meant it was all up to him, and that scared him more than anything.

"I didn't come here to sacrifice myself," Joey said. "But I can't surrender the wand either. It doesn't work that way."

"It does if you want it to," Oblivia told him. "You have the power to do anything, including give it up. You can renounce the wand. Give it to me. I'll hide it where no one will ever find it. Set down your burden, Joey. I'll take responsibility for it."

"But it's not your responsibility," Joey said. "It's mine."

"No, it isn't. I understand why you might think that. You have all this power at your fingertips and you think you need to do something important with it, but you don't have to do *this*. The truth is, you don't know what to do. You're just a child."

"That's an advantage, not a disadvantage," Jack said. "Children see things more clearly than adults because our view isn't cluttered with all the rationalizations and compromises you've made over the years."

"Your view is overly simplistic, informed by movies and comic books instead of reality," Oblivia said, rejecting Jack's logic. "You're guided by visions of the heroes you think you have to be, but that doesn't have to be your fate. Put the wand down," she told Joey. "You can forget about all this. I can help. You can still walk away and live your life."

"What kind of life would that be?" Joey asked.

Oblivia considered that. "Compared to this? A boring life. There's no shame in that. There are many people in this world who wish they had the luxury of a boring life. Deep down, I think you're one of them. Otherwise, you would have waved that wand already. You're stalling."

"I'm thinking," Joey corrected. "It's not that I don't believe in what we're doing. I just have to believe there is another way to get there."

"There isn't," DeMayne said. "This is the end of the line. She thinks she's got the upper hand, but she's underestimating you. I've seen your resolve. You can do it. Show her."

"Shut up!" Shazad told DeMayne. "You just want him to use the wand too much and kill himself, so you can pick it up next."

"Yes," DeMayne admitted. "I've been very open about that. But you'll still get what you want. A new age of magic. You have to take the bad with the good."

"And what do you get?" Leanora asked. "What's the bad thing you're not telling us about?"

DeMayne just smiled.

"You're never getting that wand," Shazad told him. "I'll pick it up and finish the job myself before I let you anywhere near it."

"We both would," Leanora said in solidarity with her friends.

Joey appreciated the sentiment, but he still racked his brain for better solutions. He wanted to search the tower with his friends and find some other way to win, but they couldn't do that. Not as long as Oblivia was threatening to kill Hypnova. The only options he could see were to surrender the wand or use it one last time.

"This isn't right," Mr. Ivory said. "A child shouldn't have to do this. There's got to be another way."

"Actually, there is," Hypnova said, coming around on the mezzanine. She rubbed her head and frowned at the sword, which was dangerously close to her throat. "Do you mind?" she asked Oblivia, pushing herself backward. Oblivia stepped forward, keeping the tip of the blade close to her jugular.

"Hypnova!" Shazad called out. "Are you all right?"

"Of course I'm all right," Hypnova said. "I'm exactly where I want to be."

Inside, Joey felt a tremendous sense of relief. He didn't understand how Hypnova could possibly have wanted to be in this position, but he was comforted to learn he had not stranded her in the mirror world after all. "I told you she'd be okay," he said to Leanora.

"Really," Oblivia said. "You wanted to be my prisoner?"

"How else was I supposed to get here?" Hypnova asked. "You didn't honestly believe I just set down the shield back in the mirror world, did you? Do you think so little of me that you actually believe I would make such a careless mistake?"

333

Joey saw a hint of concern flicker across Oblivia's face. She had called Hypnova a traitor and a liar, but she had never called her a fool.

"I'll spell it out for you," Hypnova continued. "I let you capture me."

Oblivia's eyes narrowed with suspicion. She didn't lower the blade. "I could have killed you."

"No," Hypnova said. "I knew you would use me as a bargaining chip, just in case Joey made it this far. You had no choice. His concern for his friends would be your only defense against the wand."

"And why would you want to give me a bargaining chip?"

"I needed all of us here at the same time," Hypnova said. "It was the only way I could convince you to help us."

Oblivia scoffed at the idea. "You're concussed."

"No, I'm one hundred percent clear," Hypnova said. "And you will join us. After you learn the truth."

"What truth?"

"That your sacred mission was never meant to be carved in stone. Your understanding of the Secreteers' true purpose has been flawed from the very beginning. This Order, everything you believe . . . it's not what you think."

"That's enough," Oblivia said. "You degrade yourself with your blasphemy. Don't try to drag me down with you. Just because you've lost your faith—"

"You don't have to believe me," Hypnova cut in. "The proof is standing right there." Hypnova motioned to DeMayne. "He was here in this very spot a thousand years ago. His memories can show you the truth of what happened the day the Imagine Nation was born. It's been kept from him all these years, hidden by the first Secreteer. It took everything I had just to glimpse the memory. I can't tell you what it is. You have to see it for yourself."

"How convenient that his memories are beyond my reach at the moment."

"Mine aren't. I've seen the world through his eyes. I can show you."

Joey could tell Oblivia was intrigued. He watched as Hypnova reeled her in the rest of the way. "Don't you want to know how the Order was founded? The secret to end all secrets?"

"If this is a trick . . . ," Oblivia warned.

"It only takes a moment to find out." Hypnova pointed at her own head, offering her memories to Oblivia. "You're welcome to see what I saw. If you still want to kill me afterward, go ahead. I won't stop you. But, trust me, it's going to change everything."

Oblivia was skeptical but also too curious to resist. With the golden saber still at Hypnova's throat, she reached out her free hand. Hypnova's body went stiff and her eyes glazed over as Oblivia connected with her mind. She closed her eyes, searching intently. Joey watched her eyes darting back and forth under her eyelids like a person deep in REM sleep.

Suddenly, they shot open, wide as they could. She dropped the sword. It clanged on the ground and fell from the mezzanine, landing at DeMayne's feet. "Impossible." Oblivia looked at Hypnova in disbelief as she came out of her trance. "It can't be!"

"It is," Hypnova assured her. "You know it is. You can tell a fabricated memory from the genuine article. This is real."

"How can it be real?" Oblivia demanded. "How can this be?"

"What is it?" Janelle asked. "How can what be?"

Oblivia looked like she was about to faint. She needed to lean on the wall to keep from falling over. Joey looked to Hypnova. "Tell us what's happening," he pleaded. "What did she see?"

"She saw the founder of our thousand-year-old Order," Hypnova explained. "The person whose actions formed the basis of everything she believes. Everything she's done, her whole life."

"My whole life!" Oblivia repeated. Joey could tell she was shaken to her core. "All this time . . . What have I done?"

"I don't get it," Jack said, exchanging a confused look with the others.

"You will. I promise," Hypnova replied. "First, let's give her a moment. She's dealing with a lot."

Oblivia put her head down, and when she looked up, she had tears in her eyes. She looked at Jack but had to turn away. Joey wondered what was happening in her brain. Eventually, she held out a hand to Hypnova. "I can't believe I'm going to say this, but you're right. I will help you."

21

The Clockwork Castle

"You will?" Leanora asked. "No more fighting?"

"Not everything has to be a fight," Hypnova said as she and Oblivia made their way down from the mezzanine.

"Why does everyone keep saying that?" Leanora threw up her hands. "I don't *always* want to fight."

"I don't understand what just happened," Skerren said. "Are we all on the same side now?"

"We were always on the same side," Hypnova replied. "Oblivia simply didn't realize it."

"Really." Ledger DeMayne scoffed at that and picked up Hypnova's golden sword. "Forgive me if I'm not inclined to believe this change of heart." He backed away from Oblivia as she neared the bottom of the steps.

"What you believe isn't important," Hypnova told DeMayne. "Not anymore."

DeMayne scowled. He held his tongue, but the expression on his face said, *We'll see.*

"What's going on here?" Joey asked. "Are you telling us this tower *isn't* empty?"

Oblivia shook her head. "I'll show you." She motioned for everyone to move in toward the center of the marble floor. "Come closer. Make sure you're standing on the compass." She held her arms out and spoke a magic word:

"*Descendit.*"

"What was that?" Skerren asked.

"It's Latin," Janelle said. "For descend."

A second later, the ring around the compass-rose floor design lit up with a bright bluish-white light. The room shook, and the section of the floor that everyone was standing on turned counterclockwise, disconnecting itself from a series of latches. Then it dropped like a high-speed elevator platform, plunging through the column beneath the tower.

"Whoa!" Joey blurted out, trying to keep his balance. He went down to one knee as they sank at an alarming rate, plummeting deep into the canyon. The interior walls of the

339

column seemed to fly upward as they fell. It was dark inside the column, but the walls twinkled with lines of light drawn in specific patterns. There was ancient technology in the marble, just like the magic circuits in the trees.

When they reached the base of the shaky column supporting the tower, the platform slowed and settled gently into place. That was when Joey saw what the magic circuits were plugged into. The true Citadel of the Secreteers was waiting for them, shrouded beneath a layer of fog. It was a castle, just like DeMayne had said, but it was like no castle Joey had ever seen. The hidden stronghold was a mixture of industrial revolution and medieval times. Iron walls topped with spikes rotated around the keep, sealing it off against intruders. Behind those walls, a series of turrets and spires that rose up from the steampunk fortress were also in motion. They turned in time with a sea of gears and machinery that surrounded the group. A complex network of turbines and rotors, some of them the size of houses, covered the canyon floor in its entirety. A bridge lined with footlights ran over the gearscape of interlocking metal teeth, leading to the gates of the castle.

"What is all this?" asked Janelle.

"The Clockwork Castle," DeMayne whispered, a spark of recognition in his eyes.

"What's it doing?" Joey asked.

"This is the engine that drives the Imagine Nation," Oblivia revealed. "The Clockwork Castle keeps us protected, hidden, and locked in a state of perpetual motion. It's a colossal machine, powered by magic. It never runs out of energy."

"Does it have an off switch?" Jack asked.

"It must," Joey said, coming to a realization of his own. He pointed at Oblivia. "You were going to let me use the wand to finish this? When all we had to do was come down here and turn off the power?"

"It's not that simple," Oblivia said. "First of all, I was bluffing. I knew you wouldn't sacrifice yourself and use the wand. Not because you're afraid, but because I know it's not the way you think. You're a problem solver. Escape artists always try to find another way out. Second, it's not as simple as flipping a switch. This island floats all around the world over a ring of waterfalls. I don't know what's at the bottom, but if you somehow manage to turn this off, we just might find out. The whole island could drop from the sky, killing everyone on it—including us. This place . . . this mixture of magic and technology is beyond my understanding. It's beyond all our understanding."

"Maybe not beyond Jack's," Allegra said.

"Exactly," Janelle agreed. "If we can't shut it off, can we throw it in reverse? Jack, what's it telling you?"

"Nothing I want to hear," Jack said. "It won't work with me."

"Why not?" Skerren asked. "The trees up there were friendly. Tell the castle to talk to them. They'll vouch for you."

"I tried that already," Jack said. "It doesn't care about the trees. It says it knows why we're here, and it isn't going to help us." He paused and put a hand to his ear, listening to what the castle had to say. He blinked in surprise, seeming taken aback by what he heard. "It's really angry. It says it hasn't ever been allowed to fulfill its purpose. It wants to do what it was built to do, but it won't say what that is."

Everyone looked at Oblivia for an explanation. She turned up her palms. "Don't ask me. I don't know how to turn it off or use it."

"I do," said DeMayne. "I'll tell you something else I know.

342

That wonderful shield of yours? The one you left up in the tower? We're outside of its range down here."

Oblivia gasped as Hypnova's golden saber broke through her chest. A crimson stain bloomed on her snow-white robe.

"OBLIVIA!" Hypnova shouted as DeMayne pushed the blade through. He let go of the hilt and gave her a shove. She collapsed into Hypnova's arms. "Help!" Hypnova said, catching her. "Somebody, help!"

"Stop it," DeMayne said. "Five minutes ago, she was ready to kill you."

"What did you do?" Joey screamed at DeMayne. "We had a deal!"

"I'm altering our deal." He took the Sword of Storms off his belt and aimed it at Joey and his friends. "Turnabout is fair play," he said as a violent wind blew them all off the bridge.

22

Doomed to Repeat History

"Well?" DeMayne asked.

Joey heard movement near the edge of the bridge. "I don't see them," Mr. Ivory said, looking over the side.

"They're gone," Mr. Clear confirmed.

"You're sure?" DeMayne pressed.

"I'm not sure," Mr. Clear replied. "I can't be sure. The boy could have used the wand to save himself. However, if that were the case, I think he'd be back up here already. Most likely you caught them by surprise."

"You certainly caught me by surprise," Mr. Ivory muttered.

"That was the idea," DeMayne said. "It's a shame about the wand, but it doesn't matter now. Follow me. We have work to do."

DeMayne and his henchmen turned their attention to the Clockwork Castle. Joey and the others couldn't see them, but they heard them travel down the bridge, their voices and footsteps growing fainter until they faded away completely. Everyone stayed perfectly still, waiting until they were gone before anyone said a word. They were hanging underneath the bridge. Not off the edge where Mr. Clear and Mr. Ivory had looked, but from the support structures underneath—something that should have been impossible to reach while falling.

Mr. Clear had hit the nail on the head when he suggested that DeMayne's attack had caught Joey by surprise. Joey didn't even have time to think about using the wand to save himself or anyone else. Fortunately, Allegra was there to save them all. She stretched her liquid metal arms to grab everyone as they fell and morphed her body into a wide net. She caught the whole group and held them in place like a giant hammock, securely anchored to the bottom of the bridge. Below them, the machinery that covered the canyon floor chugged along with an endless supply of pistons firing, pumps pumping, belts spinning, and gears rotating. Joey looked down at a giant toothed wheel turning slowly beneath him. Had he fallen into it, he would have been crushed under its might and ground into hamburger meat. It all happened so fast. Once Joey realized that he and his friends were safe, he let out a broken, off-kilter giggle of relief. The kind that usually follows near-death experiences. Skerren cupped a hand over Joey's mouth and put a finger to his own lips. Joey checked himself, and the group waited in silence after that. Once the coast was clear, Allegra helped everyone back up to the right side of the bridge, where they found Oblivia sprawled on the floor.

Her white robes were soaked with blood. Everyone could see she was close to death. Hypnova went to her side. Joey took out the wand. "I can help. She's still with us. I can heal this."

"Don't." Oblivia coughed. "Don't. Save your strength. You're going to need it for—"

She broke into a painful coughing fit, unable to finish her sentence.

"But you'll die," Leanora said.

"If it's . . . my time."

"This isn't what I wanted," Hypnova said, taking her hand. "I wanted you to see."

"We don't . . . always get what we want," Oblivia replied, struggling to speak. "But sometimes we get what we deserve. DeMayne was right. I would have killed you. I never would have listened. I was blind. You showed me the truth. I did see. I understand now."

At the far end of the bridge, DeMayne and his men entered the Clockwork Castle.

"Stop him." Oblivia gripped Hypnova's hand. "Do what you came here to do."

A few labored breaths later, Oblivia closed her eyes. Her grip on Hypnova's hand relaxed, and she slipped away. Hypnova set her down gently. Oblivia looked as if she were sleeping peacefully, but Hypnova's face was a mixture of grief and furious anger. Her golden saber was on the bridge, stained with Oblivia's blood. DeMayne had cast it aside, just as he had cast Oblivia aside after stabbing her in the back. Hypnova took the blade and rose slowly to her feet.

"Let's finish this," she said.

They marched on the castle with Hypnova leading the charge. Joey and Jack were right behind her, followed by everyone else.

"What do you think DeMayne's doing in there?" Jack asked Joey.

"Whatever it is, it isn't good," Joey said.

"I told you he was going to double-cross us," Jack said. "I knew he was going to try something, but I wasn't ready for him. I was too busy looking at all this."

"Don't blame yourself," Joey said. "It's hard not to be distracted by a giant mechanized castle."

"I also thought when he did make his move, he'd go after you first," Jack said. "He seemed to hate you the most. I underestimated how he felt about the Secreteers." Jack looked back at Oblivia, lying alone on the bridge. "I'm sorry, Hypnova. We both had our issues with Oblivia, but she didn't deserve that."

"No, she didn't," Hypnova agreed, striding forward. "But it's not your fault. It's mine. I wanted DeMayne to lead you here in case I didn't make it. We needed DeMayne to find this place. We needed his memory, but . . ." Hypnova trailed off, clearly angry with herself. "I've been in his head. I should have seen this coming."

"Don't you blame yourself either," Joey said. "Remember, the only reason you wouldn't have made it would have been if Oblivia had succeeded in killing you. Anyway, it's impossible to know everything that's going on in DeMayne's mind. He keeps remembering new things. The question is, what does he know that we don't?"

As they approached the gates of the castle, Joey wondered why DeMayne really wanted to come here. If he wasn't after the wand, there had to be something better in the castle. Joey couldn't imagine what that might be, but the mere possibility was terrifying.

The castle was protected by a series of exterior walls. They were three feet thick and revolved slowly around the castle in competing directions. Each wall had a single opening, and at a certain point, they all lined up to grant passage to the castle, but they never stopped moving. The gate only appeared momentarily before the walls moved on, closing off access once again.

"This is good defense against a siege," Skerren said. "You can't march an army through these gates. They only admit a small group of people at a time."

"Lucky for us, we are a small group of people," Shazad said. "We can get through this. We just have to time it right."

Jack balled a fist, and the walls came to a screeching halt.

After that, he made a few sweeping motions like he was directing traffic, and the walls rotated back into the proper position.

"Or we could just go through right now," Jack said.

"I thought the castle wouldn't work with you," Janelle said.

"I don't need its cooperation if I can understand how it works. This mechanism is simple enough. The rest of this place is a different story." Jack used his power to lock up the walls and keep them from moving while everyone walked through the outer gate. Once they were through, an interior wall, taller than any of the others that came before it, stood between them and the castle courtyard. It was made of shiny gold and bronze metal with a heavy portcullis at the center. "If DeMayne's got all his memories back, we have to assume he's in control of the castle defenses." Jack turned his palms up and raised his hands an inch, lifting the portcullis out of the way. As soon as the inner gate was open, a troop of guards wearing suits of armor came through from the other side, ready to fight. "These guys, for example."

"Who are they?" Allegra asked, morphing one hand into a shield and the other into a sword.

"Nobody," Jack said, using his powers to scan them. "They're empty suits. Drones. You don't have to hold back."

"Finally, some good news," Skerren said. He drew both swords. "Allegra, do you mind? I'd like to see what we're up against."

Allegra relaxed her stance and morphed her hands back to normal, even as the iron knights closed in. "Be my guest." She laced her fingers together and reached out to give Skerren a boost. He stepped up, placing his right foot in her hands. Her arms stretched like rubber bands as he pushed off, and she vaulted him into the air. He flipped over the armored guards and landed behind them as nimbly as a cat.

With a single slash, he cut the two rear guards off at the knees. They fell, and as they fell, he cut them again, separating them both at the waist. They clattered to the ground in several pieces, with sparks flying from their severed limbs. The other drone guards turned and immediately went for Skerren. He kicked pieces of the fallen knights across the floor to the ones that were still standing. One of them stutter-stepped to keep from tripping on a torso, and in that fraction of a second, Skerren took its head. In the same motion, he whirled around, ducking under an enemy blow and lashing out again with his swords. He never stopped moving. In a matter of seconds, any remaining mechanized suits of armor were reduced to spare parts. When he rejoined the group, he wasn't even breathing heavily.

"If that's the best this place has to offer, we've got nothing to worry about."

"Those swords are really something," Shazad marveled.

"It's not the swords," Skerren replied. "It's the swordsman."

The group stepped over the scrap-metal remains of the iron knights on their way to the castle courtyard, which was another complex network of industrial gadgetry. A field of flashing lights and electrodes crackled with energy beneath a bridge made of interlocking gears. Joey and the others walked across it as the wheels rotated beneath their feet like giant turntables. They only made it a few steps before more drone guards emerged from the machinery below, coming to block their path. The resulting battle was made more difficult by the constant revolutions of the gear bridge, but Joey and his friends would not be denied. They reached the Clockwork Castle unscathed, and Leanora beat down the doors with a firestone punch.

"DeMayne! Show yourself!" Hypnova shouted. "It's going to take more than a few tin soldiers to keep . . . us . . . out."

Her voice fell flat as the group came face-to-face with a full battalion of tin soldiers. There were hundreds of iron knights waiting in the throne room of the castle.

"Well, that's just great," Allegra said.

Fortunately, the iron knights didn't attack right away. A wide staircase led down to a sunken concourse where they stood in formation, awaiting further orders from DeMayne. Joey spotted him next to the throne, which looked like the mission control center for steampunk NASA. A series of workstations with switches, buttons, and dials were built into the back wall, going up like rows of stadium seats. Levels of industrial hardware and mechanical devices separated each tier leading up to the spot where DeMayne was standing. The throne room was like the heart of an engine. Massive gears rose halfway out of the floor, turning contraptions behind the walls. A network of pipes ran up to the ceiling, where giant steel tanks whistled and let out steam. Giant pneumatic presses rose and fell, creating the force to power more components of the great machine. The entire chamber hummed with activity.

DeMayne locked eyes with Joey across the room and scowled.

"Really?" he asked Mr. Ivory and Mr. Clear. "They're alive? You had one job. I told you to check to make sure they weren't hanging on the bridge."

"I did check," Mr. Ivory said. "I didn't see anything!"

"I specifically said I wasn't sure," Mr. Clear added.

DeMayne touched his forehead like he felt a migraine coming on. "Idiots. I knew I should have had a look myself. I was too excited about being back home." He took a breath and waved his hand, dropping the matter. "It's all right. We're nearly done here. This will all be over soon."

"You've got that right," Skerren said, starting down the steps.

The iron knights drew swords and took a step forward.

"Really?" Jack asked. "You're going to use drones? Against me? I got a look at the ones we took apart outside. They're not going to cut it." Jack held up a hand, and the iron knights halted. He wiggled his fingers, and they split their ranks, stepping aside to open up a lane and let everyone through.

"That's fine," DeMayne said, pushing the throne to the

side. "I'd rather have you focused on them. In fact, I can give you lots of them to think about."

"What's he doing?" Leanora asked.

"You'll see!" DeMayne called out. Behind the throne, a large wheel had been built into the wall. It was the size of a bicycle tire and looked like the kind of wheel someone might turn to close a hatch on a submarine. "Mr. Ivory," DeMayne called out, curling his finger. "Make yourself useful. This wheel hasn't been turned in a thousand years. We're going to need the ogre."

Mr. Ivory sighed. "I hate the ogre."

DeMayne's expression made it clear he didn't care how Mr. Ivory felt.

Mr. Ivory reluctantly dug a rotten tooth out of his bag and pressed it into the gap in his smile. He gagged before undergoing a horrifying metamorphosis. Joey watched him transform into something like the Incredible Hulk, only uglier and with less muscle definition. His skin turned gray and rough like the hide of an elephant, and his face twisted into a hideous shape with a large protruding brow, tusklike teeth, and pointy ears. He looked like a monstrous brute, but he was still himself underneath it all. Mr. Ivory grabbed

355

the wheel and gave it everything he had, straining to make it turn.

When the wheel finally budged, there was a loud hiss as jets of gas burst out of the floor in the space where the throne had been. It was the sound of an airlock decompressing. The rear wall of the throne room slid apart like elevator doors to reveal a hidden room with some kind of power core at its center. At least, that's what Joey thought it might be. There was a beam of blue light the size of a tree trunk coming out of a platform with wires and cables plugged into it.

"Hang on." Jack stopped short. "Where did that come from?"

A few of the stationary iron knights surrounding Jack and the rest of the group twitched slightly. They were free for just a moment as his concentration lapsed, but he regained control before they did any harm. Meanwhile, DeMayne was pulling levers and hitting buttons on a control panel, causing more machinery to kick into gear. Doors opened in the corners of the room, and more iron knights marched out. They were rolling off assembly lines as automated arms put them together. DeMayne had an endless supply of cannon fodder.

"So, this place is a factory?" Leonora wondered aloud.

"That's not all it is," Jack said.

"What's he doing?" Joey asked.

"I'm taking Oblivia's advice!" DeMayne shouted. "Going back to being king of the world!"

"There's too many of them," Jack said as the drones began to break free of his will. "I can't control them all."

"You don't have to," Skerren said, cutting down the drones nearest him. "You think you're going to build an army and take over?" he shouted at DeMayne. "Don't get too comfortable up there. We've taken down armies before."

"They just need to hold you for the next few minutes," DeMayne said. "I'm not going to use force. I'm winning hearts and minds. Or, just minds if I'm being honest." He made a series of adjustments to the instruments near the power core, modifying the width of the energy beam. "I knew there was something here. I knew if I could just find this place again, it would all come back to me." He keyed in a final command, and the blue beam of light grew from the size of an oak tree to something that resembled a giant redwood. A blue orb rose out of the ground in front of the power core. "It's *all* coming back to me."

Jack's control on the iron knights continued to slip as more of them poured into the room. "This isn't good," he said.

"No kidding," Joey replied as the group backtracked up the stairs, finding a more defensible position.

"You don't understand," Jack said. "It's worse than you think. The castle remembers him, and he remembers what it was built for."

"What did he just turn on?" Janelle asked. "What does all this stuff do?"

Jack turned around, taking in the place as Skerren, Allegra, and Hypnova held back the iron knights. "Everything here and everything outside that keeps the island moving . . . it generates energy that powers that beam. It's sending out a signal to the world."

"What kind of signal?" Joey asked.

"The wrong kind of signal." DeMayne tapped at the orb like someone touching a hot plate to see if it was safe to pick up. Sparks flew out every time he made contact. "That's going to change. This castle—this whole canyon—is a machine created by the emperor I once served. It took him years to build it. He was a man of science. I had to kill him.

You should thank me. I did the world a great service. He despised magic. Even after we had all but stripped the earth of its magic, he wasn't satisfied with the state of the world. He would have used this place to control it, along with everyone else."

DeMayne laid a hand on the orb. It sizzled with energy, but he was able to hold it in place.

"What is that?" Allegra asked Jack. "What does this thing do?"

"It's a mind-control device," Jack said. "His emperor built it to control people. To make everyone behave and live the way he wanted. No magic . . . no imagination."

"He wanted a world of law and order," DeMayne said. "His law. His order. I had other ideas. I taught myself to use this place, but it took too long to learn its secrets. Before I could activate the machine, they came for me. Merlin and his allies. They ripped this island free of its moorings and sank the continent, but they kept this place intact. This machine is what changed the world. It changed people's minds. The Secreteers' power gave Merlin the idea. He enchanted the machine, twisting its purpose to affect how people perceived this island—how they viewed the entire history of the world.

He took away my victory and made me forget, but they let me live. Merlin died, and the ones that came after him forgot about me. They should have known better."

He put his other hand on the orb. A wave of energy ran through his body, giving him a shock, but he managed to hold on, and the blue light in the orb swirled with red.

"Those who forget history are doomed to repeat it. I ruled the world from this spot a thousand years ago. My reign was short, but I'm going to make up for lost time. I'm going to take it all back, and I have you to thank, Joey Kopecky. More than anyone else, you're the one who made this possible."

23

Rage Against the Machine

"He's going to brainwash the whole world," Joey said, horrified.

It dawned on him that he had been played. Joey had thought that if he kept the wand away from Ledger DeMayne, everything would be fine, but it turned out DeMayne didn't need the wand after all. What he was going to do was worse than locking magic away again. He was going to set himself up as the ruler of the world, taking the place of the emperor whom he'd deposed so long ago.

"Can he do that?" Janelle asked.

"This machine can," Jack said. "He can use it to control the minds of millions."

"No." Joey reached for the wand. "I have to stop him." He was going to have to use it to finish this after all. There was no avoiding his fate. Maybe there never had been.

Hypnova grabbed his wrist before he could act. "Joey. You don't have enough energy left to stop something this big. You'll die."

"I can't let him get away with this," Joey said.

"I could say the same thing to you," Hypnova shot back. "Using that wand is the absolute last resort."

"What do you call this?"

"This isn't the end," Hypnova said. "Save the wand for later. We're going to need it for something important."

"More important than this?"

"It depends on who you ask."

"Hypnova, we don't have time to mess around," Joey said. "He's got an army."

"We've fought bigger armies," Allegra replied.

"Bigger than this?" Leanora asked.

"Much bigger," Skerren confirmed. As he spoke, he went on cutting down iron knights like he was clearing a forest, putting some breathing room between the group and the growing legion of castle guards.

"What's the plan, then?" Shazad asked. "What are we going to do?"

"See that light up there?" Jack asked, pointing at the glowing power core behind DeMayne. The blue light now had a red hue at its base. "He's reprogramming the signal. We've got until the blue light goes red."

"It's going pretty fast," Joey said, watching it rise like a thermometer someone had left on the stove.

"Let's slow things down a little." Jack raised a hand and the gears in the room stopped turning. The hydraulic presses in the walls froze in place. Even the iron knight assembly line ground to a halt.

"You're doing it!" Joey shouted as the light in the power core faded. Everything was connected. If Jack could hold the gears that moved the island, it would cut power to DeMayne's mind-control machine.

The castle shook as if an earthquake had just hit, and Joey felt the whole island drop a little. The brief plunge broke Jack's concentration, and the gears started moving again, only slower. "I can't shut it off," he said, clearly straining. "I can buy you time and slow it down, but it takes everything I've got. I can't hold these guys back at the same time."

The iron knights renewed their march, free of Jack's

control. "We can do that," Skerren said as he continued to cut them to ribbons.

"We've got your back," Allegra said, morphing her arms back into blades to do the same. "And your front," she added, stretching herself to shield Jack from harm. Leanora joined the fight, swinging firestone punches as the mechanized drones attacked in force.

"We'll cover Jack," Allegra told her. "You need to get to DeMayne."

"And wreck that orb!" Skerren added.

"No!" Jack shouted. "You can't wreck it. There's too much energy coming off that thing. This whole place will blow. And if we break the machinery outside, the island will fall. We'll all die."

"So, what do we do?" Joey asked again.

"We need to get DeMayne off the orb before he imprints himself on it. Once that signal goes out, it's going to control everyone, including us. We'll be his loyal supporters, just like Ivory and Clear."

Jack retreated up the steps, falling back as the army of iron knights stomped forward. Skerren, Allegra, and Leanora held the line at the bottom of the staircase, keeping them at bay. Joey, Shazad, Janelle, and Hypnova hung back, trying to figure out the fastest, safest route to the orb. Joey looked over the clanging army of mindless bots to Mr. Ivory and Mr. Clear. Just as Joey and his friends were protecting Jack while he worked, the agents of the Invisible Hand were there to protect DeMayne. They stood at the bottom of mission control as the last line of defense. Even with Jack slowing the machine down to a crawl, Joey could tell they wouldn't reach DeMayne in time, and they wouldn't get past the ogre and the iceman without help.

"How are we going to do this?" Joey asked Hypnova.

She didn't look sure, but Janelle answered before Hypnova could say anything. "I've got it!" Janelle exclaimed. "This is it. This is perfect!"

"What are you talking about?" Joey asked.

"The way to reveal the Imagine Nation without killing you. We can reprogram the machine ourselves!"

"How?" Shazad asked her. "We have no idea how it works."

"What about Jack?" Janelle asked.

"What about me?" Jack said, locked in a mental battle

with the Clockwork Castle. "I told you, this place won't talk to me. It likes him better."

"But you can still talk to it," Janelle said. "Can you see it too? I don't know how your powers work. Can you see the inner workings of this place?"

"I can, but I don't understand them. I'd need time to dive into them when I'm not also trying to hold them still."

"Then show me," Janelle said. "Let Hypnova connect our minds so I can see what you see. This is what I'm here for. Magic and science! You put the blueprints of this place in my mind, and I can find a weakness in this Death Star."

"Did you say Death Star?" Joey asked.

"Not now, Joey!"

"It's kind of important," Joey said. "The Death Star blows up. We don't want to blow up."

"I'll find a way around that," Janelle said.

"Whatever you do, you'd better do it fast!" Leanora yelled in between punches. "We can't keep this up forever!"

Janelle handed Joey the Staff of Sorcero. "Help them. Use this, not the wand." She turned to Hypnova. "I'm ready."

Joey ran down the steps to join Skerren, Allegra, and Leanora in battle. Shazad stayed with Janelle and Jack, standing guard as their last line of defense. Sparks flew out as Joey swung the Staff of Sorcero at the iron knights, tearing through them like they were made of tinfoil. Over his shoulder, he saw Hypnova use her power to build a bridge between Janelle's mind and Jack's.

"Wow." Janelle staggered a step. "It's so complex. . . . I can't believe someone built this a thousand years ago." She turned around, studying the throne room as if she were looking through the walls with X-ray eyes. "Is this how you see the world?" she asked Jack, marveling at the view. "It's amazing."

"Can she sort through all this fast enough for it to matter?" Allegra asked.

"If anyone can, she can!" Joey said.

As if on cue, Janelle froze in place. "I've got it. There!" She pointed to the center of the throne room floor. It was overflowing with iron knights.

"There?!" Shazad said. "What's over there?"

Janelle started down the steps without pausing to answer. She made a beeline for the edge of the melee like she was on a mission. One of the iron knights went after her, and Shazad rushed in with a kick that sent it stumbling backward to be crushed in one of the giant gears protruding from the floor. Janelle forged ahead, in a world of her own.

"Cover us!" Shazad shouted, taking her arm and staying by her side. Joey, Leanora, and Hypnova formed a protective semicircle around them, and together they fought their way forward. Once they cleared a space at the center of the room, Janelle found an access panel in the floor—a trapdoor. She opened it and jumped down into the guts of the castle without any hesitation or explanation.

"Where's she going?" Shazad asked, peering down into the gear works.

"Wherever it is, I'm going with her," Hypnova said, lowering herself down after Janelle.

"We need to keep moving," Leanora said as the iron knights swarmed around them. Meanwhile, up at the power core, DeMayne had already managed to turn half of the blue light red.

"Shazad, I think it's time for you to go into beast mode," Joey said.

"That's going to be a problem." Shazad grabbed the edge of his cape and held it out. His trademark magical object was in tatters, torn by the clawing hands of the iron knights.

"My parents are going to kill me—if these things don't do it first."

"These things aren't killing anybody. Not if I can help it." Skerren slashed his way to the center of the room. The sword in his right hand was a blur, shredding any metal soldier that got within striking distance. The sword in his left hand, he offered to Shazad. "Here. Work your magic with this."

"Your sword?" Shazad took the blade as if he were being handed a priceless work of art. "Really?"

"Take good care of that," Skerren ordered.

"Don't worry," Shazad said. "Protecting magical objects is what I do." Skerren eyed his ruined cape, looking unconvinced. "Usually," Shazad added.

"If you two are finished, I could use some help back here!" Allegra shouted. She wrapped a silvery arm around Jack and dragged him back to the door in a strategic retreat. He was straining hard to slow down the great machine and was no help to her as she fought off the iron knights alone.

"Duty calls," Skerren said. "We'll buy as much time as we can. GO!"

Using his other sword, Skerren cut a swath back toward Jack and Allegra while Joey, Shazad, and Leanora pushed

369

forward toward DeMayne. It was pure mayhem as they crossed swords, fists, and staves with the iron knights every step of the way. Their magical weapons gave them the advantage over the mechanized drones, but for every one of them Joey, Shazad, and Leanora took down, there were ten more to take their place. It was the wildest fight Joey had ever been caught in the middle of. Absolute bedlam. He had more than his share of close calls as several killing blows nearly found their mark, but he was rescued by Shazad or Leanora just in time. Joey came through for his friends in a similar fashion, taking out enemies in their blind spots as they struggled against the iron knights. Punch by punch and swing by swing, they made it across the room to the mission control workstations. Mr. Ivory and Mr. Clear were there waiting for them. Magic energy coursed through DeMayne's body as he gripped the orb, locked in a dogged attempt to reprogram the Clockwork Castle. It looked terribly painful, but he refused to let go. Joey got the sense DeMayne didn't expect he would have to hold on so long. Jack had managed to hurt him by slowing down the machine, but it was up to Joey, Shazad, and Leanora to stop him. The power core was now almost 75 percent red.

"You're too late," DeMayne grunted through clenched teeth. "In a few minutes, you won't be fighting me. You'll be bowing down before me. Ivory! Clear! Keep them back!"

Mr. Ivory and Mr. Clear stepped up to block for DeMayne as Joey, Shazad, and Leanora came up the steps. Mr. Ivory was still an ogre, a giant with thick muscles and hands like cinder blocks. Mr. Clear was there behind him, rubbing his hands together and trying to keep warm. They were formidable obstacles, even if neither of them looked like he wanted to be there.

"We don't have to do this," Joey said.

"I'm afraid we do," Mr. Ivory replied.

"Let us pass," Joey pleaded. "We don't want to hurt you."

"Don't worry. You won't."

Mr. Ivory reached forward and shoved Joey, hitting him hard in the chest. All the air left Joey's body, and he went tumbling back into Shazad and Leanora. They fell down the steps, nearly landing back in the arms of the iron knights. They were still coming off the assembly lines and massing at the base of the steps. One of them grabbed Leanora, but Shazad cut it off at the wrist before it could drag her down. Joey brought the Staff of Sorcero down on its head as if he were driving a railroad spike into place with a sledge-hammer.

"Just stay down," Mr. Clear told them. "This will be over soon."

"We can't do that," Joey said.

Mr. Clear sighed and covered the steps with a slippery sheet of ice. He also put a thick wall of ice in the middle of the staircase. Leanora put a fist of fire through the wall, smashing it to bits.

They climbed the steps with care. The iron knights couldn't follow. After repeatedly slipping and falling, they abandoned their pursuit of Joey, Shazad, and Leanora and instead focused their efforts on reaching Jack. At the top of the steps, Mr. Ivory swatted at Shazad, who dodged the attack and responded with one of his own, slicing Mr. Ivory's palm open. It wasn't a terrible wound given his giant size, but it still had to hurt. Mr. Ivory pulled his hand back in surprise, and Joey saw an opening. He darted forward and swung the staff as hard as he could at Mr. Ivory's knee. Sparks flew out, and there was a sickening crunch. Mr. Ivory cried out in pain. That one *definitely* hurt.

Mr. Ivory clutched his knee and wobbled in place before

he fell. Joey had to move fast to avoid getting crushed beneath him. Unable to support himself, Mr. Ivory collapsed and pounded the floor in anger. He hit it so hard the tremors knocked Joey, Shazad, and Leanora off their feet.

"Stay back!" he shouted from the ground, blocking the way to DeMayne.

"Why are you fighting us?" Leanora shouted back. "You can't be on board with this. DeMayne wants to brainwash the entire world and everyone's minds. You really want him ruling the planet like a king?"

"What's the difference?" Mr. Ivory asked, clutching his broken knee. "He's been doing it for years already."

"And how's that working out?" Leanora demanded. "The world's a mess—that's why we're here! You could help us!"

"You can't beat him," Mr. Ivory said. "He always has an ace hidden up his sleeve. Look around. You never saw this coming. Only he did. This is what I was talking about. You let magic loose in the world, bad things happen."

"Like what happened to me." Mr. Clear appeared over Mr. Ivory's shoulder. He raised a shaky hand, and his bracelet lit up again. Ice formed around the ankles of Joey, Shazad, and Leanora. It materialized around their wrists like handcuffs, weighing them down toward boulders of ice that were growing up from the ground. Within seconds, they were trapped, just like they had been in Gravenmurk Glen.

"It's like he s-s-said," Mr. Clear said, with his breath appearing as a frosty white vapor. "It's too late. S-stop fighting. I'm already so cold. It's going to take me days to warm up now. After what I did to get us all to the tower?" He shook with a pitiful convulsion. "I don't want to do this anymore. There's no point. In a few minutes we'll all be on the same side."

"We're already on the same side," Leanora argued. "DeMayne's side only has room for one. That's why he never helped you. That's why you're the only two fingers left on the Invisible Hand."

"That isn't true," Mr. Clear said. "There are hundreds of us."

"Then where are they?" Shazad asked. "They don't exist. It's just the two of you left. We were in his mind. We saw every one of his followers through the years. There are only two active members. You two."

"It's true," Leanora said. "He needs you more than he lets on. It's all smoke and mirrors with him. He's got no one

374

else! That's why he has these metal soldiers down there. It's why he needed us to get here! DeMayne's not as powerful as he makes himself out to be, and it's his own fault. He won't trust anyone enough to let them get close. He won't help people who need it, because he knows if he did, he might lose them. It doesn't have to be that way." Leanora charged up her firestone, breaking her right hand free of the ice. "Magic isn't about keeping secrets. It's meant to be shared." She didn't melt the ice around her other hand or free her feet. Instead, she held the firestone pendant out to Mr. Clear. "I'll show you. Here."

"Lea, what are you doing?" Joey asked. "We have to keep fighting."

"I am," Leanora said. She kept her arm out, offering the firestone to Mr. Clear. "Take it. I'm giving it to you. You look like you could use it."

"What is this?" Mr. Clear asked. "Some kind of trick?"

"No tricks," Leanora said. "Just magic. The way it's supposed to be."

Mr. Clear approached with caution. Once he was close enough, he snatched the pendant out of Leanora's hand, jumping back before she could try anything. His caution was unnecessary, his suspicions unwarranted. Leanora's offer was genuine. Standing at what he no doubt considered to be a safe distance, he held the pendant up by its chain, staring at the orange stone.

"Put it on," Leanora told him. "Go ahead. You've seen me use it. You know what it does. What are you waiting for?"

Mr. Clear hesitated but ultimately decided he had nothing to lose. He placed the pendant around his neck and wrapped his left hand around the firestone. Soon his right hand began to glow. It was a tiny light, no bigger than a flame dancing on the wick of a candle, but it grew. Mr. Clear flared his fingertips, and the orange-red light began to move up his arm. It didn't stop at the elbow the way it always did for Leanora. It spread across his entire body, traveling through his veins and warming his blood. For a moment his entire body was illuminated, and when he let go of the stone, he was a new man. His skin had gone from a frosty white to a rosy pink. For the first time since Joey had met him, Mr. Clear looked to be on the verge of life instead of death.

"I don't believe it." Mr. Clear looked at his hands as if they belonged to someone else. "I'm warm." He took off his coat and threw it down. "*I'm warm!* I haven't felt like this in . . . I don't know how long! I forgot what it was like!" His voice cracked as he spoke. Tears fell from his eyes and they didn't freeze in place. "I didn't think this was possible."

"Anything's possible," Leanora said. "I think those stones were meant to be together."

"I don't understand." Mr. Ivory pulled himself up. He limped forward, clutching his knee. "You're just going to give that to him?"

"I don't want to fight anymore," Leanora said. "I'm tired of fighting. Maybe we could try to be friends instead."

Mr. Ivory was quiet for a moment. His face was inscrutable due to his monstrous appearance, but when he spoke it was clear Leanora's words had touched his heart. "I never had any real friends."

"Just speaking for myself," Shazad began, "I've never had better friends than these two." He gave a nod to Joey and Leanora. The heartfelt moment was spoiled by the sound of a hard-fought battle that was still raging across the room. Allegra and Skerren were still fighting to keep the iron knights away from Jack. They were standing their ground, but they were losing steam. So was Jack for that matter. "The rest of our friends need help. You can do something. You can make a difference."

Mr. Clear and Mr. Ivory looked up at DeMayne and then at each other. In that moment, their minds were made up. Mr. Ivory hobbled over to Joey, Shazad, and Leanora and smashed their ice block restraints with his ogre strength as Mr. Clear reached out to freeze the iron knight assembly lines and bury any finished drones under a massive iceberg.

"Excellent! Now do him!" Shazad said, pointing at DeMayne.

Mr. Clear tried to encase him in ice, but the magical energy that was pouring out of the orb had formed a bubble that couldn't be penetrated.

"What now?" Mr. Ivory asked.

"Throw me," Joey said. Mr. Ivory turned in confusion, but Joey urged him on. "There's no time! Get me up there!"

Mr. Ivory took Joey and heaved him up to the top of the steps. It wasn't a perfect throw. Thanks to Joey's assault on Mr. Ivory's knee, he had no strength in his legs, even as an ogre. Joey landed a few steps short of his target. He scrambled to his feet and ran the rest of the way to the orb, but he was too late.

Across the room, one final, very determined iron knight scaled the iceberg and leaped from the peak, flying over Skerren and Allegra. It landed with a shoulder roll that propelled it forward and sprang up to ram into Jack. Skerren and Allegra swooped in to demolish it before it could hurt him, but the damage was already done. With Jack's concentration broken, the Clockwork Castle kicked back into high gear.

"YES!" DeMayne rejoiced.

"NO!" Joey screamed.

He took out the wand. He didn't pause or ask permission this time. He was going to use it no matter what the consequences were for him. He had to act before it was too late. Joey threw his arm forward, pointing the wand at DeMayne, but before he had a chance to say anything, something happened.

Behind DeMayne, the red portion of the power core raced to the top of the beam and stopped an inch before it got there. One inch away from victory.

"What?" DeMayne said, baffled.

Joey looked at the wand in his hand. He checked the power gauge on his arm. It was steady at ten percent. He hadn't cast any spells. Whatever had stopped the machine had not been his doing. He was looking around for someone to thank when he realized the machine had not truly stopped.

The Clockwork Castle was still running like a Swiss watch, only nothing was happening. DeMayne slapped at the orb, ordering it to work, but the red light refused to climb any higher. In fact, not only did the red light fail to overtake the blue, but both lights began to drop and fade. All around the great machine hummed along uninterrupted, but someone had pulled the plug on the power core. Joey saw his chance, and he took it before the moment passed him by.

"No! Don't touch him!" Jack shouted as Joey dove headlong at Ledger DeMayne.

Jack was all the way on the other side of the room. Joey didn't hear a word he had said, but if he had, he would have understood the reason for the warning the second he crashed into Ledger DeMayne's body. He was overflowing with magical energy, and when they collided, there was an explosion of light brighter than anything Joey had ever seen.

The force of it blew him back into the wall and sent DeMayne sailing in the opposite direction. Joey's vision blurred, and he felt like his entire body was on fire. Everything hurt. His hair. His teeth. Everything.

After that, things got a little hazy. Joey was ready to pass out, but he looked around before he lost consciousness and saw his friends were safe. The machine was still running, but the red light continued to fall. He also saw Ledger DeMayne across the floor, looking about as bad as he felt. Joey took some comfort in that.

He closed his eyes. When he opened them back up, he saw Janelle and Hypnova coming out of the gear works.

"wHat HAppEned?"

Joey saw Janelle's lips form the words, but her voice sounded distorted. She looked concerned. He leaned his head back, resting. Time seemed to jump forward, and the next thing he knew, he saw Jack being helped up to where he was by Skerren and Allegra. Shazad was shaking him, trying to keep him awake. He heard someone say the machine was putting out so much energy, it had practically electrocuted him.

That makes sense, Joey thought. He started to feel woozy

and strangely disconnected. Like he was disconnected from his body sinking into the floor. He saw Shazad, Leanora, and Janelle leaning over him, but with every passing second, they were farther and farther away. They were telling him to stay with them. They were calling him back. Where did they think he was going?

Where am I going? Joey wondered.

He knew he wasn't moving, and yet he couldn't stop his descent. Soon, he could barely see his friends' faces.

He couldn't hear them.

He couldn't hear anything.

He couldn't see anything.

He was gone.

24

System Crash

There was something in front of Joey's face. Something red. A shroud of some kind. He pushed it away. It was soft, with a fuzzy, velvety feel. He was tangled up and turned around inside it, but with a little effort, he threw it off.

That's when he saw he was standing on a stage. He was back in the theater, the fully restored Majestic. He wasn't wearing a tuxedo this time, and he didn't have the wand with him, either. However, Redondo was there again, wearing his tux.

"Hello, young Kopecky."

"Oh no." When Joey saw Redondo, a sobering realization sank in. "I'm dead. Aren't I?"

Redondo held his thumb and forefinger very close together. "A little bit. I hate to say I told you so, but I told you this would happen."

Joey sighed, resigned to his fate. "Congratulations. You were right."

Redondo took no pleasure in seeing his prediction come to pass.

Joey thought about everything he had just been through. The lengths he and his friends had gone to, trying to make sure he didn't wind up in this position. He hadn't used the wand more than his body could handle, but here he was. Dead anyway. "So much for Heraclitus."

"What?"

"He was a Greek philosopher. He said 'Character is destiny.'"

"I know who he is. I'm just surprised to hear you quoting someone who doesn't wear a cape and fight crime at night."

"I guess I've grown," Joey said. "Not that it matters now. It turns out destiny is destiny. There was no avoiding it after all."

Joey looked around the empty theater. It felt strange to be back there. The situation was surreal and hard to comprehend.

"Is Oblivia with us?" he asked.

"No. She's not dead yet," Redondo replied. "She's getting there, I'm afraid. DeMayne got her good."

"Did we stop him?"

At this Redondo smiled. "You did. You did it. The student has officially become the master."

"Student?" Joey repeated. "Didn't you tell me, back when we first met, that you weren't going to teach me anything?"

"Quiet. Don't embarrass me in front of the others." Redondo waved to the audience. The theater was suddenly filled with old members of the Order of the Majestic, Harry Houdini and Merlin among them. Joey had seen their faces before. They'd flashed in his mind when he'd first picked up the wand. Former masters of the wand and leaders of the Order. He was one of them now. They rose from their seats to give him a standing ovation.

"What now?" Joey asked Redondo once they finished.

"Now? It's time for me to retire. For good this time. No more comebacks. I belong in the audience with them." He offered Joey his hand. "It's been a pleasure working with you, Joey. You were truly magnificent."

Redondo turned to exit the stage. Not knowing what else to do, Joey followed him, but Redondo wouldn't allow it. "What are you doing? Haven't you ever been to the theater?

After the performance, you take a bow, and you go back-stage." He pointed to the curtain. "That way."

"I'm not coming with you?" Joey asked.

"Of course not, silly boy. You've got your whole life ahead of you."

"My whole life?" Joey squinted at Redondo. "What are you talking about? I'm dead."

"And yet the show must go on. There are other audiences, fans of yours—big fans—eager to see you return. You mustn't disappoint them."

"I don't understand. What am I supposed to do?"

"That's for you to decide. You're free now."

"Free?" Joey took out his magic deck of cards. Once again, he drew three blanks.

Redondo took the cards away from him. "If it's all the same to you, I'd like to have those back. For sentimental reasons. You don't need them anymore."

"Because I have no future."

"No, because of what you said before. You've grown." Redondo held up the blank card. "This isn't your fortune. At least, not the way you think. It's a blank slate for you to fill in with whatever your heart desires."

"How?" Joey asked. "As a ghost?"

Redondo laughed. "Joey. You're not a ghost yet. You're more of a visitor."

"A visitor?"

"That's all. Just a visitor. Think about it. I said you were going to die before this was over. I never said you had to stay dead." Redondo gave Joey a friendly tap on the cheek with the tips of his fingers. It hit like a hard slap with an open palm.

"OW!" Joey shouted. "What the heck?!"

He blinked and saw that he was back in the Clockwork Castle, surrounded by his friends. He sat up slowly. Everything still hurt. Janelle was by his side and looked like she had been crying. Shazad and Leanora also had red, puffy eyes, but they were all smiles now.

"I'm back," Joey said, equally relieved. "Oh my God! I'm back! How long was I out?"

"You weren't out," Janelle told Joey. "You were dead. Your heart stopped."

"How long was I dead?" Joey asked.

"Long enough," Leanora said. "Too long. Don't do that again."

"Deal," Joey agreed. "How did you bring me back? We

don't know any magic that could do that. Do we?"

"It wasn't magic. It was CPR," Janelle said. "Well, maybe a little magic. I handled the compressions. Shazad provided the defibrillator."

"Really? Thank you both." Joey needed both of their help to stand up. "Ow," he said, feeling a pain in his chest. "What did you do, hit me with the Staff of Sorcero?"

"Actually, I used this." Shazad held up the wand.

Joey was shocked to see it in someone else's hand, let alone hear they had been able to use it. The wand had only one master at a time. That was the rule.

"That means . . ." Joey checked his arm. It was unmarked. "I'm not the master of the wand anymore?"

"You carried that weight long enough," Hypnova said. "Now it's someone else's turn. You're free."

"That's what Redondo said." Joey understood now. He had died. It was only temporary, but it still counted. That meant the wand could choose someone new.

"You saw Redondo?" Leanora asked.

"He said I was free. He said I . . ." Joey checked his pockets for the fortune-telling deck of cards. They weren't there. "He took the cards back."

"I hope you're not upset," Shazad said. "I could try to give the wand back."

"Upset?" Joey asked. "Shazad, I'm alive thanks to you. I couldn't be happier."

"You want to see happy—wait until my parents find out about this."

"It's definitely going to make up for what happened to your cape," Leanora said.

"And that bag full of magical objects Joey lost," Shazad added.

Joey cringed. "I forgot about that."

"They won't," Shazad said. "But don't worry. It's going to be all right." He held up the wand. "Better than all right."

"Be careful with that thing," Joey said.

"You know me—safety first." Shazad revealed a green power gauge mark on his arm, just like the one Joey used to have.

Joey nodded in approval. "You're stealing my act?" he joked.

"Just a little," Shazad said. "Don't worry. I'm not going to start quoting comic book movies or anything."

Joey smiled and looked around at the aftermath of the battle—the disaster they had just avoided. The Clockwork

Castle was humming along, keeping the island afloat and on the move, but the power core at the center of the throne room had been switched off. There was no red or blue light coming out of it.

"What happened to the machine?" Joey asked. "Did you reprogram it?"

"We didn't have to," Hypnova said. "Janelle cut its power supply."

Janelle held up a small gear wheel. It didn't look like anything special. It was just another cog in the machine, but it was a very important one. "All the wheels turning in this place . . . they turn gears that turn other gears, and on and on, all the way into this room. But this little gear connects everything out there to everything in here. At least, it did." Janelle tossed the gear to Joey. "Once I took it out, this thing powered down fast."

"It went even faster after you rammed into DeMayne," Jack said. "You released a lot of energy in a hurry. A *lot* of energy."

"I noticed," Joey said.

Jack tapped the dormant orb. "It's just a hunk of metal now. That was quick thinking, Janelle."

"Sometimes you have to think small to think big," she said with a wink.

"You realize what this means," Joey said. "We did it. We won. If this thing isn't working anymore, people can see the island. The Imagine Nation won't be hidden away. Ledger DeMayne and the Invisible Hand can't sweep this under the carpet."

"There is no Invisible Hand," Mr. Clear said. "Not anymore."

"Where's your boss?" Joey asked. "Did you put him on ice?"

"Our former boss," Mr. Ivory corrected. Joey noticed he was no longer in the shape of an ogre. His wounds seemed to have healed when he reverted to his human form. He was walking without a limp, and even the cut on his hand was gone. "He could probably use some ice. The shock fried him too. Not as bad as you, but pretty bad."

Joey saw DeMayne sitting with his back against the wall, looking deserted and defeated. For the record, he was both. DeMayne wouldn't look at Joey. His eyes were on the wreckage and ruin of the room. Joey suspected he was replaying the battle in his head over and over, wondering where he'd gone wrong.

It started about a thousand years ago, Joey thought.

DeMayne wasn't moving. His labored breathing sounded painful. That made Joey smile. He was glad to see DeMayne hurting. He deserved it, but Joey was also glad to see that he was still alive. It gave Joey the opportunity to gloat.

"It's over, DeMayne." Joey hobbled over to where DeMayne was sitting. "It's done. The world is a magical place again. It's going to stay that way, and everyone's going to know it. You lost."

DeMayne finally looked Joey in the eye. "You think that means you won?" He spat on the ground. "You haven't saved the world. You've doomed it. The things you've unleashed . . . You don't get to choose what magic you set free. You have to take the bad with the good. Everything's going to change, but not necessarily for the better. You'll see."

"There's more good out there than bad," Joey said. "And the good magic is stronger."

"Not in my experience."

"Says the guy who looks like a fried drumstick."

"Magic is chaos. It needs a strong hand to control it. It needs order."

"Stop it," Joey said. "Just stop it. You already told us that was all bull. You only care about what magic can get you, but that's over. Your game is over. And there will be order. There'll be us—protecting people, not controlling them. The world is always in between chaos and order. That's life. That's the way it's supposed to be. Too much control from people like you, and that's not living. Too much chaos and things fall apart. But as long as there are people like us, that won't happen."

"People like you," DeMayne muttered. He saw his former henchmen, Mr. Ivory and Mr. Clear, standing alongside Joey and the others. He gave them a look of pure hatred. "Traitors."

"Takes one to know one," Mr. Clear said. "You didn't exactly inspire loyalty."

"What can I say?" Mr. Ivory turned up his palms. "You should have been a better friend."

Ledger DeMayne shook his head. "You're going to regret this, all of you. I would have fixed the world. I would have even taken on your pet project and fixed the environment," he said with a nod to Janelle.

"Please," she said, not believing a word.

"It's true," DeMayne said. "When you rule the world, you want to make it last forever."

"That's an . . . interesting choice of words," someone said.

The voice was weary and strained. Joey didn't recognize it at first, but when he turned around, he saw Oblivia standing on the steps. She was covered in blood and about to fall over.

"Oblivia!" Hypnova said, rushing to catch her. "I thought you were dead!"

"You weren't wrong," Oblivia rasped, leaning on Hypnova for support. "Just early. Give me a couple of minutes." Hypnova started to tell Oblivia she was going to make it, but Oblivia cut her off. "It's all right. No one's going to miss me. I know. I didn't have any friends either." She nodded to DeMayne. "Both our lives revolved around our missions. His mission was himself. Mine was . . . equally flawed. Bring me over there, will you?"

Hypnova helped Oblivia over to where DeMayne was sitting and eased her down beside him. Oblivia exhaled hard. She looked like a long-distance runner who had just completed a marathon. "That's better," she wheezed.

DeMayne snorted. "It doesn't look better," he said,

eyeing her blood-drenched robes—his handiwork.

"You don't look so hot yourself," Oblivia countered. She made the mistake of chuckling, which set off an ugly coughing fit. When it was over, she let out a painful sigh. "Aren't we a pair? I knew about you and your Invisible Hand for a long time, Ledger DeMayne. A very long time. Of course, I didn't know who you really were. I thought, on some level, we were doing the same work. I was wrong."

DeMayne turned away from her with a petulant groan. "I should have cut your throat. At least then I wouldn't have to hear this. If it didn't hurt so much to move, I'd kill you again."

Oblivia clutched his shoulder. "Listen to me. This is important. I may have been doing the wrong job, but I was good at it. Keeping secrets . . . learning secrets. Right up until the end." She smiled a crooked smile. "I have an idea what's kept you alive all these years. The Forever Stone. Isn't that what you call it?" She ripped his shirt open, revealing the black stone pendant that hung around his neck. "There we are."

DeMayne's eyes widened in terror. He tried to push Oblivia away, but he was too late. She had a tight grip on the stone and she wasn't letting go. When he shoved her, she fell over on her side, and the chain around his neck snapped. Desperate, he lurched forward, grabbing for the stone. She held it out of his reach.

Then she threw it away.

DeMayne bleated out an anguished cry as the shiny black stone skipped across the floor. It bounced into the gear works, where it was promptly crushed in the teeth of the Clockwork Castle.

"Forever isn't what it used to be," Oblivia said, triumphant.

DeMayne whimpered. "No."

Whatever strength he had left seemed to leave his body all at once. He slumped down in a heap and looked up with the doomed eyes of a dead man. He looked so pathetic, Joey almost felt sorry for him. After that, things happened fast. His handsome face stretched tight, as if he were dehydrated, but it wasn't water that he needed. He needed protection against the passage of time, and that protection had just been ground into dust. His skin shriveled and cracked as the weight of a thousand years caught up to him. Within seconds, he was a pile of bones, and then, he too was dust.

Joey turned away as the last remnants of Ledger DeMayne disintegrated. When he looked back, there was nothing left but a pile of clothes.

Nobody said anything for a few seconds.

Allegra was the one to break the silence. "That was intense."

"Seriously," Joey agreed. "Like the end of an Indiana Jones movie."

"I don't know what that means," Allegra replied.

"I do," Mr. Ivory said. "I'm just glad he didn't go out like *Raiders of the Lost Ark*. That face-melting scene freaked me out as a kid. I don't think I could handle seeing that in person. Not even with him."

"Quiet. She's trying to talk," Jack said, moving toward Oblivia.

She reached out a frail hand, beckoning him to come closer. He knelt beside her as she struggled to undo a golden clasp that held her cloak around her neck. "Take this," she said, pressing the clasp into Jack's hands. "It . . . it belonged to your mother. When you see her, Jack . . . tell her I said I'm sorry."

"What are you talking about?" Jack looked up at the others. "She's delirious."

"No," Hypnova said. "She isn't."

Jack scrunched up his face. "What do you mean?"

"We can deal with that in a minute," Shazad said. "Right now I need you to step back, Jack."

"What are you doing?" Jack asked.

"I've had this thing five minutes, and already I'm on my second emergency." Shazad pointed the wand at Oblivia.

"PANACEA!"

With that, Oblivia's body lifted off the floor with a whoosh. She began to spin around, twirling in the air like a ballerina. As she turned, the crimson bloodstains faded from her robes, and color returned to her cheeks. Eventually, she stopped whirling and returned to the ground. When her feet touched down, she was dizzy at first, but she steadied herself. She stood tall, not hunched over like before. Oblivia poked at the spot on her chest where DeMayne had stabbed her with Hypnova's blade. She was delighted to find there was no pain. She was healed.

"Panacea?" Leanora repeated with a smile on her face.

"I was thinking about those magic bandages you used on Joey last year," Shazad explained. "I was wishing we had them with us now."

"They were in the bag Joey lost," Janelle said.

Joey grumbled. "Do we have to keep bringing that up?"

"You did this?" Oblivia asked Shazad, surprised to see him holding the wand. "But I thought Joey—"

"You missed a few things while you were dying," Joey told Oblivia. "I'm out. Shazad's the man now."

"He certainly is," Oblivia agreed. "You saved me. Thank you."

"That's what he does," Leanora said, patting Shazad on the shoulder.

"In that case, we've got a job for you," Oblivia said. "There's one more person who needs to be saved."

25

The Right Place
at the Right Time

"What's this all about?" Joey asked Hypnova. "Does this have something to do with what Oblivia saw in your memory?"

"It has everything to do with that," Hypnova said. "It's time."

"For what?" Jack asked.

"Time to put things right," Oblivia said. "I'm ashamed to say it's long overdue. You have no idea how long."

"I don't understand," Leanora said. "What did you see?"

"She saw the same thing you saw," Hypnova said. "DeMayne's final memory of the first Secreteer. Unlike you, Oblivia recognized the person under the hood. She knew her."

"She knew her?" Shazad asked. "Someone from a thousand years ago?"

"It's hard to believe, but it's true," Hypnova said. "The first Secreteer called herself Rasa. Tabula Rasa."

"What?" Jack said. "That can't be . . . It doesn't make any sense!"

"What doesn't make any sense?" Leanora asked. "Who's Tabula Rasa? What kind of name is that?"

"It's a code name," Hypnova said. "The name she chose when she first became a Secreteer."

"The name who chose?" Joey asked.

"Jack's mother."

"What are you saying?" Allegra asked. "Jack's mother is the first Secreteer?"

"How?" Skerren added, trying—and failing—to wrap his brain around the idea. "That doesn't . . . *How?!*"

"What is this?" Jack asked Hypnova. "My father told me my mom became a Secreteer a few years before they met. How could she have founded the Order a thousand years ago?"

"This is the same Order that kicked her out?" Skerren asked.

"It's not possible," Allegra said.

"It may not be probable, but it is possible," Hypnova said. "Anything's possible. The people in this room know that better than most."

Jack rubbed his head. "I guess so, but—"

"But nothing. This isn't the first time your life has been upended by time travel," Hypnova told Jack. "You think your mother died when the Rüstov first invaded Empire City." She shook her head. "She didn't die. She was lost."

"What's the difference?" Jack asked.

"I don't know about you, but I'm lost," Mr. Clear said.

"Who are the Rüstov?" Mr. Ivory wanted to know.

Hypnova ignored their chatter, keeping her focus on Jack. "Fifteen years ago, when the Rüstov armada invaded, a future version of you calling himself Revile came back in time to kill you as a baby. He wanted to erase himself from existence. You know this. What you don't know is that your mother was with you when he attacked. It was the first time he had ever seen her, but he knew she was his mother. He told her who he was and what he was there to do. He told her all of it. As I'm sure you can imagine, it was hard for her to hear. She had already lost your father.

Losing you would have been too much to bear."

Oblivia cringed in shame.

"What did she do?" Jack asked Hypnova.

"Your mother saved you. She stopped Revile. Not by fighting him. Just by being there. She hit him with something he'd never expected, something he'd never had before . . . a hug from his mother. That embrace bought precious seconds for other heroes of the Imagine Nation to arrive and join the fight. After it was over, your mother was gone. Everyone assumed she died in the battle."

"Everyone assumed?" Jack repeated. "What do you mean assumed? Are you saying my mother's alive?"

"You have to understand, it was chaos after the invasion. There was so much death and destruction, so many people missing. . . . Nobody realized what really happened."

"What happened?" Jack asked, his voice going up an octave.

"Revile was overloaded with temporal energy from his journey through time," Hypnova explained. "When your mother embraced him, that energy was transferred to her. She became unstuck in time. Dislodged from her place in the natural order of things, she went rocketing back through the timestream. Her first stop was a thousand years ago, when Merlin and his allies were making plans to fight back against Ledger DeMayne and the emperor who tried to rid this world of magic. She was there for that battle, and when it was done, she helped Merlin hide this place away. She founded the Secreteers before vanishing back into the timestream once again.

"Ever since then, she's been bouncing back and forth in a state of temporal flux. Lost in time. Unable to stay in one place, she's altered the course of history and glimpsed endless possible futures, all in an effort to create a timeline that could lead her back home. But she couldn't do it alone."

Jack put his hands to his head, struggling to process everything he had just been told. A moment passed before he could speak. "Hypnova, I want to believe you, but . . . how could you possibly know all this?"

"How do you think?" Hypnova replied. "Your mother told me, of course."

Once again, Jack was speechless. "She visited me after I was drummed out of the Order of Secreteers," Hypnova explained. "When I was lost and in need of a new purpose. She has appeared throughout history, influencing events where she could, including a 'chance encounter' with a young man named Melvin Kamitsky."

"Melvin who?" Mr. Ivory said, tracking the conversation as best he could.

"Redondo the Magnificent," Shazad said. "Our mentor."

"Our friend," Leanora added.

"Jack's mother introduced Redondo to magic and put him on his path, just as she put me on a path before I sought you out last year," Hypnova said. "She didn't tell me everything. Just enough to get us all in the right place at the right time. Once the spells that hid the Imagine Nation were broken, a window of opportunity would open up for her. This has been my mission. For me, this was never just about bringing the Imagine Nation back to the world. It was about bringing my friend back. My best friend. My sister. The family I chose. I orchestrated all this to give you two the time that was stolen from you."

"I . . . I don't know what to say," Jack said. "I came here hoping I could learn more about my mom. Can we really bring her back?"

"I'm sorry I couldn't tell you sooner," Hypnova said. "This is your mother's plan. You'll have to take it up with her."

"How?" Jack said. "How does this work?"

"Magic, of course," Hypnova said. "I was hoping Joey would have enough energy left over to do the job, but it seems the wand has a new master now."

"You will help us, won't you?" Oblivia asked Shazad. "It's within your power?"

"It's more than that." Shazad checked the power gauge on his arm, which was still in the 90 percent range. "After everything we've been through together, it'll be my pleasure."

"I can't believe this is happening." Jack handed Shazad the golden clasp, full of hope. "Take this. Maybe if you have something that belonged to her, it'll be easier for you to find her. Is that how it works, or am I just making things up?"

"Let's find out," Shazad said. "Are you ready?"

"Are you kidding? I've never been more ready for anything in my life."

Shazad held the clasp in an open palm, waved the wand over it, and cast what was arguably the longest anticipated and most deserving spell in the history of magic.

26

The New World

It was done.

No more spells needed to be cast. The world had been changed forever. Magic was free, and the Invisible Hand was gone. There was no one left to hold it back. The Imagine Nation was free, and the Secreteers were through. No one would try to hide it away ever again. Everything was going to be different from now on.

Joey and the others left the Clockwork Castle and headed back up to the tower. Oblivia led them up to the very top to get a proper look at the new world. Joey, Shazad, Leanora, and Janelle stood on a wide terrace, looking out at the beauty of the Imagine Nation. The rest of the group took in the view with them, except for Jack, who was off to the side, engaged in deep conversation with his mother. The two of them had talked the whole way up the tower and showed no signs of slowing down. Joey was happy for him. Everyone was. It was impossible not to be. After everything Jack's family had been through, they deserved this moment. It was too much to hope for, but it was here just the same. The fact that it was impossible just made it that much better. Not unlike the view in front of Joey and his friends.

"Look at that," Joey said, marveling at the massive crystal mountain floating on the horizon. "It's incredible."

"A world of pure imagination," Shazad said.

"I can't believe we did it," Leanora said. "We really did it."

"Wait until we show you around," Allegra said. "You haven't seen anything yet."

"Speaking of which," Skerren said. "What next for all of you?"

"I don't know," Joey said. "What do you guys usually do after you save the world?"

"Personally, I like a big breakfast," Skerren replied.

Joey rubbed his empty stomach. "I *am* starving."

Skerren clapped his hands. "That settles it! You'll be my guests at Castlevarren. We'll have a feast to celebrate our victory and Jack's family reunion. Everyone here will be guests of honor."

"I wish we could," Janelle said. "As amazing as that sounds, and as much as I want to go explore Empire City, we have school in a couple of hours."

"School?" Joey was incredulous. "Are you kidding? I'm not going to class today."

"We have to go," Janelle argued. "We're not students anymore. We're the new teachers. We have to tell everyone how the world works now."

"Can't I take one day off?" Joey asked. "I did die, you know."

"For, like, a minute." Janelle rolled her eyes. "Don't make such a big deal out of it." She punched him in the shoulder and smiled. "Come on, Joey. You can't call in sick the first day on the job."

"Speaking of jobs, I think we're out of one," Mr. Clear said.

"It's for the best," Leanora told him.

"You could always work with us," Janelle said. "Changing the world was just the beginning. We still have a lot of problems that need fixing. The polar ice caps in particular could use a man with your talents."

Mr. Clear smiled. "Count me in."

"Me too," Mr. Ivory said. "You never know when you might need an ogre."

"You're not an ogre." Allegra patted him on the back. "Welcome to the superhero life."

"Superheroes?" Mr. Ivory said. "Really? Us?"

"If you want to make a difference in the world," Allegra said. "That's all it takes to be a hero."

"I have a feeling we're all going to be very busy," Skerren said. "That Ledger DeMayne of yours was a liar, but he wasn't wrong. You let magic back into the world, you have to take the bad with the good."

"I wonder what our families have been dealing with," Shazad said. "There's no telling what's out there waiting for us."

"There never is," Hypnova said. "There's no telling what the future holds."

"Except you did know," Joey said. "If this was all part of a plan . . . was it always going to happen this way?" He looked at Hypnova. "You sent us to the Imagine Nation on a day when you knew Jack, Skerren, and Allegra would be there to meet us. It wasn't a coincidence. You let DeMayne keep his memory on the ship. You let Oblivia catch you. . . . You took a lot of risks, including me dying."

"Ugh." Hypnova sighed. "You're not going to let that go, are you?"

"The point is, you knew it would work, because Jack's mother saw it all in time."

"And it did work. What's the problem?"

"It's not a *problem*. I'm just wondering . . . was it fate after all? Was it destiny?"

"No," Jack said, joining the group alongside his mother.

She was dressed in a tan Secreteer's cloak with the golden clasp that up until recently had been worn by Oblivia. It matched her golden hair, and Jack's as well. It was obvious he was her son. He looked just like her, especially around the eyes. Jack was also nearly as tall as she was. Joey thought it must have been hard for Jack's mother to see her son so big, but she didn't seem bothered by it. She just looked happy to be home.

"I keep telling you," Jack continued. "We make our own destiny. You gotta trust me on this."

"But how do you explain—"

"My son is right," Jack's mother said, cutting Joey off.

"This isn't fate. None of this was guaranteed. It took a lot of work for me to get back here, and I had a lot of help from all of you. This moment has been a thousand years in the making. You couldn't just wave a magic wand and make it happen. Not like this. I showed Hypnova a vision of the future, but she had to believe in it. You all had to work to make it a reality. We have to fight for the future we want. That's the way it is. That's the way it's always been." She pulled Jack close to her. "Sometimes if you're lucky, the future turns out to be everything you imagined it could be."

Jack hugged his mom back. "I never imagined this. I never dreamed it was possible. Not with any amount of magic. I can't ever thank you enough."

"We did it together," Leonora said. "The world is a magical place, full of possibility and promise. That's what Redondo told us. People forget that, but magicians remind them."

"This island is going to be a reminder the world can't ignore," Shazad said. "I only wish Redondo were here to see it."

"He was," Joey said. "Don't be surprised if you see him

again, by the way. Now that you have the wand. If you do, tell him I said thanks. For everything. I never got to say thank you."

"Don't worry," Shazad said. "He knows."

Joey caught Shazad looking at the power gauge tattoo on his arm. "You're going to be okay," he assured him. "I can't think of a better person to wield that wand."

"It depends on what needs doing," Shazad said. "I think the wand chose you first to get us to this point and me to watch over things from here."

"Just promise me one thing," Leanora said. "Make sure I don't get a turn anytime soon."

Shazad laughed. "Don't worry. I'm the responsible one, remember?"

Below the tower, the gears of the Clockwork Castle continued to turn. The magic machine kept the Imagine Nation in motion, and it continued on its course, floating over the sea to a familiar destination. Up ahead, the New York City skyline came into view.

"Have you thought about what you're going to say to your parents?" Leanora asked Joey. "You're going to have to give them an explanation now."

"I guess I'll start by teaching them a magic trick or two," Joey said. "My dad always did like magic."

"Magicians revealing their secrets." Mr. Ivory shook his head. "What's the world coming to?"

"Good question," Joey replied. "I can't wait to find out."

Acknowledgments

Writing a book is never easy. It's a process. For me, a very long process. There *was* one time I managed to write a book in less than a year, but it didn't turn out very well and never got published.

That's the way it goes. There are lots of hurdles to overcome. Lots of things to figure out. Like how to make people care about your characters. That's a big one. Or how to make a story set in a magical world feel real. Or how to fill up the pages with moments that matter and keep people guessing until the end. Most of the time, I'm doing a fair amount of guesswork myself.

It's a nerve-racking experience, especially as I close in on the end of a story. I feel a lot of pressure to stick the landing and write an ending that's worthy of everything that came before it. That pressure is amplified when the book is the finale of a series. On this book, I felt more pressure than ever because it involved two different series, Order of the Majestic and the Jack Blank Adventures.

I'm glad I got the chance to write this book. I always felt I had unfinished business with the Jack Blank Adventures, but at the same time, going back to the Imagine Nation was scary for me. I was confident the story in those books held up, but it felt like a tower of cards I had assembled long ago that was somehow still standing after all these years. Connecting Jack Blank's world with Joey Kopecky's world meant going back to the tower and stacking more cards on top. If I wasn't careful, the whole thing could come crashing down.

What if the new book didn't turn out well? What if it flat-out stunk? Even worse, what if it stunk so badly that the stink rubbed off on both series? I'm not above worrying about such things. Hopefully, I avoided that fate with this book. The final verdict is up to you, but if you're reading these pages, I'll take it as a good sign that you enjoyed the ride.

Thanks for coming on this journey with me. It's a strange experience, writing a book. You live in your own weird fantasy world the whole time you're writing it, spending an hour or two out of every day detached from reality. And 10 percent of your brain stays in that place when you head back to the real world, always trying to work things out, so you can pick things up quickly without too much of an onboarding process when you return.

At least that's how it is for me. The writer part of my brain is always on, but this was a strange year to write a book, living through a global pandemic and staying locked down at home. We all had real concerns we would have liked to escape from. A dire reality that was hard to forget and hard to avoid. It was overwhelming at times. Like most of you reading this, I found it hard to motivate some days. It was hard to try and be creative or deal with another thing on my plate. Another thing to figure out and work on. At the same time, the creative process was a welcome escape when I needed it. Like most things we love, this book simultaneously drove me crazy and kept me sane.

It's been a privilege sharing these stories with you. For the first time in a long time, I don't know what I'm going to do next, but I do know I have some talented people to thank for helping me get this far.

First, I have to thank my agent, Danielle Chiotti, who was the first person outside my family to ever hear me talk about Joey Kopecky or Redondo the Magnificent. A little over six years ago, we met for coffee in New York, and I pitched her the outline of this series based on my notes and sketches. She was instantly on board, and here we are, a full trilogy later. Danielle, you have been in my corner since day one. I am so grateful to have you and everyone at Upstart Crow on my team.

My editor, Liesa Abrams, acquired the Jack Blank and Majestic books for Simon & Schuster/Aladdin, and she didn't blink when I said I wanted to connect the two series in a shared universe. She just trusted that I would figure out a way to do it and make it work. I'll always be grateful for the faith she had in me and her guidance on all the books we worked on together. Liesa, I couldn't have done it without you. I hope you enjoyed the Batman references!

Kara Sargent also edited this book, and her insights helped me carry it across the finish line. Together we solved story problems, fixed scenes, and tightened things up to produce the book you're holding right now. Kara, it was a pleasure working with you, and I'm excited about the future!

Samira Iravani was an essential partner for the entire Majestic series. I cringe at the thought of these books without her input. Samira, I learned so much working with you and will push myself to keep learning. Thanks for leading the way.

I also want to thank art director Karin Paprocki and artist Owen Richardson for another fantastic book cover. I have to say I absolutely LOVE all the covers for the Jack Blank and Majestic books. It makes me so happy that the same artist and creative team produced all six of them.

I've been lucky to have great people at Simon & Schuster/Aladdin behind me every step of the way: production editor Rebecca Vitkus, copyeditor Penina Lopez, proofreader Kathleen Smith, and publishers Mara Anastas and Valerie Garfield. Thank you all for everything you have done and continue to do on my behalf.

Of course, I have to thank my family. My mom and dad instilled a strong work ethic in me and filled our house with books, comic books, and art supplies that filled my head with ideas. They gave me the gift of imagination, and I love them for it.

My amazing wife, Rebecca, is a creative wonder in her own right and my partner in passing that same gift of imagination on to our two boys. Rebecca, I couldn't do these books (or much of anything else) without your love and support. Let's never stop making magic together.

Finally, to my readers, where would I be without you? You're the heroes of my story, and I can't ever thank you enough.

Now it's time for the next adventure. Until then . . .

MATT MYKLUSCH

is the author of the Jack Blank Adventure series and other books for children (including grown-up children like himself). He lives in New Jersey with his wife, Rebecca; his boys, Jack and Dean; assorted pets; and other forms of magic. Find him online at MattMyklusch.com.